KING'S
RHAPSODY

KING'S RHAPSODY

By Hester W. Chapman

Based on the play by Ivor Novello

Houghton Mifflin Company Boston
The Riverside Press Cambridge

L'amour est aussi le grand refuge de l'individu contre la solitude, l'immense solitude muette que lui ont imposée la nature et les lois éternelles

HENRY BATAILLE, *La Femme Nue*

CONTENTS

I. HOW IT ALL BEGAN   1

II. HOW I AWOKE FROM THE DREAM   18

III. HOW I STAKED TO WIN   35

IV. HOW I SPENT THE DAY OF THE BALL   50

V. HOW I LEARNT MY LESSON   65

VI. HOW I BECAME A QUEEN   80

VII. HOW ONE AGREES TO DIFFER   93

VIII. HOW I BECAME A POPULAR FIGURE   110

IX. HOW TO DEAL WITH A CRISIS   127

X. HOW I FOUND A FRIEND AND LOST AN ENEMY   147

XI. HOW WE DID WHAT WE COULD   169

XII. HOW WE CAME TO THE DARK RIVER   187

XIII. HOW WE LEARNT TO ENDURE   213

XIV. HOW WE REACHED OUR HAPPY ENDING   236

EPILOGUE   243

KING'S
RHAPSODY

CHAPTER ONE

How It All Began

I'VE NO PATIENCE with reporters. It's almost impossible to make them understand what it was like to be a Princess of the Blood Royal in the eighteen-eighties; and of course they're not interested in the Kingdom of Murania—my kingdom, Nikki's fate, Paul's heritage—for the very good reason that it no longer exists.

"Won't you tell us about the King, Ma'am?"

"Which one?" I answer, wondering how many times I must go through it all again. "My father, my husband, or my son?"

And then they look so embarrassed, poor dears! I can't make them see that I came here, to Mentone, as many people of my age do, to die: and that I've lived on, beyond regret and sorrow, far from hope and desire. It generally ends with my saying, "I can't talk about the past, because I live in it—so you must really leave me in peace."

But once, about a year ago, one of them got into my garden somehow, walked up to the villa, saw me on the terrace, and blurted out, after half an hour's beating about the bush: "What was it like in Norseland, Ma'am, before they had a republic? Were you happy? Why did they call you the Snow Princess?"

And then I began to remember. . . .

I was born in 1862, in the Summer Palace of Kraken. My mother died a few hours after my birth, and my father, Peter IV, refused to marry again; they used to say that he turned his back on life when he lost her. But I remember him as gay, kind, and gentle; he was a conscientious, hard-working ruler. To me he was indulgent and tender, even spoiling. He had been partly educated in England, and was, I suppose, something of an Anglophile. His library was filled with English books; his grooms, his valet, even his secretary, were English; he and I always spoke English when we were alone, or with Countess Vera. It was Vera who insisted on my learning to speak French equally well, so that I became—as was often the case with persons of my standing—trilingual; I owe her that, and many other things. She was more than a mother to me; she was my companion, my protectress—but I realize now that I was inclined to take her for granted.

Vera had been a singer. She had been born in Wales, and brought up in France and Germany, where she was trained by the best masters in both countries. It was in Paris that she met my father's friend and most valued counsellor, Carl Lemenken, for whom she gave up a magnificent career. She arrived at our Court as a bride, and became my mother's dearest friend. When my mother and Lemenken died within a few months of one another, everyone thought that Vera and my father would eventually make a morganatic marriage; she was an amiable edition of Madame de Maintenon, and my father an enlightened Louis XIV—that was the popular verdict. But, whatever their relationship really was, it never gave rise to more than momentary gossip or surmise.

By the time I was eight years old, Countess Vera was an institution. Where should we have been, all of us, without her? I say "all of us," because it was at this time that my little cousins, Hulda and Kirsten, came to live in the Palace, at my father's wish, and, I conclude, at Vera's suggestion. Their parents, my father's sister and her husband, had been drowned in a yachting accident. I can imagine Vera's managing, vehement approach to my father as soon as the funeral was over. "Poor little things! Of course you'll have them to live here, with Christiane, Father Peter. That child's too much alone. She's getting spoilt. She must learn to share her toys and her treats and get on with other children. I'll arrange it all. I'll speak to Christiane. Poor little dears—but they'll get over it, you'll see. I'll fetch them tomorrow, shall I?" And my father's answer: "Do what you think best, my dear Vera. I suppose Christiane does need companionship—but she seems quite happy. You do think she's happy, don't you?" And I can see his wistful, worried look. He was always wondering if I were happy.

He needn't have; I was. I had a perfect childhood; too perfect; it was the worst possible preparation for life in Murania.

Kirsten and Hulda were twins, and two years younger than I; I got quite fond of them, but they always rather bored me. We didn't care about the same things; I liked reading poetry, and singing, and playing long, dramatic, imaginative games—and they had to have everything explained to them. "But how can you be the Ice Maiden, Christiane? You're not old enough, and you'd drown under the water." "Why do you call your pony Pegasus? He can't fly, and you'd fall off anyway." And so on. I used to order them about, and then Vera would say, "Now, that's not nice, Christiane—princesses must be unselfish"; and I'd say, "But they're princesses too—why can't *they* be unselfish?" and she'd purse up her lips, and her eyes would twinkle, and then we'd both laugh, and she'd pretend to slap me.

How I loved her—what a darling she was! I came to her with all my troubles, all my wants; I believe she'd have given every drop of blood in her body to please me and my father. She was a little like one of those scolding, kind old Nannies you read about in English novels, and a little like an elder sister. She was short and plump, with wonderful dark red hair and a grand, sweeping way of coming into a room. She had plenty of sense, but she was inclined, like many Welsh people, to dramatize situations—and so was I. My father knew this, and it irked him, especially when Vera and I combined against him.

And that brings me to the morning of my eighteenth birthday—my coming of age. That was when Vera made her one great mistake.

As I look back down the years, I can see myself as I was then—a pretty little blue-eyed creature, with a mop of golden-brown curls, pink cheeks, neat legs, and an icicle instead of a heart. The Snow Princess—what bitter irony, what a hideous, grinning fate lay in wait for that Christmas-card picture of a girl in her teens! I was dressed in pale blue velvet and white fur, too; nothing had been forgotten. I might have posed for a picture of Innocence or Virginity, or the Maiden's Prayer. No wonder my people loved me. I was everything that a young Princess should be—ignorant, reasonably accomplished, blithe and happy and good and gay, as the old rhyme says. I ran into the Palace—we were always very informal in Norseland—through a crowd of cheering people. Hulda and Kirsten and

Countess Vera were in the presence-chamber, where I was to receive my birthday gifts. An argument was going on.

2

I'd been ski-ing since dawn on the slopes that lay behind the Palace, all by myself. I was not, as a rule, allowed to go out alone, but this was a special occasion; those hours of solitude were a birthday treat. Now I had the feeling that this was to be the happiest of all my birthdays—that something wonderful was going to happen. I waited, almost afraid. Hulda and Kirsten were standing with their backs to the door; Vera was arranging my presents on a table by the window.

"Mr. Trontzen's rather sweet," Hulda was saying. "I wonder if I shall ever dance like him."

"Not if you don't practise," said Kirsten. "It's sheer waste of time having lessons from one of the best masters in Europe if you——"

"Mr. Trontzen's a very patient man," Vera put in. "But even he can't make you dance unless you put your heart into it."

"If I wasn't royal," Hulda went on, in a languid tone, "I might consider marrying him." She yawned, and added, "Countess Vera, who will Christiane marry?"

"The man of her choice."

"We don't know any eligible Princes."

"There's always the Balkans," Kirsten put in.

"Oh," said Hulda, opening her eyes, "but they're so—so lascivious."

"Hulda! That's not a nice word——" began Vera, and I burst out laughing.

Then they were all round me, wishing me a happy birthday, and I unpacked their presents. Everything was wonderful, just as I'd hoped it would be. But all the time I wanted to get back to the glittering silences of the slopes, and the secret life I led when I was alone.

The man of my choice—what a ridiculous expression! Kirsten and Hulda were always chattering and sighing in corners about some young man or other—Mr. Trontzen, who was happily married; my father's new equerry, who didn't care for young girls; the Danish *chargé d'affaires*, who had a mistress. I despised them for it—and Vera's cosy way of arranging my entire future irritated me a little.

As a matter of fact, I'd only met one eligible Prince—Maximilian of Styria—and he had a boil on his neck, and a stutter. How could I choose, when there was no one to choose from? And besides—I'd already disposed of my heart. I'd set myself apart, and thoroughly enjoyed feeling superior and icy. There was a song I used to sing, "Some day my heart will awake"—and whenever I sang it I remembered my secret. Poor silly little Snow Princess, living in a daydream! If I hadn't been so pathetic, I should have been ludicrous.

The whole background of my girlhood sheltered me from the world of everyday. Our simple, democratic way of life; the cool, fresh spaciousness of the Summer Palace, in its setting of mountains and fir trees; the cheerful, unpretentious elegance of the Palace in the capital, with its gay frescoes and pink colonnades and bubbling fountains; the little dances, the games, the skating parties in winter, the picnics in summer; the love and kindness which surrounded me always; the public duties which no one thought of neglecting; the obedience to high principles and ancient beliefs—all these things had made me truthful, serious, and loving, but they had brought me neither discernment, sophistication, nor subtlety.

And here I was at eighteen, the perfect product of an outmoded civilization—a survival, an anomaly; and also an extremely obstinate and wilful young person.

Just as I'd finished thanking Vera and the cousins, my father came in. He took me in his arms almost before I'd had time to make my curtsey, and sent Hulda and Kirsten away as soon as he'd given me his present—a diamond necklace from Lacloche. I put it on, and he kissed me again, smiling rather sadly at my breathless thanks.

Then he looked over my head at Vera and said abruptly: "No, Vera, don't go away; you've always looked after Christiane. I should like you to hear what I have to say to her."

"Oh dear," I said, still absorbed in my necklace, "am I to be scolded?"

"No, my dear, not scolded," said my father, stroking his beard. "Frightened a little, perhaps."

"No——" I began, half laughing, and then stopped as I saw his expression.

He went on hastily: "Well, not exactly frightened."

"I'm frightened now," I said pettishly. "Do please tell me what it is I've done."

There was a pause. Then my father said gently: "You've done

nothing. It's——" Again he broke off. "Christiane, you know that some day you will—you must marry."

I said quickly, carelessly: "Oh, yes, some day—but not for ages."

"Sooner than that."

I would not look at him now. "Not too soon . . ." The offhand manner was wearing rather thin. "Besides, I've met no one I want to marry."

"No, my dear, you haven't," said my father, a shade of impatience in his tone. "But Princesses seldom do. These things are arranged. Of course, one always hopes . . ."

"What does one hope, Father?" I said innocently. Still I could not look at him; I was staring out of the window.

"That the husband will—will be sufficient—— Vera, this is so difficult . . ."

"It isn't difficult, Father," I said, turning, emboldened by the helplessness in his voice. "What you are trying to tell me is that some day I must make a suitable marriage. I realize that."

I was rather pleased with the worldly manner in which I rattled off the last sentence.

There was a long silence. Then my father said, in an expressionless voice: "Christiane, some day is—*now*."

We were staring at one another.

I said, "Now?" in a breathless whisper.

"Yes."

"But——"

"Let me tell you in my own words," said my father, with sudden volubility. "Our country has for some time been in negotiation with another country for a great increase in mutual trade. These negotiations have proved successful—they will bring an enormous increase in prosperity to both our countries—our people will benefit greatly." He paused and cleared his throat. "Murania—has certain commodities which—"

"Murania!" I said, in a shrill, unnatural voice. "But the King of Murania is old and married. His son"—the words stuck in my throat, but I forced myself to go on—"his son is exiled."

"The King is dying, and his son is to be recalled," said my father. His voice seemed to come from a very long way off.

"But he's been away for twenty years—he gave up his rights . . ."

"He is ready and willing to return on one condition—you."

I put my hands to my head. I felt sick and hot. "Nikki . . ." I said, and I became aware of Vera's hand on my arm, her anxious eyes on my face. I burst into an hysterical laugh. "But he doesn't know me— he's never seen me!"

"No, that is quite true," said my father, turning away. "But—he too must think of his country's welfare."

Suddenly I felt desperate—had I dreamed all this, was I going mad? With a tremendous effort I pulled myself together, and began to speak in what I imagined was a very grown-up, cynical manner. "He didn't twenty years ago. He thought of himself—and someone else."

For a moment I thought my father was going to tell me not to be vulgar. He merely looked rather anxious.

"That little affair, I am assured, is over and done with," he said, glancing at Vera.

She nodded.

"It can't be," I persisted, rather pleased with the way I had risen to the occasion. "He gave up his rights to the throne for her. How can it be over and done with?"

My father sighed; then he smiled. "It's twenty years—a long time, Christiane."

"It wouldn't be a long time for me if I loved anyone," I said, feeling like the heroine in one of my favourite novels.

My father looked at Vera, and they both laughed. Then I was suddenly furious. If I was old enough to be married, surely I was old enough to be treated like a grown-up person. After all, I should never see seventeen again.

I ran to the chest on which my birthday presents had been placed and began to throw them onto the ground, heedless of Vera's agitated "What *are* you doing?" and opened the lid. I dived into the chest, sneezed, and produced an album. I have that album still. It is of red leather, decorated in blue and gold. "Look!" I said, holding it open in front of my father and glancing up at him.

It occurred to me then that I need never be in awe of him again. I was practically a married woman. A sudden blinding ecstasy swept over me. The shock of my father's opening words had stunned me. Now I was beginning to realize that the unbelievable had happened.

My father put on his gold-rimmed glasses and peered at the album. "This is most extraordinary," he remarked, after a long silence, adding, in a dazed voice, "it's full of—him."

I burst into a wild laugh. "Yes—nothing but him! Every word that's ever been written about him, every photograph, every drawing—I've kept them all!"

My father put the album under his arm and his spectacles in his pocket. He said very gravely: "Then there's nothing more I can tell you, except that the final decision will rest with you. Your happiness comes first."

I began to feel guilty. Eighteen years of training stood between me and my own wishes.

I mumbled, "You want it—don't you?"

"Yes," said my father, and he gave me back the album.

"Then I want it too," I said, putting my arm in Vera's—and my eyes were suddenly full of tears. I cried out, "It's too good to be true!" and flung my arms round her neck. "Oh, Vera—Vera darling——"

The album fell to the floor, unheeded.

"There, there, my pet—it's all been too much for you . . ."

"And I," said my father, "was looking forward to an hour of apologies for his character. There are still things you must know——"

"I don't want to know anything——"

"My child, my child," said Vera's warm Welsh voice in my ear, "what is all this? You've never even seen him."

I looked at her. I couldn't say anything. I'd never lied to Vera in all my life. But my heart spoke—couldn't she hear it, beating out the words? "Ah! but I *have* seen him—Nikki of Murania—the man who threw away his kingdom for a woman . . ."

3

I first saw Nikki—or, to give him his full title, Paul Alexander Nicholas, Crown Prince of Murania—when I was eleven years old. I'd developed, and couldn't throw off, a sort of nervous asthma, and the doctors advised my father to send me to the South of France for a cure. I was to lie in the sun, do no lessons, bathe, and drink *tisanes;* so I set off for Nice with Vera, my French governess, my nurse, an equerry, and three maids. We were to take the first floor of the Hôtel Splendide, and remain there for a month.

At first I was happy. Then, as I grew stronger, I got rather bored and a little out of hand. At the end of a fortnight, I'd read all the books we'd brought with us and was begging Vera to buy me some new ones. "It'll be good for my French," I said; Mlle Dacquemine broke in with a remark about suitable literature, and they set off for the shops, leaving me in charge of my old nurse. She dropped asleep as soon as she saw me settled on the balcony.

It didn't take me a moment to steal out of the suite and down through the ground-floor rooms to the terrace. It was the hour of the siesta. A man and a woman were sitting at a table in one corner, looking out over the sea. Two waiters were yawning and gossiping in another. There was no one else in sight.

I sat down and ordered a *sirop à l'orange*. No one recognized me; it was the first time I had appeared in this part of the hotel. The waiters were, I think, rather amused by my careful French and unchildish aplomb; after I had been served, they exchanged glances and laughed; then they seemed to forget all about me.

That very morning I had been surreptitiously poring over the story of Prince Nikki in a weekly paper. Although it was nearly ten years old, the romance was still popular. "Crown Prince gives up his throne for love—Muranian Don Juan runs away with Hungarian prima donna—all for love and the world well lost"—the stale, dreary phrases had held for me all the drama, all the poetry, that life could offer. I knew that Nikki and his mistress were at the Splendide, because I'd overheard Vera scolding my maids for talking of them when I was in the room. In fact, they could have told me nothing I didn't know already. (I knew, for instance, that they always sat on the terrace at this time of the day.) Here were the hero and heroine of that thrilling story, sitting so near me that I could almost hear what they were saying.

I am old—old, and weary of life. But it is impossible for me to recall that moment of wonder and delight without some recurrence of the awestruck happiness that then was mine. I fell in love, then and there, with beauty, grace, and charm. I regret nothing. And I can at least say that, having given all my heart, I neither grudged the gift nor asked for another in exchange.

But I am going on too fast. Here I am, sitting on the terrace, looking at Nikki and Marta. I can see them as plainly now as if I had returned to the past and was once again an eager, curious little girl. They didn't see me; they were looking at one another.

Marta was then, I suppose, about thirty-four, and in the prime of her beauty. Her hair, fair to whiteness, was swept up in a smooth, glistening wave under a straw hat trimmed with yellow roses; she wore a primrose muslin dress, decorated with bunches of silver-grey ribbon. She had a charming, delicate nose, with a tilt, and a short, full upper lip. Her eyes were grey. She looked happy and kind. She had beautiful hands.

The world has forgotten Marta Karillos. But I never shall: because, although I envied her, with an agonizing, hopeless envy, I couldn't hate her. I couldn't hate anyone whom Nikki loved, and who had been able to make him happy.

Well, there he sat, looking at her, his profile outlined against a creamy mass of oleanders—dark, arrogant, melancholy, severe. Suddenly he smiled; and then he was like a nice, rather shy schoolboy. It was a vague, pleading smile—the smile of a man who hopes that everyone's happy, but isn't quite sure that they can be. The sculptured, noble beauty of his head, the tossed richness of his black hair, the brooding, heavy line of eyebrows and eyelashes, the curl of his lip when he laughed, the quick movements of his hands—all these I saw, and treasured, as I do the memory of them.

But I wanted to hear his voice. Surely if I waited, I should be able to. The wind got up, and the sound of the waves rose between us. Still I sat on, gazing at them, and sipping my orangeade.

They had been talking gaily and, it seemed, casually, as people do who are everything in the world to one another. Then suddenly he frowned and tapped on the table. The waiters hurried up, and were peremptorily dismissed. Marta leaned forward, smiling, her eyebrows raised, as if she were teasing him. He shrugged his shoulders and turned away, his lips compressed, his eyes half closed. She leant back and appeared to consider.

I don't know how long it took her to persuade him out of that fit of gloom or bad temper—half an hour, perhaps; but she did it in the end, and he began to laugh, and then to look round, as if for some other distraction. At once she got up, put her hand on his, straightened her hat, stifled a yawn, and trailed across the terrace, her yellow flounces shimmering in the afternoon sun; she gave the impression that she had been wanting to make a move for some time. He strolled after her, his hands in his pockets—a little bored, but somehow appeased, and at peace with himself and the world. (I don't know how I was so sure about all this, but I am still certain that it took place just as I saw it.) Then they both caught sight of me; he stared, and she smiled; I suppose they thought I was a funny little thing. A moment later they were gone.

I went upstairs, and found my nurse still asleep; Vera and Mademoiselle came in a few minutes later. I told no one what I had been doing.

It was after that that I began, secretly, to collect the photographs and drawings of Nikki—and to talk to him when I was alone. In these conversations he was, of course, just on the point of leaving Marta. "It's gone on too long," he'd say. "Don't you think so, Christiane? I'm not the faithful kind—not really. What do you advise? I suppose you—but what am I saying?—you're only a child. Perhaps some day . . ." Then I would make a prim but encouraging reply, and he'd kiss my hand and exclaim, "At last I've found you! Why have you kept me waiting so long?" And then, somehow, we'd find ourselves married. . . .

Yes: I was playing a fool's game; but even so, I don't think I quite deserved the fate that was meted out to me.

4

A few days after that strange birthday, my father sent for me to read and sign some papers. By this time I was too much occupied with my trousseau—of which the greater part was to be made by the peasants living on the Kraken estates—to be able to concentrate on what he laid before me. I sat down and ran my eye over the first few lines of the marriage contract. Sapphire mines, coal, silver, forestry—these were to be a part of my dowry: could anything be duller?

My father, who had been standing with his back to me, half turned, and said, "I can feel you're not reading those, my dear."

"Father, how can I? I keep wondering——"

"What?"

"Has he"—I couldn't bring myself, at that moment, to call Nikki by his name—"has he asked, personally, for my hand?"

"All our correspondence has been with his mother, Queen Elena."

"Oh."

"Are you disappointed? He has not yet succeeded—he can't ask for himself. In fact, he's still in exile."

"Yes—I see."

"Have you changed your mind?"

"No!" I exclaimed, my eyes filling with tears. "How can you ask?"

"Upon my life," said my father, with his great laugh, "I've never seen a lady so willing."

A little offended, I took up another paper: but I couldn't take in a word of what I was reading. I sat still. My hands were trembling so much that I had to put that particular document back on the table.

My father began to walk up and down.

"Christiane," he said abruptly, "you must prepare yourself for what may be an ordeal."

I looked at him helplessly. I was beginning to feel as if I'd been caught up by invisible hands and was being whirled through space. Already my home seemed far behind me.

"An ordeal?"

"Yes. The Muranian Prime Minister, Count Misia Vanescu, is arriving tomorrow to make the final arrangements for the marriage."

"Oh," I said vaguely. "Is he very alarming?"

"I don't know. I shouldn't think so. But he—he has, during these last years, been virtually governing Murania—he and Queen Elena. He is—she will be guided by his opinion."

"I see," I said slowly. "But I thought—won't the Crown Prince— doesn't he even want to know if I'm—I mean——"

As I broke off, my father put his hand on my shoulder.

"You've idealized him, haven't you?"

"In a way. I've always felt he has been misunderstood. I shan't misunderstand him," I said dreamily.

"Suppose—suppose he's not—kind? If he were—selfish, for in-stance——"

"But why should he be? He gave up——"

My father made a despairing gesture.

At this point Countess Vera came into the room, and he turned to her with a look of relief. "Vera—I can't make this child under-stand. She knows something of Nikki's reputation—and yet . . ."

"Oh, it's no good going on, Father Peter," said Vera comfortably. "Good girls always think bad men wonderful."

"But why should he be bad?" I exclaimed.

"They're all bad, that family," said Vera, in her matter-of-fact, pleasant voice. "Look at his mother—she's been a scandal for forty years."

I couldn't help laughing. "Vera, darling—she's an old lady."

Vera gave me a look of pitying humour. "She's fifty-seven, I believe," she said, in a dry tone.

"*Cela n'empêche pas,*" my father murmured; then he seemed to pull himself together, and began to go through the marriage contract with me, point by point.

When Count Vanescu was presented to me, I was agreeably surprised; I had expected to find him dry, stiff, and unapproachable —he was handsome and amiable. The only disappointment was that he could tell me so little of Nikki. The old King of Murania was not expected to live for more than a few weeks; then Nikki would be recalled. "Officially," Vanescu added, "he will spend the night at His Majesty's bedside, praying for his recovery."

We were standing in the throne-room. The reception given in Vanescu's honour was nearly over, and we had been left alone in the embrasure of a window in the marked manner that in Courts indicates a discreet watchfulness. We were both used to being watched.

I found myself saying, quite naturally, "How do you mean, Your Excellency, 'officially'?"

"The news of His Majesty's death will be suppressed until His Royal Highness has had time to return."

"Why couldn't they really meet? Just to say good-bye?"

"Your Highness is charmingly direct," said Vanescu, his cold blue eyes narrowing as he smiled. "The relationship between the reigning monarch and the heir is not usually a happy one."

"But if his father's dying—surely . . . "

"Your Royal Highness must forgive me if I find myself unable to dwell on this tragic but inevitable loss," said Vanescu, very smoothly indeed. "I have been a devoted servant of His Majesty for more than twenty years."

"I beg your pardon, Count Vanescu."

"Your Highness is most gracious."

Of course, I was much too excited by all the preparations and by my highly coloured visions of the future to give this conversation another thought. The days of Vanescu's visit went by in a round of formal entertainment and long conferences between him and my father and my father's Ministers.

Vera took what I considered to be the most absurd dislike to our distinguished guest. "He's like a toad," she said, when I pressed her for a reason.

"What can you mean? He's extremely handsome."

"I know, I know. But his eyes——"

"Toads don't have dark blue eyes and beautiful straight noses, and——"

"Don't be foolish, my child. I was thinking of his expression."

"I hadn't noticed anything about that."

"Exactly. He hasn't got one. He gives nothing away. I don't trust him."

"Queen Elena does," I said pertly. "Shouldn't that be enough?"

Vera glanced at me, and walked out of the room. People seemed to be doing that rather a lot at this time, especially when I spoke about Queen Elena. I began to feel strangely isolated. Even my father appeared ill at ease when I mentioned her.

What did any of it matter? Soon the old King would be dead, Nikki would be proclaimed, and then—no, it was all too wonderful to be believed. I'd wake up sometimes, having dreamt that the King of Murania had recovered and that I was to be married to Maximilian of Styria. Once I was so frightened that I ran into Kirsten's and Hulda's room, and they wrapped me up in an eiderdown, and we talked till morning about Murania. "Of course, you'll come to stay with me," I said grandly. "I shall give some balls for you." But even then I didn't want to talk about Nikki. He was marrying me for my dowry—what of that? After a week or two—perhaps less—he'd fall in love with me. And then we'd live happily ever after, and Murania would be the best-ruled and the happiest country in the world.

I read a great deal of poetry at that time. There was one poem I learnt by heart—Nikki and I would, of course, read poetry together when we were alone, and I would say to him:

"*I had wealth and ease,*
  Beauty, youth—
Since my lover gave me love,
  I gave these."

"Isn't that a perfect description of our marriage?" I'd say, and he'd laugh, and lean back, and look at me as I'd seen him look at Marta Karillos.

And then I'd sing to him; I'd already begun to learn some Mura-

nian songs; I'd sent for a Muranian phrase-book, too, and a diction-
ary.

On the fourth day of Vanescu's visit there was a ball, and when
he asked me for the honour of a dance, I answered, "With pleasure,
Count Vanescu," in Muranian.

It was a square dance. As we went down the line, I said, rather
timidly: "I haven't had much time to learn your language. But
I'm getting on."

"Your Highness is a remarkable linguist. You speak French perfectly."

"My Muranian——"

"If Your Highness will permit me, I would advise you"—he
paused as we turned, saluted the opposite couple, and came back up
the middle—"I would advise you not to bore yourself with learning
Muranian."

"But I must——"

"At Court, Madame, we speak French. Muranian is only spoken
by the peasants and shopkeepers. Even the merchants——"

"Do you mean that my husband won't speak his people's language?"

"I know so little of His Highness. He is, if Your Highness will
permit the expression, a cosmopolitan."

"But won't any of the people round me speak Muranian?"

"None, Ma'am. It is not our custom."

"But that must estrange you. I mean, it's like two nations. Isn't
that——"

"If Your Highness will forgive me—our customs are as ancient as
your own."

I was silent for some minutes. We had reached the bottom of the
dance and were standing still when Vanescu spoke again. He was
smiling, and had assumed his most deferential, most insinuating
manner.

"If I might be so bold, Ma'am, as to suggest—we were speaking
of languages . . ."

"Please go on."

"Your Highness speaks Italian?"

"Very little. Almost none."

"Ah!" He put up his hand to his perfectly trimmed imperial,
while his eyes wandered across the ballroom; then he said, in a
casual tone: "Her Majesty Queen Elena is Italian. She is of the

House of Bourbon-Parma. But Your Highness is no doubt aware——"

"Surely the Queen speaks French, as you all do?"

"Naturally, Madame, yes. But Her Majesty and the Prince have the habit, when *en petit comité,* of speaking Italian."

I stared at him. "But have they met since he was exiled?"

"Frequently, Madame. Her Majesty travels a great deal."

I was suddenly frightened. I seemed to be gazing into an abyss. It was then that I began to realize—how, I don't know—that I was going into some sort of hateful battle—and that I was unarmed.

An infantile, hysterical desire to break up the reserve of this polished, undefeatable courtier made me say, with an attempt at a laugh, "I suppose, then, that Queen Elena knows Madame Karillos?"

Vanescu glanced at me. He appeared as inscrutable as ever. Then he said, with a faint smile: "Her Majesty is a woman of the world, Ma'am. She has made a point for many years of being most gracious —I might almost say, friendly—to that lady."

"And now?"

"Now—everything has changed."

"You mean, they've parted. Is that really true?"

"It is indeed, Your Highness. I should hardly be here if it were not," said Vanescu imperturbably.

I knew that I had made a fool of myself. "And so you advise me to brush up my Italian?" I said, after a pause.

"If I might presume, Your Highness. It would be a matter of no more than a few weeks in the case of so talented a linguist as yourself."

The dance was over. He was leading me back to the dais. I was silent. I couldn't speak when he bent over my hand, but I managed to smile.

Then the band began to play a waltz. I wasn't, of course, allowed to dance round dances, and so I sat down by my father, who was looking at me rather anxiously.

Suddenly I longed to be alone, to get away from those crowds of solid, well-behaved, warm-hearted people. "Her Majesty and the Prince have the habit of speaking Italian——" There was something rather sinister about the manner in which that simple statement had been made. It haunted me—and yet, why? As the weeks went by, I was afraid whenever it came back to my mind. I couldn't any longer lose myself in the imaginary conversations with Nikki.

They didn't materialize, somehow—and neither did he. It was oddly alarming.

Then, at last, the news came of the old King's death and Nikki's accession. I was formally summoned. With tears and exhilaration, I said good-bye to my home and my father, and with Vera (Heaven knows what he sacrificed in letting her go), I set out for Murania. We travelled by sea. The voyage was calm and without incident. I arrived in the harbour of Bledz on the twentieth of April, 1880.

CHAPTER TWO

How I Awoke from the Dream

By the time I reached Murania my future husband was Nicholas VII. His coronation had coincided with the eight-hundredth anniversary of the rule of the Orosvars. Nikki was, I think, a fairly representative member of that ancient and now almost forgotten House. The Orosvars had not only a long history but a sinister one; during the last two hundred years they had acquired—and ignored—a reputation for tyranny, pride, and lust; but no one had been able to accuse them of stupidity or degeneracy. The male members of the House of Orosvar were remarkable for their ability to move with the times and outwit their enemies; they chose their wives for their looks as well as their dowries.

I knew that Misia Vanescu had been sent to Norseland to report on my appearance; the King and his mother would not trust the flatteries of artists and photographers, preferring to rely on his powers of description. In those days it was not considered necessary, or even desirable, to appeal to the populace by the dissemination of their future Queen's likeness in the newspapers. The King of Murania made his choice, and that was enough.

The arrival of the yacht in the harbour was greeted with a burst of gunfire. I was to remain below until we reached the quayside, where the Archbishop of Bledz, the Officers of the Household, and the Prime Minister were waiting to receive me. The King and the Queen-Mother would greet me "within the Palace precincts." This was the custom of Murania, and I was glad of it. I did not want to meet Nikki in front of a staring crowd—for the quayside and all the streets leading from the harbour to the Palace were lined with people.

It was a brilliantly fine, still afternoon. The sun blazed down on the tall, ancient white houses encircling the harbour; these were decorated with flags, streamers, and gilded shields. Every window was bursting with people, waving coloured scarves; the space behind the quayside was crowded with cheering, gaily dressed townsfolk, carrying flowers or holding up their children to get a sight of me. Immediately in front of the landing-place, under a canopied dais, stood the dignitaries of Church, Army, and State. On either side of them were placed the ladies of my household; for I had persuaded my father to let me arrive with only one gentleman-in-waiting, Vera, and my personal maid, Astrid, who was also my foster-sister. All the other members of my suite, of whatever rank, were to be Muranians.

The announcement of this decision had already made me popular; but I had not required it of my father with that end in view—I had always taken popularity for granted in my own country. No—I had had the romantic idea of arriving almost unattended, and so giving myself up completely to the care and service of my new subjects. That, I thought, would please my husband and make him see that I was devoting myself to his interests and desires.

The first half-hour of my arrival was spent in formal presentation of, and converse with, the personages on the dais. I received a confused impression of dark faces, exotic decorations, heavy scents, and richly elaborate toilettes. The Muranians are a handsome race; this, my first contact with them, made me feel perfectly unsophisticated and, as it were, colourless. I was dressed in a white muslin gown trimmed with apple-green ribbons and a green straw hat ornamented with one pale pink rose; I wore no jewels but the string of pearls that had been my father's parting gift.

I had been feeling horribly nervous. But as soon as I left the yacht, the sick tremors left me and I became ecstatically excited. Nikki was within half an hour's drive now; soon I should hear his voice and touch his hand. My cup of expectation was full. I am sure that I appeared as radiant, as happily receptive of all the compliments and speeches that were being made to me, as a bride in a dream—a dream in which nothing can go wrong.

Nevertheless, I was thankful to see Vanescu; in this group of bowing, curtseying strangers he took on the semblance of an old friend. As he handed me down the steps of the dais to the open carriage drawn by six white horses in which I was to progress through the city, I said, in a low voice: "We arrived two hours early. I hope that the King and Queen Elena have not been put out in any way?"

He made a complimentary rejoinder; but I seemed to detect a faint shade of embarrassment in his courteous impassivity.

A moment later I was in the carriage; we ascended a slope, and passed through the medieval gates of the old town, where the mayor and the city fathers were waiting with an address and the gift of a Bible and prayer-book of gilded leather decorated with the Orosvar arms, quartered with those of my own House. A little girl in yellow silk gave me a bouquet of dark red roses; a very small boy in brilliant scarlet recited a poem in Muranian, of which I understood one word in three—but that wasn't bad, considering. Then we drove on, through the old town, to the residential quarter.

Presently the cheering and the shouts gave way to silence as, from a stage that divided to reveal a triumphal arch, two young men, dressed in medieval garments of purple and silver, descended to give me a gold key—the key of the capital. They also spoke in verse, but in French; they represented one of the ancient guilds of the city. Just as the first of these had bowed and was preparing to bend over my hand—I had to lean out, but not down, from the carriage, rather a feat for a person of my small build, but I managed it—I heard him mutter to his companion, "By God, she's a beauty, after all!"

Well, of course, I was delighted. I knew that I was reasonably pretty, but no one had ever called me beautiful. (Vera always said I was a nice-looking little thing.)

Vanescu remarked, as we drove on, "You have conquered all hearts, Madame—but that was only to be expected."

"I'm so grateful, so happy!" I exclaimed. "I wish I could thank them properly. What's the use of just bowing and smiling? I never knew people could be so kind."

He glanced at me, his blue eyes glittering oddly. "Your Royal Highness's opportunities will be—limitless," he said gently. "We are all convinced—and I speak for Her Majesty Queen Elena as well as for these others—that you will use them for the good of your people."

Just for a moment I wondered why he hadn't included Nikki. Then I forgot everything as the carriage swung into the long avenue of trees bordering the road that led up to a vast oval; round this the colonnades of the Palace swept in curves of yellowish-grey stone. I could discern in the distance a group of splendidly dressed officers standing at the top of the double staircase that wound up to the huge baroque doorway. Nikki must be standing in the centre of these. Five minutes more, and we should be face to face.

2

Yes! One dark face, one tall figure, stood out above the rest. I continued to bow and smile. I like to remember that I was sufficiently well trained to go on talking to Vanescu—or, at least, to be able to answer his murmured explanations, although I couldn't take in what he was saying.

Now we came through the Palace gates; there was a crash as the sentries presented arms. As I was handed from the carriage I perceived, out of the corner of my eye, Vera and the Mistress of the Queen's Household; their carriage must have come by another route. In this climax of fearful excitement my powers of observation were momentarily sharpened; I saw that Vera's hat was a little on one side and that Madame Racovitza was unbecomingly flushed.

I could not look at the faces immediately above me. Afterwards, when I read in the newspapers half a dozen eulogies of my modest demeanour and shrinking delicacy of bearing, I burst out laughing. I kept my eyes lowered because I was frightened.

Then that tall central figure stepped forward, and I sank into a deep curtsey. I had ceased to think. I could not look up. Now—at last, at last!—I felt his hand on mine. With a tremendous effort, I raised my eyes. He had drawn me towards him. We were looking at one another.

I stood there as if I had been turned into stone. It was impossible to utter a word. A bleak, blank horror, a wave of misery and revulsion, swept over me and took away my breath. For it *was* Nikki's face—but so much aged, so unspeakably ravaged, swollen, and reddened, that I wanted to put my hand over my eyes.

What had happened? Where was the brilliant, noble creature of my dreams? Then Vanescu's voice came from behind me; it was grating and harsh, as though he were suddenly agitated.

"His Royal Highness Prince Cyril of Murania has the honour to welcome you, Madame."

I couldn't immediately disassociate Cyril's face from the one I had been holding in my memory. Then I remembered. Cyril and Nikki were first cousins, and had been, I knew, very much alike. Cyril was the heir-presumptive to the Kingdom of Murania. Standing there, young, healthy, eager, and already beloved, I represented the downfall of his ambitions.

I pulled myself together and said what was expected of me, wondering rather crossly why no one had warned me that Cyril would be there, or of that disconcerting family likeness. Cyril's wife, Princess Anna, stood with her ladies and her twelve-year-old son (a plain, spotty child) behind the group of which her husband had been the centre. She was presented to me. More compliments were exchanged. Then I left Vanescu's care and entered the Palace between Cyril and his wife. They were to lead me to Queen Elena's apartments.

I realized at once what had happened. After years of freedom, informality, and exile, Nikki had revolted against the publicity required by such an occasion as this. I should be received by his mother; then he would come in, and we should be left alone; or perhaps she was going to take me to him. I was glad of this unexpected delay, for it gave me time to recover.

Cyril, Anna, and I, followed by the most important members of our respective suites, walked slowly through a long corridor, hung with crimson and silver brocade and with life-size portraits of the Orosvar family. The Prince and Princess were very large and fat, and towered over me like a couple of gaolers. Every now and then I seemed to catch a frown, a smile, or a leer from one of the sombre canvases above us. So, watched by the dead, escorted by the living, Orosvars, I was drawn on towards my destiny.

I was suddenly sick with anxiety as my thoughts took another turn. What had I heard about Queen Elena? Suppose she was like a mother-in-law in a a story—jealous, watchful, prying? Might she dislike me at sight? What if she were already preparing to stand between Nikki and me?

Now we paused in front of a pair of white-and-gold doors, painted with garlands of flowers. They flew open. I was standing at the end of a long white-and-gold room; there were one or two great mirrors, framed in *rocaille*, bowls of lilies, more family portraits, some silver-framed photographs, a narrow sofa covered in pale-blue satin, and two vast Venetian chandeliers, in which the colours of a hundred flowers seemed forever impaled. Some ladies stood round the sofa; one, taller than the rest, was standing apart by the window.

The doors shut behind me. Prince and Princess Cyril drew back. I advanced towards that motionless, glittering figure. I had hardly begun my curtsey before she swept down on me, took my hands in hers, and kissed me on either cheek. A deep, gay voice said: "My dear, you're exquisite! What a piece of luck!"

I couldn't think of an answer to this extremely unconventional greeting. As if aware of my confusion, my helplessness, Queen Elena went on, "My dear child, welcome—welcome to Murania."

At last I had a moment to look at her. I saw that she was not nearly as tall as I had imagined; she was so delicately slender that she made everyone else look clumsy and squat. What else did I see in those first few seconds of agitated scrutiny? She had Nikki's profile—high-bred, aquiline; his long, fine hands—but there the likeness ended. Her face was narrow; her features small. There were shadows under her brilliant dark eyes; her mouth was full and pouting. She had been a black-and-white beauty—indeed, I remember it was one of her boasts that she never put rouge on her cheeks. Now her magnificently thick hair was grey, drawn back from her face and arranged like a coronet on the top of her small, exquisite head. I suppose she had wrinkles, lines—all the marks that are usual in women who have reached their fifties; but somehow one never noticed them. Queen Elena was so ageless, elegant, and serene that when she was standing still she looked as if she were made of ivory or porcelain; when she moved it was as if she were walking through a minuet.

She spoke French perfectly, but with the warm, slurring intonations of the Italian; there was a faint harshness, a croaking, ironic note, in her tone, more like that in the voice of a young man than in an elderly lady. When she said, "I expect you are very weary from your journey," and drew me down beside her on the sofa, I felt as if I were with someone of my own age.

We got through the formalities easily enough. I presented Vera to the Queen; she presented her ladies-in-waiting to me. Prince and Princess Cyril begged permission to leave. Tea was brought in. I swallowed two mouthfuls, and crumbled a biscuit. I couldn't taste anything. I sat on the sofa, dazed, only rising when Queen Elena did. She motioned me to remain seated, and continued to talk, walking about the room (I wondered if she too was nervous, and then decided that she couldn't possibly know the meaning of the word), glancing at her ladies, smiling, touching the flowers.

She was so strange, so fascinating, that for ten whole minutes I forgot all about Nikki; I ceased to conjecture as to the circumstances of our meeting. Queen Elena chattered on. I replied in a glib, hypnotized manner.

3

"Tell me," she began, "are you pleased with your reception?"

"Overwhelmed," I said quickly. "I hadn't expected such affection."

"Ah!" said Elena, looking at a bowl of flowers with her head on one side. "Our people are so easily moved, they are almost too demonstrative at times. I expect you will find them quite a change."

I was so absorbed in looking at her that my attention was wandering. "In what way, Ma'am?"

"Well"—she replaced the flowers and moved to the window again —"South and North, you know."

"I have never known anything but affection from my people," I said, wishing that I could speak more graciously. Determined to contribute something interesting to the conversation, I added, with an effort, "Surely the human heart is the same all over the world?"

She looked at me, her eyes half closed. Then she said, in a very calm voice, "I hope you'll find it so." After a short silence she added, "I hope the Palace pleases you? But you've not yet seen your own rooms."

I murmured something about looking forward to that, when she interrupted me in a much brisker tone, with a glance at Vera, who was standing like a monument of disapproval. "Have you any hobbies?"

"I sing a little."

"Good. Now—tonight." My heart began to beat very fast. I said nothing, and she went on, speaking rather jerkily. "I have arranged nothing for you—I knew you'd be tired—you would like to dine quietly in your own apartments, and perhaps an early night——"

She broke off, and then resumed with a perceptible effort. "Tomorrow you will of course show yourself in public again. We will drive through the city together."

I gazed at her. I thought she was trying to conceal something terrible. Was Nikki ill?

Queen Elena threw a glance at the lady-in-waiting nearest her, and went on rapidly, "And we must talk about clothes. I see you go in for simplicity—that's good. But it must be the right kind."

I made up my mind to help her, and replied, in as conversational a tone as I could manage: "I have quite an elaborate trousseau. Our people were generous. They embroider very beautifully."

Queen Elena looked amused. "Embroidery? Does that still go on? It reminds me of my girlhood in Italy—I had a great many embroidered dresses there." She paused, one hand on her cheek, scrutinizing me. Then she said coolly, "I'm sure you would like to retire early."

I heard Vera gasp. The sound destroyed such control and tact as I had left.

I burst out: "Retire, Ma'am! Before my meeting with the King?"

As soon as I had got out the words I felt better. Queen Elena gazed at me, her eyebrows raised. Then she said casually: "The King? He's dead."

I thought I was going to faint. Horror pinned me to the spot. Suddenly Queen Elena's face cleared, and she laughed in a tinkling, artificial manner. "Oh, Nikki—how stupid of me. I was thinking of my husband. I'm still in mourning, as you see. Ah, yes—well——"

She picked up a tall vase of tiger-lilies, and moved it from a bracket to a bureau. Then she continued, in an offhand tone, her eyes wandering everywhere but in my direction, "I cannot tell you how excited he has been—he has made himself quite ill—oh, he has such a nervous temperament." Here she threw me a very sharp look indeed, but I remained impassive and stunned. "And then there's been this unfortunate trouble in the Eastern Province. He actually had to go himself, to quieten things down." (She was now engaged in replacing the lilies on the bracket.) "He's so beloved there, you see. I said to him, 'Nikki, go yourself, even if you're not back for Christiane's arrival. I will explain everything to her.'" She was standing like a graceful Renaissance statue, another vase of flowers in her hand. "After all, what is a day when you've all your lives together? Oh, yes, he had to go . . ." Her voice faded away, and silence fell.

"But, Madame——" I began.

"Good gracious, what am I doing with these things?" she exclaimed. A lady-in-waiting removed the vase from her hand. Then she continued, speaking rather faster: "You know what the personal touch means. I know you're disappointed; it's only natural you should be"—she had lost her breathlessness and the words were coming smoothly now—"but when you see him it will all be forgotten."

I found it hard to speak, but after a moment more I managed to produce some kind of polite reply. Queen Elena then made one of her serpentine movements in my direction and, looking more than ever like a beautiful black snake—for her mourning was pleasantly relieved by a necklace and bracelets of emeralds—took her leave, followed by her ladies. For the first time that day Vera and I were left alone.

"I don't like her," Vera announced, plumping herself down beside me on the sofa. "She's as hard as nails. Dear me! I shall be glad to get out of these stays."

"Do be careful," I urged. "She's coming back to show us to our rooms."

A long silence fell, during which Vera did not look at me. At last I said, in a low voice, "She was lying, wasn't she?"

"Oh, well, my dear, Italians, you know—and there has been unrest in the Eastern Province."

Suddenly all the disappointment swept over me at once, and I became feverishly eloquent. "Enough to take him away from the capital the day his bride arrives? Oh dear!"—I buried my face in my hands—"Perhaps it's just as well. I'm tired and hot, and he'd hate that."

"We're all tired," said Vera repressively. "And very nervous——"

At this moment the door opened, and the Queen-Mother, Prince and Princess Cyril, and their attendants appeared to conduct Vera and me to our apartments. Here we found Astrid—I had never been so glad to see anyone, for she and I were more like sisters in our treatment of one another than employer and employed—waiting to undress me. I put on a tea-gown—the first I had ever worn, but I hardly noticed what I looked like—and presently Vera and I were alone once more.

There was a life-size painting of Nikki above the mantelpiece. I went up to it. Vera came and put her arms round me. For a moment we stood looking at it in silence.

"He's older than I imagined," I said at last.

"Well—he's getting on for forty."

"And his mouth smiles, but his eyes . . ." Suddenly I turned away and buried my head on her shoulder. "Oh, Vera, it's all been a failure! He doesn't want me—let's go home! Tell them—say I'm ill, that I've changed my mind. The yacht's still in the harbour. Vera, I'm afraid, I'm afraid . . ."

Of course, I didn't really mean to run away. But the long day, the strain, the excitement, above all the suspense, and the hideous disappointment on top of everything else, had been too much for me. I cried myself into a racking headache in Vera's arms.

She soothed me, as she always had in the past. But there was an aching misery in my heart. Why—why wasn't Nikki there? The more I thought about that trouble in the Eastern Province, the less I believed in it. Then a strange thought came to me—was all this suffering part of the preparation for being a queen? I tried to be sensible, and behave as my father would have wished.

Vera sent away my maids and put me to bed herself. She sang me to sleep, as she used to do when I was a little girl. "Fly home, little heart"—that was the burden of her song. But I didn't really want to fly home, or be anywhere but in the Palace of Bledz. Soon Nikki would come to me, and then I should be happy.

4

I woke up early, quite rested and strangely calm. It was as if my arrival and reception had formed part of the dreams from which I had just arisen—dreams in which Nikki's face, distorted or ghostly, had superimposed itself on the shadowy lineaments of his mother and his cousins. That ordeal, those visions, were now behind me. I crept out of bed, put on a dressing-gown, and began to explore the rooms immediately surrounding my bedchamber. This was my private suite; it was connected by a corridor with the State apartments that Nikki and I would occupy after our marriage.

The first sight of these interiors bewildered me; I could not at once appreciate what I saw. This baroque style of decoration had never been introduced in Norseland; if it had, it would have been characterized as decadent and affected. But there was something in me—the same instinct, perhaps, that had rejected the fair-faced, rather stolid young men of my own race and drawn me towards the dark, tempestuous beauty of an Orosvar—that found gaiety and contentment in the curves, the delicate colours, and the sophistication of these eighteenth-century rooms. As soon as I had taken it all in, I was delighted by the fluidity of the designs that were swept up as though by a whirlwind, surging round the paintings of nymphs, shepherdesses, and *amorini*. I was charmed by the background of citron, rose, and palest turquoise that set off studies in *grisaille* of birds and monkeys, which were encircled in their turn by swirling arabesques of silver and gold.

There was something very satisfying about this rococo elegance; when I came into the boudoir and drew back the shutters, I gazed fascinated at the fragile mushroom-pink of the brocaded curtains and the grey-green damask that covered the Empire chairs and sofa. A piano, painted with garlands of wild flowers, stood by the window. In the rack which was gilded and shaped like a harp stood some of the folk-music of Murania. This room, like all the others, was filled with bowls of lilies and carnations. Surely I could not fail to be happy in such a refuge as this, whatever the trials that awaited me beyond it?

As I stood there, wondering, a maid put her head in, curtsied, and ran away. I went back to bed and rang for Vera; but somehow I didn't want to talk to her. Then I was informed that the Queen-Mother would like to see me, if I were sufficiently rested. Her arrival was preceded by a bouquet of orchids in which a diamond and emerald brooch lay concealed; this was a part of her wedding present to me.

Coffee was brought in, and Queen Elena and I were left alone. We were in the boudoir, sitting opposite the portrait of Nikki. She saw me looking at it, and said, with her trilling laugh, "You poor dear patient child—if he weren't so popular, he'd be sitting here between us."

I didn't much care for the patronage in her tone; but I was determined not to give way to the resentment and agitation that had overwhelmed me the day before.

I began, "May I ask you something, Ma'am, about him?"

"Of course—anything."

"Is it because he has been away for twenty years that he is so much beloved?"

She glanced at me, and lowered her eyes. Then she produced a charming smile. "Upon my word!" she said, tapping my cheek with a long, jewelled finger. "Isn't that rather an odd question for a girl who's hardly out of the schoolroom? Well—yes. We had to prepare the ground, Vanescu and I (his father had nothing to do with that; between you and me, my dear, poor Nicholas was a very unco-operative creature), by making Nikki into a romantic figure. 'He gave up the throne for love'—you also know about that, I conclude?"

"Yes."

"It's so extraordinary what girls know nowadays," she went on, moving restlessly about the room. "No, don't get up, Christiane, I want you to be quite informal when you're alone with me. When I was your age I had to find out everything for myself. Dear me! How these celebrations bring it all back!" She wandered over to the window and looked out. "The same crowds—the same music—yes, and the same flags, by the look of them."

I laughed. She was really very delightful.

She turned, with the lithe grace that I was beginning to look for, and said, still smiling, "I feel we're going to be friends, Christiane, don't you?"

"Yes—please," I said, rather confused.

She contemplated me for a moment, her head on one side. "I know whom you're thinking about—Marta Karillos," she said abruptly.

"I couldn't help wondering——"

"She's gone, you know—gone for good," said Elena, rather sharply. "I agreed with your father that you were quite right to insist——"

"I insist? I don't understand."

"My dear child, you signed the paper demanding that she be expelled from Murania."

"I signed such a lot of papers——"

"Without reading them?"

"Well—yes."

"Ah—how charming!" she exclaimed, her black eyes sparkling with amusement. "You were too excited about being a queen to think of anything else, I suppose?"

"Not quite about being a queen . . ." I stopped, realizing that I had begun to blush.

"Now, don't tell me you fell in love with the romance! How very——"

"I don't know very much about love," I broke in, speaking low and fast. "I only meant that I didn't expect—I mean——"

"Expect what? Do go on, you dear, delightful child."

"To—to be the first——" I blurted out, after an agonizing pause.

Queen Elena burst into a peal of laughter, and clapped her hands. "You're too refreshing for words, Christiane! The first! How sweet—do you know, I think you're going to be a tremendous success here. Muranians like novelty. Ah, well!"—she became wistful again—"*I* was a novelty once. My branch of the Bourbons-Parma, you know, was connected with the Borgias. Oh, wrong on both sides of the blanket, of course—don't look so bewildered, you sweet thing—but I mustn't run on like this; in a moment we shall have to get ready for our drive, and you simply must put on another of these dear little embroidered gowns." She walked to the door, and then turned to look back. "How pretty you are, Christiane—so fresh. Such a contrast to—by the way, this evening we should have news of Nikki. In fact, I think he may very well be back by then." And, brushing aside my attempts to answer, she swept from the room.

Nikki did not appear that evening—nor the next, nor the next. At last, when a week had gone by, and several public engagements had had to be put off, it was given out that he was ill and confined to his hunting-box in the Eastern Province. I knew that this could not be true, and so did Vera. By this time I could neither eat nor sleep, and was very near collapse.

On the seventh evening, which was to have been spent at the opera, I begged to be let off, and, with Vera, shut myself up in my rooms. Then I remembered the promise I had made two days before to receive Madame Kasha, the most—I should perhaps say, the only—fashionable dressmaker in Murania. She had by this time been waiting with her models, her dresser, and her troupe of mannequins for two hours. When I spoke of her, Vera protested.

"You're worn out—you can't——"

"Nonsense," I interrupted, rather wearily.

"But——"

"Vera—don't you see? There's one Muranian fashion I must never adopt." She raised her eyebrows, and I went on, with a shaky laugh: "Breaking promises. I promised Madame Kasha I'd see her gowns, and I'm going to—now, before I have time to think how ironical . . ."

"Well, you can't receive her like that," said Vera, with a smile.

I looked down at my dress. I had quite forgotten that, turning away from the smart, tight-laced tea-gowns which had been part of my trousseau, I had reverted to a simplified edition of a Norseland peasant costume—a sleeveless bodice, a full, embroidered skirt, and a lace apron—that I often wore in my own country. I had put it on as soon as I came in from a military review; it made me feel less homesick and strange.

"She must see me as I am," I said, after a moment's silence. "Will you tell them I am ready for her now?"

Madame Kasha was French; she designed her own models, and had always, I discovered, been somewhat piqued that Queen Elena imported every stitch she wore from Jean Worth. As I see them now, Madame Kasha's gowns were far too exotic for a girl of my age; then, however, they appealed to a new and disturbing consciousness of my own inadequacy. Perhaps, if Nikki did arrive, and saw me in one of these rather insistently provocative toilettes, he might not despise me.

"I want them all," I said, when the display was over.

Madame Kasha threw up her hands. "Your Royal Highness is too gracious."

"No," I said; already the gloom was lightening a little. Once more uneasily aware of my own appearance, I added: "My poor embroidered trousseau—made so lovingly—how ridiculous it looks before all this! I wonder why I troubled to bring it." I caught Vera's warning glance, and went on hastily, with a smile: "Take everything to my bedroom. I shall wear a different dress every day."

Madame Kasha sidled up to me, and said, in an insinuating tone: "Your Highness—may I be impertinent, and make a very personal request? That little dress you are wearing—it is quite delightful."

"This? But this is what our peasants wear."

"But the shape, and that exquisite embroidery! It has real *chic*. I assure Your Highness that it could set a fashion. After all, everything Your Highness wears everyone will want to wear. Could I presume?"

"You mean you would like to copy it?"

"If Your Highness would do me so much honour."

I consented, and, when her raptures were over, began to speak about the dress that she had sent some days before for my approval, and that I was to wear in twenty-four hours' time at the State Ball. This Madame Kasha considered her masterpiece, and I think she was right.

A few more compliments were interchanged. Then Madame Kasha, her eyelids lowered, begged to express her sympathy with me over the King's illness. I reassured her with a courtesy that had become extremely formal, and she took her leave.

As soon as we were left alone, I glanced at Vera and said, in a dry, tearless voice: "Well? It's almost funny, isn't it? What if he never comes at all?"

"Christiane——"

"The royal romance that ended in smoke——"

"Smoke?" said Vera, in her most vigorous manner. "If he doesn't come soon, it'll end in a bomb."

"Why is he humiliating me like this?" I burst out. "I've never done him any harm. I only said yes. Perhaps that's why he hates me so much——"

I broke off at the sight of Vera's face. She gazed at me, and then burst into tears. "There's—there's another reason," she said at last. "Oh, my dearest child—and I believe it's my fault."

"Well?" I said coldly. Her grief irritated me; I could feel none of it. Anger and humiliation had frozen my tears days ago.

Vera went on, in a choked voice: "You were told that his—romance, with that—with Marta Karillos, was over. It isn't. She's here, in Murania, and he's with her now."

There was a long silence.

"Go on," I said steadily. It was quite easy to be calm. I felt nothing. "How is it your fault?"

"I was quite sure he'd given her up. You see, Queen Elena sent your father a letter, assuring him—I felt it must be all right. I wanted so much for you to be a queen, Christiane—I persuaded your father not to take any steps—Oh dear . . ."

"You mean, you persuaded him to take her word?"

"Yes—oh——"

"It's all right. Don't cry any more. We've been fooled, that's all—Father and you and I."

I sat down on the sofa. Vera's sobs gradually faded away. I thought of those six nights I had spent lying awake in the dark; of the seven days that I had got through somehow, smiling, chattering, being charming, being grateful.

"It's as good as a play," I said slowly. "Isn't it?"

"You must decide," said Vera, with a gasp. "Are you staying?"

"Staying? Here? I don't know."

"A message to your father, and he'd——"

"He's with her now," I said, staring at the ground. "He never wanted me, except to be of use. I'm beaten before I start."

"Royal engagements have been broken before now," said Vera, reviving a little. "Everyone will blame him—not you."

"Does it matter who is blamed?" I said dully, looking at her.

She buried her face in her hands. We sat there for a long time, saying nothing.

"Vera—will you please go now?" I said at last. "I must think it out alone."

"Of course." At the door she turned, her face all blubbered with crying, and said timidly, "You were bound to know some time, and it might have been too late."

"Perhaps it's too late now."

"Oh!"

"Good-night, dear Vera. Tell my maids—Astrid, everybody—to go to bed. I can manage for myself."

She gave me one last miserable look and went out. I began to walk up and down.

In those hours of solitary despair I grew up. The Snow Princess—that fairy-tale figure—became a woman. Presently—I don't know how much later it was—I found that I was standing underneath Nikki's portrait. The painted eyes gazed into mine. What if this were all that I should ever know of him? What if we never found one another?

And yet, hatred was far from me. I knew now why he looked at me so sadly—poor, trapped Nikki, sold for a couple of sapphire mines and a few acres of forest! I said, half aloud, "Now I know why your eyes don't smile."

I stood there a long time, trying to take it all in, to understand. Then I moved—carefully, stiffly, as if I were made of glass—to the piano. My eyes still on the portrait, I began to play. I didn't know what I was playing. Misery, anger, suspense, bewilderment, following relentlessly upon one another, had turned me into an automaton. I began to sing, softly, as if I were asleep. I seemed to be listening from far off to the voice of another person in another world.

Then, very gently, the door opened. Was I never to be left alone? I started up from the piano.

A tall man, in a long, dark cloak, stood before me. He shut the door, and leant back against it, smiling.

This—this was real. I was not dreaming. Nor had the portrait suddenly come to life and stepped down from its frame.

I had loved him since I was a child. And as I looked at him I knew that I loved him still—hopelessly, irreparably, forever. He was all the romance that I had ever known, or dreamed of—all that my heart had long desired.

He glanced round the room and loosened his cloak. Then he said, in a faintly ironical tone, "That was charming—won't you go on?"

CHAPTER THREE

How I Staked to Win

FROM MY VERY EARLIEST YEARS I had been taught—rightly or wrongly, I don't pretend to know—to conceal my deepest emotions. As soon as I realized that Nikki did not know who I was, I decided not to reveal myself until I had found out what his attitude was going to be.

So I stood looking at him in silence. He glanced at me carelessly, but with a certain awakening of interest, as a man eyes a girl whose looks have momentarily caught his attention.

"Who are you?" I said, coming round the piano, so that I stood facing him.

He looked me up and down, and his expression changed a little. "An audience of one, clamouring for more," he said lightly.

That was the first time I really heard Nikki's voice; when he came in the shock of his appearance had prevented me from taking in anything more than the mere words.

His voice was warm and gentle—not so much deep as insinuating and persuasive; everything he said had quality and interest, no matter how trivial it was. I sometimes think that I shall hear his voice in my grave as I heard it then: with a sound of amusement and—yes!—anticipation, in the casual, half-mocking, half-gallant phrase. Suddenly I made up my mind to surprise him, or at least try to take him at a disadvantage.

"I know who you are," I said abruptly.

His smile disappeared, and he looked blank and cold; for a moment I thought he was going to speak sharply. Then he said, in a rapid, contemptuous manner: "Why? Have the new stamps come out?" I laughed nervously, and he went on: "But they're only profile. They always say my face is two profiles stuck together."

I found nothing to say to this odd witticism; there was something bitter and harsh behind the easy coolness of his rallying tone.

He went on with a laugh: "So this is my bride's apartment. And are you my bride—or has she retired to bed, like a virtuous young lady?" As I stood there, silent and terrified, he added brusquely: "And if she's retired to bed, why are you playing the piano?"

Before I had time to answer, he sat down, rather suddenly, with his back to me.

Now, I had never seen anyone the worse for drink, as it's called, in my life; but the peculiarity of the circumstances was stimulating me to a knowledge that I had not hitherto possessed. I became dimly aware that Nikki had been struggling to free himself from some very disagreeable emotion—that he was overstrained, exhausted, on the verge of an outburst. His reputation had never been that of a drunkard; tonight, for some reason that I was beginning to guess at, he had deliberately dulled his capacity for unpleasant feeling, and was seeing in me someone who might be a companion —perhaps even a friend.

I told him that the Princess Christiane allowed me to play the piano in her absence, and he looked as much amused as if I had said something brilliantly witty.

"Oh, she does!" Now he was sitting with his head thrown back and his eyes half closed. I was so near him that I could see the sweep of his dark lashes, the hollow of the cheek that was turned to the light. He glanced up at me, and said lazily: "You're being very disrespectful, you know. You should be calling me 'Your Majesty.' But don't if it disturbs you—after all, we're both off duty." I permitted myself a discreet smile, and he went on, making as if to look underneath his chair, "Where *is* my bride?"

I made a deep curtsey, and said, speaking with exaggerated respect, that if His Majesty had been here for the last week His Majesty would have known that Her Royal Highness had gone to the opera.

"Oh, come—that's enough Majesties to last the whole night," he interrupted. "The opera—let me see. That gives us at least two hours."

"If I may so far correct Your Majesty——"

"Well?"

"After the opera Her Highness is going to a reception at the Old Palace, where Their Royal Highnesses Prince and Princess Cyril have the honour to entertain her for the night. She will return here tomorrow morning."

He leaned forward, and put his hand on my wrist. I couldn't move or look away. He said, in a slow, thick voice, "Here—let me look at you." His eyes travelled over my face and figure. Then he said idly: "You're beautiful—very beautiful. How wrong people can be! I was told that the Countess Lemenken was—by the way, you are Countess Lemenken?"

"Not even that," I said, looking away. "The Countess would hardly wear a peasant's dress."

He released my hand, and leaned back. "If she looked like you she would," he said, with a smile.

This remark sounds impertinent. But now his tone had changed from that of the too successful *coureur de femmes*; his smile was as I had seen it once before, pleading, a little vague. He seemed to be saying, "I've been so bored—can't we have a good time together, just you and I?"

Then he went on: "It's good, that dress. It shows off the ——" He made a gesture with his free hand. Then suddenly he threw back his head and laughed like a schoolboy. "I've made you blush! I didn't think they could blush, north of the Danube."

"I assure you we can," I said, withdrawing my hand and speaking with an assumption of pertness, like a waiting-woman in a play. "We can do most things as well as you." Then I forced myself to move away.

By this time I was almost composed. It was so wonderful, so unbelievable, to be with him at last! A fog of misery and doubt had cleared from my brain, and my mind was working quickly and easily. I seemed to know just what to do to lift the gloom that had been hanging over him.

He said, as I had hoped he would, "What, for instance?"

I walked over to the sofa and perched on the arm. (I had never sat on the arm of a chair or a sofa in my life; Princesses didn't do such things in my day—but I knew that heroines in novels did, when they wanted to appear nonchalant and gay.)

"Well—we keep our promises, for one thing," I said, smiling.

His eyes narrowed. "Ah," he said slowly. "My family is, as you may know, notoriously unreliable."

"But Her Majesty Queen Elena——"

"Oh, Mamma! She was there, I suppose, saying what a pity it was—yes, I can imagine." His expression changed completely as he spoke of his mother; there was amusement and sympathy in it, but bitterness too, as if he knew and accepted the whole range of her ingenuity. Then he added, "How did the arrival go off?"

"I can hardly remember," I said demurely. "It's so long ago— seven whole days."

He laughed; then he yawned and stared round the room. Immediately all my confidence left me. I was going to bore him—I knew how easily he got bored. I could think of nothing to say. But I must not look anxious; I got up and walked away, humming a tune. Nothing happened.

What could I do? Suppose I offered to play to him? And, supposing I did, what if he didn't like my playing? Now I could feel his glance, no longer interested, straying to the door. Perhaps the situation was already lost, and he was near the point of departure.

2

Then I had to turn and look at him. His hands were clasped behind his head, and he was staring in front of him. Suddenly I realized that he had changed in these last seven years—and not for the better.

It wasn't that he had aged, or coarsened (though I hadn't seen until this moment that there was grey hair on his temples). He looked disgusted, and defeated; sickened of himself, and perhaps— ah! could it possibly be so?—of her for whom he had given up, as the world thought, a throne. Inexperienced as I was, I knew, somehow, that he had been unhappy for a long time, and that he had come now to the edge of an abyss—marriage. And yet I, standing on the other side of the gulf and holding out my arms to him, could do nothing. He might talk to me, to pass an idle hour, he might flirt with me, he might even make love to me—though I couldn't believe, as I contemplated his blank expression and lounging attitude, that that was very likely.

Well—I had set myself to play a part—that of the acquiescent, sharp-spoken waiting-maid—and I must go on with it, or I should lose what I had already gained, little though it was. How could I distract him? Then that warm, caressing voice broke in on my frenzied conjectures.

"I should like some wine."

Of course! How could I have expected to provide all the stimulation that he needed?

He went on: "I know I've had enough. But I want"—he stretched out his arms—"too much. Get me some."

"I'll ring for a footman," I said; I was so pleased at being provided with a solution that I forgot the part I had assigned myself.

"What? And spoil our *tête-à-tête*?"

"No—I mean—there's some wine in the cupboard."

"Then get it, my dear child—get it," he said, with good-humoured impatience. "I shall make myself comfortable. It's rather pleasant here." He got up and stretched himself. "I see this room has been redecorated—for my bride, I suppose," he added, looking round. "A sort of virginal bower—cupids, flowers, nymphs, shepherds—quite delightful." And, throwing off his cloak, he lounged over to the mantelpiece and leant against it—but now he was looking at me, not at the wall-paintings.

"There's one bottle," I said, after a moment's scrutiny. "But it's very dirty."

"Oh—what's it called?"

"Tokay—Imperial Tokay."

"And you've never tasted it?"

"I've never heard of it," I said, turning, the bottle in my hand.

Now he appeared more animated than I had yet seen him. "Tokay," he repeated, as if speaking to himself. Then he looked at me, half smiling. "Yes. It will be a—an experience for you—won't it?"

Unsophisticated though I was, I could not help grasping the implication in his voice. I laughed, and nodded; I longed to be able to answer wittily, pleasantly, but speech was impossible.

"Is there a corkscrew?"

"There is."

"Then give it me," said Nikki, his eyes still on my face. "This —Tokay—must be opened very delicately."

I gave him the corkscrew; his fingers lingered a moment on mine.

Still looking at me, he said quietly: "Yes, you're very beautiful, aren't you? Glasses—bring two."

It was a relief to turn away; unbearable joy to watch him pour out the wine and know that in a moment he would be looking at me again.

"It's a pretty colour," I said, determined to appear at my ease.

"Try it," he said, looking at me over the rim of his glass. Now his eyes had lost their mocking look, and were very kind.

"It's quite nice——" I said faintly.

"Nice! It's as well the peasants who bottled it can't hear you. Not so fast! Now—look at me . . ."

"I can't look at you, and drink."

"Yes, you can. It should be sipped, not gulped. Everything pleasant ought to be taken slowly. Did no one ever tell you that in your own country?"

"No," I said, feeling my colour rise again. "Like this?"

"Yes. It's good—don't you think so?"

"Yes, I——"

"But dangerous."

"Dangerous?"

"I mean, for me." He seemed amused at my alarmed expression. "I haven't eaten, you see, since breakfast."

"You mean, it might——"

"It might make me"—he waved his hand—"foolhardy—talkative, even. I might tell you some of my secrets."

"I'd keep them," I said, in a low voice. "Tell me."

"Not I. You'd tell your Snow Princess. Aren't you her confidante?"

"She has none."

"A heroine without a confidante—impossible!" he went on, with a faint sneer. "By the way, I'm the villain of the story. Have another glass."

"I don't think——"

"Afraid?"

"I'm not afraid of anything."

"Ah! it's gone to your head already." As he filled both glasses he went on: "Your cheeks are a good deal pinker than when I first came in. What shall we drink to? The bridegroom? Happy man! No, I know—let's drink as they do in my other country."

"Where's that?"

"Italy. I'm half Italian—didn't you know? My mother never lets me forget that. Now—I'll drink to what I see in your eyes, and you drink to what you see in mine—that'll be rather amusing, if your thoughts are what I think they are."

"You should not be drinking at all," I said, emboldened by the increasing bitterness in his tone. "You've had a fever."

"Was that the story?" said Nikki, moving rather unsteadily towards the sofa. "Well—it's as good as another."

He sat down, staring into his glass. I leaned over the back of the sofa, my hand hovering above his black hair.

I said softly, "Was it really a story—nothing more?"

He glanced up at me. "Where are you? Stand where I can see you."

I obeyed. He drained his glass, and then said, in a vague, expansive tone: "I'm not going to lie to you—there's something about you that I like. You're Northern—nothing dark and deep and devious about you." He paused, and pointed his finger at me solemnly. "I'm going to tell you something, but you must keep it to yourself— do you hear me?"

"I hear you."

"You see," he went on, leaning forward, one hand on his knee, the other holding the empty glass downward, "I stayed away deliberately."

"Why?"

He waved his hand impatiently. "I'd have stopped away—sent her back to her frozen North—but I discovered something." He waited, and then went on, as if speaking to himself: "I was trained to be a king—and now the job's mine. Do you know the Villa Flora, on the Hervat Road?" As I stared at him, bewildered, he shook his head. "No, of course you don't. But that's where she is—Marta."

"I know," I said defiantly.

"How do you know? Oh, well, of course everyone knows. Does your Snow Princess think I'm going to give up Marta? If my plans didn't include her, let me tell you, there wouldn't be any. But Marta knows that I have to be King," he added, speaking in a dreamy tone that alarmed me far more than his irony, or his abuse of me, "and that they like me."

"You mean," I said, speaking very low, "that if you sent us—the Princess—back, they might not like you so much?"

He looked at me rather absently. "How right you are," he said, after a pause. "This marriage, you see, is supposed to be my salvation. I'm a reformed character—well, I wish they could see me now, that's all."

"But the Princess——"

"She means nothing, and never will," he broke in fiercely. "I was prepared to accept her—I need an heir. She could have given me one. Now she's not going to have the chance."

Perhaps the wine had gone to my head a little. As he spoke I seemed to follow his thoughts with knife-like intuition. I felt that I could bear anything from him, and yet turn it to my own advantage. I knew what to say, how to act.

"It's rather an amusing story," I said. "The Princess that nobody wanted. Give me some more wine, won't you?"

"Of course. Hold your glass steady, child. There. As I was saying, I'll have nothing to do with her—now."

"But why? You don't even know her," I said in a casual tone.

"Perhaps not," he said slowly, turning his glass in his long brown fingers, "but I know her signature. You're not her confidante, you say. So much the better for you. Her signature"—he sat up, and seized my hand—"was on a shameful, arrogant scrap of paper. 'If the Countess Marta Karillos is not forthwith expelled from Murania . . .' Ah! you didn't know about that, did you?"

"But listen—the Princess might not have——"

He rushed on. "Good God—doesn't she know that this is purely a marriage of convenience? How dare she dictate to me how I shall behave to the only utterly loyal person I've ever known?"

"Yes," I said, with sudden bitterness, "so loyal that you had to give up your throne for love of her."

He stared at me. His expression was grim; his eyes glittered. "No, I didn't," he said. "I gave up the throne for hate."

"I don't——"

"Hate—hate, do you understand? I hated my father so much that I would have killed him if I'd had the courage. What are you staring at? It's a very common situation."

To tell the truth, I did not understand—then. One question only obsessed me.

"But the Princess," I persisted, after a pause. "She might not even have known about that paper. She might have signed it without reading it, mightn't she?"

He had been gazing at the ground. Now he raised his eyes

and looked at me curiously. "What do you know of such things?"

"Nothing. But—I know her almost as well as I know myself."

"This is very interesting," he said, dropping back into his idle, mocking tone. "And what's your name?"

"Astrid."

There was a long silence. I was trembling; I thought he had discovered me.

At last he said slowly, "Give me some more wine—Astrid."

I took his glass and filled it. Now my hands were steady again. "You don't know——" I began.

He stretched out his hand. "Give it me."

"Here."

"No—come nearer. Are you afraid of me?"

"I was, when you were angry. And you're the King, after all."

"Yes, I'm the King," he said, with a dreary laugh. "Poor devil! Do you know—can you guess—what it's like being a king?"

"I can imagine."

"You're too far away still. Come and sit by me."

"I'll sit on the floor," I said, and knelt down beside him.

He put his hand on my hair. Another long silence fell. Then he began to speak—slowly at first, hesitating for a word, contradicting himself every now and then. I leant back against his knee, and listened. . . .

3

The story that Nikki told me was an old one. It is to be found in the history of many countries. The heir, the adored only child, grows into a handsome, charming young man, with ideas and ideals of his own, and forms a following with liberal views. Thereupon his father's doting love turns to hate and jealousy; his mother—in this case Queen Elena saw her opportunity to take all the power into her own hands—foments the discord. When Nikki came of age, he was denied such freedom as he had already enjoyed, and sent for six months' "military training"—a euphemism for imprisonment— to a dark, deserted old fortress in the mountains. There, sick for his home and his friends, disillusioned, rebellious—in fear, some- times, of his life—he ceased to be the Prince Charming and came back an embittered, desperate man. His mother—on whom above

all others he depended—had failed him. She never came to see
him; she had used his absence to win over his weaker friends to
her side.

Then he met Marta, and they fell in love. He turned, with all
the frustrated passion of his ardent youth, to her beauty, her tenderness, her devotion. He defied his father's prohibitions and, with
Marta, left Murania for twenty years, giving up his rights to his
cousin Cyril. They wandered about Europe, happily enough. But
his was a difficult, stormy, fluctuating temperament, and Madame
Karillos sometimes had her hands full. "I wasn't even faithful to
her," he said, "but she was in my blood, I suppose."

That was all he told me of her then. Of course, I felt a pang; but
at least he was with me now, and not with her. Soon we should be
married. And when he discovered that I was the girl with whom he
had got on so well, surely things would come right. I was very
innocent. I came to the conclusion that he had been unfaithful to
Marta because he wasn't really in love with her.

But there was another side to the story that I found much more
upsetting, and that was Nikki's relationship with his mother. It
puzzled me. He spoke of her in such an odd way—disrespectful,
affectionate, ironic.

I began to say something about her looks, and he interrupted me
with an impatient exclamation.

"Oh, she's been a beauty all her life—if there's anything she
cares for more, it's power," he said bitterly. "And she's devoted to me
too, of course—yes, she's a wonderful mother." After a pause he
added thoughtfully: "She has a large heart—Mamma. It's like the
kingdom of heaven, a place with many mansions—or perhaps it's
more like a fashionable restaurant, with a great many *cabinets parti-
culiers.*"

I was too bewildered to question him. The wine was finished; he
was sobering down; but the top layer of his reserve was gone. And
the fact that I was a stranger and that we might never meet again—
for I had told him that I was going back to my own country to be
married—made me the perfect repository. I should not be there
when he came to himself and realized how much he had given away.
(I had some scruples over this lie, but they didn't last.)

All these considerations came to me gradually, later on. As I
listened, I was thinking of one thing—how to make him stay with
me. I couldn't see beyond the next minutes; they were going by so

quickly. Nikki continued to speak—in halting, broken phrases—of his mother.

Then I began, as I thought, to understand. In fact, Queen Elena was a charming, if rather frivolous woman; but I didn't at once realize that she was also a power-maniac, and something of a Messalina. Not for a year together had she been faithful to her husband, whom she treated with good-humoured indifference. Once, when he was seventeen, Nikki had discovered—how, he did not tell me— her way of life; when he turned his eyes away, revolted and speechless, she laughed in his face.

"She reminded me," he said slowly, searching for words, "of those pictures of the patrician ladies of Rome, watching the defeated gladiators sprawling in their own blood on the sand. I told her so, and she said something about an unconscious tribute, and looked in the glass. And I flung out of the room. I shan't easily forget that conversation."

Long afterwards, when my last illusion about Nikki was taken from me, I remembered it too, and used it as a guide. Now, recalling it again, I see that his treatment of women—and of myself, among others—sprang from a fierce and undying resentment of his mother's behaviour. Nikki was no Orestes—but the Furies were behind him, now and again, urging him to revenge his mother's attitude on other, less fortunate women. This was his fate, and his torment. And he suffered as much from self-disgust as from the disappointment of a man who has been trained for a unique position, and is then denied it. I see all this quite clearly now; then, as he told me about it in harsh, elliptic sentences and derisive allusions, I thought of Queen Elena as wicked but clever, and of him—I was sentimental, blind, and naïve, like most girls of my age—as a martyred hero, a crowned and sceptred victim of circumstances.

It would be for me, I had decided, to bring him happiness and peace. He had wanted a son—he told me so. "Of course, he'd have been a Prince—but to me he'd probably have been just a son," he had said. I said nothing about daughters—though I couldn't help thinking that Nikki was being rather *exigeant*—and at last silence fell.

We looked at one another. Then, softly at first, music welled up from below the window. Some men were singing a love-song, one that I knew. The creeping, wailing, wistful melody filled the room.

Nikki started to his feet. I went towards him. The lamp had gone out, and moonlight was streaming through the window. He turned, and I saw his face, lit by that icy radiance. He burst out laughing; the sound froze my blood, and I buried my face in my hands. I felt as if I had lost everything—what had happened? Why had he suddenly turned against me?

4

"Good God!" he exclaimed, shaking with laughter. "Why do you look so horrified? Those are my serenaders—serenaders under her window. You see, I was going to do the thing properly. Why, aren't you enjoying it?" He came nearer, holding out his hands.

I shrank back. "I don't understand . . ."

"Don't you? The press will—and my mother. Ah; that's the Italian manner! Guitars—moonlight—swooning, sentimental music— the whole filthy——"

"Don't!" I burst out. "You were so kind—now you're horribly frightening. Please . . ."

The music poured into the room with the moonlight. We stood looking at one another.

"Are you crying?" he said abruptly.

"No—I——"

"Most women's tears flow as easily as that," he said, in a gentler tone, with a gesture towards the window. "Why won't you let me come near you?"

"I will—only——"

"Well?"

"I must know—please tell me——" I broke off; my lips were shaking, my hands, clenched behind me, were like lumps of ice.

"Haven't I told you enough?" he said, with a hard smile. "You've heard my life-story. What more do you want to hear?"

"Do you—do you love Marta Karillos?" I said at last.

I just managed to force out the words; as I did so the song throbbed to a crescendo, and my voice was drowned.

"What did you say?"

"Do you love Marta Karillos?" I repeated, in a harsh, strained tone.

"With all my heart and soul."

The words sounded like a knell. I turned away; there was one stupid sob that I couldn't keep back. The music was softer now. He put his hand on my shoulder.

"Are you answered?"

"No!" I said sharply, speaking very fast. "I wasn't thinking of your heart, or your soul—what have I to do with them?"

His hand dropped to his side. "What an extraordinary girl you are," he said softly, amused. "How old are you? Eighteen, or eighty?"

"Don't laugh at me!" I burst out. "Answer—tell me!"

"You mean, I suppose, am I faithful to her? I've told you—I've betrayed her many times. Why do you ask?"

As I looked at him hope rose within me. "Couldn't you betray her once more—with the Princess?" I said, in a hoarse voice.

"We shall marry—no getting out of that—and go our own ways," he replied, a little impatiently.

"And—the heir?"

"Oh, yes—well—he must be an unrealized hope, for the moment. If my bride has got any sense she'll betray me with a handsome equerry—I shan't object to his doing my work for me."

Now we were so close to one another that I could see my own face mirrored in his eyes.

He put his arm round me. "Don't you think that's a good plan? I've only just thought of it."

"I can't hear anything but the music now," I said.

My head dropped on his shoulder.

He laughed softly. "Take no notice of it—it's only part of the mixture. Music—moonlight—Tokay—the cheapest spell in the world. Listen to the words they're singing . . ."

"I don't understand them—tell me what they mean."

"'If This Were Love . . .'" He took my head between his hands, and stared at me. "Well—perhaps it is. One kind of love. Do you know about it? Or are you as cold as your countrywoman?"

"I—I might be."

"I don't think so, somehow—but if you were? As cold as the Ice Maiden—what then?"

"I might freeze you to death."

He held me at arm's length, and his look darkened.

"Now you look like your portrait," I said, trying to smile.

"What game are you playing?"

"No game," I said, in a whisper.

"How can I tell?"

"Feel my heart—it's beating so fast that I can't hear the music any longer."

"Yes—I see. So I'm to make love to you, am I?"

"Do what you like—only don't—don't . . ."

"What?"

"Don't look at me—don't let me see . . ."

"I'll shut your eyes." He kissed my eyelids. Then he kissed my lips.

Suddenly my heart seemed to stop beating. The music sobbed and died. Nikki picked me up in his arms and carried me over to the sofa.

"One kind of love"—for me it was the first, the best, the only kind I had ever known. In the tempestuous, breathless darkness there came a moment when he realized that, and murmured the reassurances, the endearments, that one gives to a frightened child. Oh, Nikki, my darling, my own, only love—you were neither as selfish nor as gross as you would have had me believe . . . how could I be afraid?

Slowly the moonlight faded from the painted walls and sunrise boiled over the edge of night. And the tender colours of the dawn paled before the violence of morning. The supremest joys are not savoured, but endured. So I, yielding to an ecstasy of passion, and sinking thereafter into a spellbound languor, and rising again to the delirious onslaught of a love that would not be denied, bore longing and delight and pain for the first time.

It was broad daylight when he bent over me to say farewell. "Good-bye, Astrid—don't forget me. I shan't forget you."

I smiled, and pushed back the hair from his forehead. Our lips met in a long, quiet kiss. When he had gone, I fell on my knees and thanked God that nothing could take those hours from me. If I were to die now, I should die with the gift of happiness in my hand.

Later, when I had slept and eaten and had had time to think, I knew the certainty of triumph. In a few hours Nikki and I were to meet again, at the ball. I should no longer be the stranger he had dreaded and despised, and so he would forgive me the trick, because he would understand—none better—the motive and the desire that lay behind it.

Now I belonged to him completely. Marta, the past, my supposed demands, his resentment—these were all part of the night-wrack and the storm. It was morning at last. The clouds were gone, and sunshine flooded the world.

CHAPTER FOUR

How I Spent the Day of the Ball

Nikki left me in the early hours of the morning.

I thought of Marta with luxurious and wondering pity. Well— she'd had twenty years of him. It seemed to me a fair allowance. Then I fell to reminding myself of everything he had said to me. At last I sank into an exhausted sleep. My dreams were amorous; in them I alone was loved.

Later on, when I had had breakfast and could bring my mind to bear on my engagements, I saw that for the first time since my arrival in Murania, I had what was very nearly a free day, allowing, that is, for my usual visit to Queen Elena. No doubt this had been arranged so that I might appear at the ball looking neither harassed nor fatigued.

I then wrote two notes—one to Queen Elena, asking when it would be convenient for us to have a private talk, and the other to Princess Cyril, whom I proposed to visit later in the day. I knew that there was no possibility of these engagements clashing, for Queen Elena would be sure to spend the hours immediately preceding the ball shut up with her masseur, her hairdresser, and her maids.

I was very anxious to establish myself with Nikki's family. True, I had already had a week in which to do so, but so much of that week had been wasted in pretence and anxiety that it seemed to me as if I had been speaking to them from a long way off and seeing them through a glass partition. Now, with my mind free and alert, my spirits at their highest, and the certainty of success in my heart, I could really begin to be on friendly terms with them. Surely when Nikki became aware that I was getting on well with his mother and his cousins he would find it easier to continue with the relationship that had begun, so to speak, from the wrong end.

Queen Elena and I had luncheon alone together—alone, that is, except for three footmen and a major-domo. None of them, she assured me, spoke a word of anything but their own language. Nevertheless, I did not feel able to converse on the subject that really concerned me until we were sitting unattended in her boudoir.

"Do you know, Christiane," she began, leaning back in her *chaise-longue*, "I've just had a note from Nikki. He really is going to be at the ball this evening. Oh, the relief! He's perfectly well again."

"I'm so glad," I murmured.

A wave of scent enveloped me, as she leant forward and put her hand on my arm. "I'm going to treat you as if you were already my own dear little daughter—I always wanted one, you know—and smoke a cigarette. It's my only vice. I daren't eat or drink much, because I'm vain enough to think my figure's worth looking after. By the way, my dear child—of course, you're as slim as a wand; but can you expect to remain so with such a very healthy appetite? I merely ask. Don't take any notice. Now, what was I saying?"

I had never seen a woman smoke before, and it took me a moment or two to get over the spectacle of my future mother-in-law lying back in a blue-grey cloud, her eyes half closed, her expression feline, but friendly. I wonder what my father would have said.

I began, in a hesitating tone, "When Count Vanescu came to our Court to make arrangements for my marriage, he spoke to me very frankly about—about Madame Karillos."

"Vanescu sometimes exaggerates. What did he tell you?"

"That you had in the past known her quite well."

Queen Elena contemplated me for a moment without speaking. She seemed to be making up her mind.

Then she said, in an extremely deliberate tone, "You never knew your own mother, Christiane, did you?"

"No, Ma'am. But——"

"That's so sad. I want you to think of me, if you can, as your adopted mother—will you?"

"You're very kind——"

"And, as your mother might have told you, married life can be
—oh! so difficult, sometimes."

It seemed to me that this was rather an arbitrary way of changing
the subject, but I said nothing.

She continued, twisting round to look at herself in the mirror:
"I wasn't happy with my husband. So I had to make a life of my
own. Nikki and I were the dearest companions—everything in the
world to each other."

I made a sympathetic murmur, and she went on: "So when he
fell in love with Marta I couldn't make an enemy of her, you see.
She was good for him. She kept him out of mischief, for one thing.
The temptations are very great for a young man in his position—
but you wouldn't know about that, of course."

"I think I can imagine."

"What a sensible little thing you are! Girls nowadays seem to
understand everything. Well—Marta was sensible too."

"Please go on," I said, as she seemed to be sinking into a reverie.

"You see, when poor dear Nikki ran away with her, I couldn't
just cut him off, could I? A few months later I visited him—in Nice,
I think it was—and, really, she was so very gentle and—and reassuring——"

"Is she still?"

"What do you mean?"

"When you last saw her, Ma'am—was she still gentle and reassuring?"

"Who's been talking to you?" she said sharply.

I gazed at her without speaking. "I really want to know," I said
at last, in a low voice. "Won't you tell me, please? I'm thinking—
after all, that's what I came here for—about the future. I want to
be an understanding wife, as well as a loving one. Please help me.
I've no one else."

She sat up, and looked at me for a moment. Then she put out
her cigarette. As the smoke that had hovered between us thinned
and cleared away she said briskly: "Very well. I saw her a month
ago. Cyril and I went to Paris. That was after the doctors told me
that my husband couldn't live for more than a few days. Nikki was
staying in a hotel near the Place Vendôme. She came in while I
was talking to him."

2

In the silence that followed, I looked at the ground.

"Is she still beautiful?" I said at last.

"You wouldn't think so," said Queen Elena, rather amused. "She's over forty, and of course that must seem to you——"

"She's younger than he is?"

"I believe they're much of an age." She paused, a little embarrassed.

"Please tell me what happened then."

"Oh, well, Nikki was in one of his moods that morning. It was nearly midday, and there he was not shaved, and in his dressing-gown; but he was looking very handsome—very." She sighed. "I told him about his father, and begged him to come back. 'You're an idol still,' I said. And—well—he has rather a satirical way of talking sometimes, and—I don't mean that he was disagreeable, of course——"

"Perhaps he'd been up late, and was tired."

"Yes—I expect that was it," she said, with a faint smile. "He would go back over the past—his father's treatment of him—his own liberal views. By the way, Christiane, I hope you won't encourage him in all that nonsense—dangerous nonsense, it is really. We don't go in for democracy in Murania—it doesn't do. However, I expect Nikki's abandoned all that by now."

"In Norseland we're——"

"Oh, my dear, that's *quite* different. I assure you, if we'd listened to Nikki there wouldn't have been any sort of a life for us. Our people have to be kept down. And they wouldn't appreciate privileges. They're barbarians."

As I looked at her, I remembered what Nikki had said about the patrician ladies of Rome; it occurred to me that she might have been able to trace her descent from one of the great families of that cruel age.

"Did he speak at all about politics?" I asked.

"Very little. He knew perfectly well that if he'd insisted on staying where he was, and Cyril had taken over, there'd have been civil war. That was partly why he decided to come back. Poor dear

Cyril behaved very well, I must say. By the way, he's taken a great fancy to you, Christiane."

"He's been very kind. So has the Princess."

"Poor Anna—she does put on weight so. I said to her, 'Anna, if you don't take trouble over your appearance, you can't expect to keep him.' I suppose you've guessed that that's not a very happy marriage."

"I had heard——"

"The truth is that the Orosvars are not monogamous. Of course," she added hastily, "I'm quite sure that Nikki's really longing to settle down. But you will have to be a little patient at first."

I looked at her, and then at the decorations of the room, which was of fairy-like, glittering elaboration; one or two small gilt tables were covered with knick-knacks, enamel boxes, models of animals in semi-precious stones, miniatures, mother-of-pearl hand-mirrors, fans with diamond handles. Suddenly I felt submerged and stifled; I decided to speak out, and put up with the consequences.

"You mean I shall have to shut my eyes to Marta Karillos? To the villa on the Hervat Road?"

Queen Elena sat up and stared at me. Then she said, in a shocked voice, "Christiane! Have you been listening to some horrid gossip?"

"No. I know where he has been this last week—that's all."

There was a short silence. "Oh," she said softly, leaning back again. "I see. Yes. But I must beg you, my dear child—what you said just now was a little bit vulgar."

"I'm sorry. What I should have said was that I understand. I have no resentment—no bitterness—against Madame Karillos."

"Haven't you, indeed?" she said, very gently, looking at me from under her eyelids, much as Nikki had. "You're a most remarkable girl, I must say."

"Is she—I suppose she's a very clever woman?" I went on, after another pause.

"Marta? Not exactly clever. She's quiet and domestic."

"Did he ever—did they think of marrying?"

"At one time I believe they did. But—well—not to put too fine a point on it, that really wouldn't have been safe. You see, when they ran away, it was Marta who got all the blame. And Nikki was afraid. 'A live Marta is better than a dead one,' he said to me once. That was just his way of putting it——"

"Do you mean that she might have been murdered?"

"Well—it was *just* possible. There's a fanatical streak in our people, you know."

She was looking away from me. I leant forward, and saw her smile; she didn't know I was watching her. In that smile I perceived her amusement at her own very neat version of Marta Karillos's danger. I guessed then, and rightly, that if Nikki had married Marta he would have lost her, and through his mother's agency.

It wasn't really much of a shock, after what Nikki had already told me, but it deprived me of speech for a moment or two. Queen Elena went on talking.

"You see, Nikki wasted twenty years in exile—twenty years of futility, he called it. His father—really, Nicholas was a most difficult, tactless person—said to him the last time they met, 'I shall outlive you—don't think you'll ever get back.' And in a strange, superstitious way Nikki believed him. 'I really thought he'd live forever,' he said to me, that time in Paris."

"But didn't he see his father at all before he died?"

"Oh, yes. But Nicholas was unconscious by then. Dear me—that was a very trying few hours. I kept on thinking he might come to and curse Nikki with his dying breath, or something equally *outré* and impossible. However, he didn't. He just ceased to breathe, without a word or a sigh. Then Nikki said such an odd thing. He got up from his knees, walked over to the window, and said, 'So the job's mine. Can I do it? Perhaps it's too late. We'll see.' And of course the Archbishop was there, and I'm sure he heard—oh, it *was* awkward. There's no doubt about it, the Orosvars are a most eccentric family."

"Had he already sent for Madame Karillos?"

"Now, Christiane, let me advise you. It's a great mistake to dwell on these things. We all hope you're going to be very happy here. And you will be, if you make up your mind to be sensible. After all, you'll have everything," she added, in a pathetic tone. "I shall just sit in a sunny corner out of the way, and watch you both making a splendid success."

"The sun will always be in your corner, I think," I said; and in a way I meant it. Whatever else she was, Nikki's mother could never be boring.

She laughed, as delighted and amused as if she had never received a compliment in her life, and we began to talk about the ball. I was not to be announced until everyone, including Nikki, had arrived. Then the music would begin, and he would open the ball with me. Queen Elena had already seen and approved of my gown.

"I'm sure you'll look quite exquisite," she said, with the sincerity of one who has never for an instant doubted her own charms. "Oh, and there's one other thing. Shortly before the ball you'll receive a bouquet of flowers, with the betrothal ring of the Orosvars, from— that is, on Nikki's behalf. Between you and me, dear, it's *hideous*. But never mind. I'm giving you a nice cabochon emerald to make up. Now, what flowers would go best with your gown, do you think? I always prefer to see to these things myself."

"I think, white roses——" I began.

Queen Elena's expression changed completely. For the first time since I knew her, she looked both nonplused and alarmed.

"Oh, no, Christiane," she said faintly. "No."

"But——"

"You must forgive me, but really, you know, in Italy white roses —well they're only used for funerals. They mean—now don't think me superstitious, but I can't help feeling that would be a little ominous, for a first meeting. Be a dear good child and think of something else. I hope I don't sound too silly—but I do want you and Nikki to meet in the happiest possible way——"

"Please—any flowers will do," I interrupted, between confusion and amazement, and she smiled and patted my hand.

"I only thought of white roses because we wear them so much in my—at home," I added.

"Of course—but you're not homesick, I trust?"

"Oh, no, Ma'am—not in the least."

3

The conversation at the Old Palace was quite different, and much less interesting. Princess Cyril had a mania for lapdogs. Vera and I had to shout at her above the yapping of three pekinese, two griffons, and a spitz.

The Prince was late. When he came in, he kicked the dogs out of the room and sat down without looking at his wife.

"Well, Countess Vera," he began, as soon as the preliminaries had been interchanged, speaking with heavy jocosity, "are you looking forward to your first Muranian ball?"

"My dancing days are very nearly over, sir," said Vera composedly. "And in any case, a Court ball . . ."

"Far from being a pleasure, eh?"

"Well, sir——"

"It will be the first time I have ever danced round dances in public," I put in, as Vera showed signs of becoming embarrassed.

"I shall have the pleasure of leading you out for the second round dance—a polka, I believe," said Cyril, adding, with a leer, "I'd rather it was a waltz. More swing and less spring, if you know what I mean."

"Countess Vera and I have got to the chaperone stage," said Princess Cyril, with a nervous smile. "I dare say we shall find ourselves looking on together."

"I suppose the King is an excellent dancer?" I asked, in the pause that followed.

All day I had been testing myself by bringing in Nikki's name with what I hoped were the correct inflections—timidity, eagerness, humble enthusiasm.

"He used to be—when he was a young man," said the Princess. "It's a long time since he attended a function of this kind."

"They bored him then—they won't now," added her husband, with another meaning look in my direction.

"I do hope he'll be well enough to enjoy himself," said Vera, in her warm, motherly voice, and there was a short silence, broken by Princess Cyril, who suggested that the young Prince Michael should be sent for.

"You haven't got to know each other yet, Christiane," she added, when she had given the order. "He's asked about you a great deal. 'Mother,' he said, 'do you suppose all that hair is her own?' He's rather a noticing child."

"Talks too much," his father put in. "Spoilt and greedy. Otherwise he's a fine little chap."

At this point Prince Michael came in—or, rather, burst in, a flustered tutor at his heels. He rushes up to the tea-table, treading on Vera's train, and exclaimed, pointing at me: "Aha! There's the new cousin! The one you said was going to put all our noses out of joint!"

"Sir—your jacket," came in a whisper from the tutor, now crimson with confusion and shame.

"Be quiet. It isn't lesson-time. Mother, can I have one of those?"

"You haven't said how-do-you-do to Cousin Christiane."

"Oh," He turned and sketched a bow, seized my hand, and implanted a damp kiss on my forefinger. "How are you? Have you brought me a present?"

"Now, Michael——"

"If you haven't, it doesn't matter. Next time will do. Mother, can I have that cake now?"

"Yes, dear. You may leave us, Mr. Kohary."

"I say," the boy went on, as soon as his tutor had disappeared, "do you know what? I heard something very funny about Cousin Nikki. Perhaps you'd like to hear it, as you're going to marry him?" turning to me.

"Tell me."

"Michael, dear, don't speak with your mouth full——"

"Don't nag the boy, Anna—you're always nagging——"

Now the centre of attention, Michael fixed his eyes on me, sniffed, scrubbed his hand over his nose, swallowed, and announced: "He wasn't ill at all. He was hunting, in the Racovitza Forest."

"I know," I said, with a bright smile. "Don't you wish you had been allowed to go with him?"

Michael looked at me, and then went on, in a snuffling monotone: "I was with Great-Aunt Elena when she was talking about it to Madame Varsov. 'He's a madman,' she said. 'One gesture—that was all that was expected of him.' What's a gesture, Father?" Glancing at his father's empurpled countenance, he continued, without waiting for an answer: "I don't like Cousin Nikki. He smacked my head last time he came here."

"Hold your tongue, you young ruffian," said his father, now rather delighted. "I expect you deserved it. What did you do? Come on, now, tell us."

"Cyril, I don't think——"

"Anna, how many more times must I tell you not to *nag* the child!"

"I said," Michael went on, his shrill voice rising above his parents' asides, "I said, 'Why don't you live in the Palace, now Great-Uncle Nicholas is dead? Don't you like it? It's much nicer

than that house on the Hervat Road. Why do you always go there?'
And *he* said, 'How the devil do you know I always go there, you
little beast?' And *I* said, 'Because I heard the grooms talking about
it,' and then he smacked me. But I didn't mind. I kicked him, quite
hard. And then Mr. Kohary came in and took me away."

We had all listened to this monologue in fascinated horror. Michael glanced round at us, and then, without a second's warning,
plunged his hand into the centre of a cream cake, tore out
the greater part of its semi-liquid contents, and stuffed them into his
mouth. His father seized him by the arm.

"Put that down, sir—do you hear me?"

"I can't."

"Put it *down*, I say!"

"I can pull it out—some of it, at least," Michael expostulated. "I
can't put it down, though—it's too soft."

"Come here, darling, and let me wipe your mouth and hands,"
his mother interposed.

Prince Cyril was roaring out, "I will *not* have the boy babied,
Anna," when his aide-de-camp came in, bowed, and announced the
arrival of Count Vanescu.

"Of course—we asked him to call," said the Princess distractedly.
"Oh dear me—now, Michael, if I let you stay down here you must
be a good boy and not interrupt the conversation; do you hear me?"

"All right, Mother," replied Michael; he was now sticking out
his leg with a view to tripping up the nearest footman.

Vera exclaimed, "Your Highness, be careful—you'll hurt yourself!" and snatched back the offending limb before the mischief
was done.

Vanescu's manner of dealing with Prince Michael was quite mas-
terly, and no doubt the result of long practice. When his bows had
been made, and he had been waved to a chair and given a cup of
tea, he evidently found himself rather too near the youngest member of the party. He asked, with charming courtesy, whether he
might move away from the window—his rheumatism had been
troubling him a little, and he could ill afford to be incapacitated at
this pleasant moment in his country's history (this was said with
a bow and a smile in my direction). Having moved into a zone of
comparative safety, he fixed in his eyeglass and gazed, with severe
amazement, at the young Prince, as if he could hardly believe his
eyes. Then he removed his glance, and began to converse in meas-

ured and pontifical tones about the arrangements for the wedding, which was to take place in a fortnight's time.

"Mother"—the irrepressible whine penetrated at last—"I don't want to be a page. Why must I be?"

"Ask the Count, darling," replied the Princess, in a low voice—it was plain that this branch of the family was very much in awe of the Prime Minister.

"It will be your duty, sir—unfortunately," said Vanescu, with a glacial smile.

"But why? I don't *want*——"

"Not to put too fine a point on it—and we in Courts must accustom ourselves to the increasing bluntness of speech as now used in the outside world—it will be expected of Your Highness," said Vanescu, speaking as if to a man of his own age whom he neither liked nor respected.

The contempt and frigidity of his manner had the desired effect. Michael spoke no more. Presently he crawled under the tea-table and bit Vera's ankle. She gave him a sharp kick, but before he could cry out, Vanescu, who had been watching him out of the corner of one cold blue eye, rose to take his leave, and somehow managed, with a flow of compliments and speeches delivered in the sonorous voice he used for public pronouncements, to drown the whines and mutterings of the unpleasant little creature.

"That child!" exclaimed Vera, as we drove away.

"I know," I replied, in an abstracted voice. I was thinking about something else.

4

As soon as we had turned out of the avenue that led up to the Old Palace, I said: "Pull the check-string, Vera. I want to change our route." As the groom came to the carriage door, I went on: "Dismiss the outriders, if you please. I wish to return to the Palace through the Old Town."

"But, Your Highness——"

"Are the streets too narrow for the carriage to get by?"

"No, Your Highness."

"I will take all the responsibility. Please do as I say."

"You're attracting a good deal of attention as it is," said Vera, in a low voice. "Is it wise?"

"I've only been allowed to drive through one part of the Old Town. It's the side-streets I want to see."

"We should never get through."

"I know, Vera, darling. But I want just to look down them."

"The crowds won't be very——"

"We must get used to crowds different from those we knew in Norseland," I said, putting my hand on hers.

That was the first time I saw below the surface of my new capital, famous, then as now, for the beauty of its baroque buildings, its fountains designed after—rather a long way after—Bernini, its little medieval churches, its long avenues of plane trees.

I'd never seen a slum in my life, until then. There weren't any in Norseland. I have wondered since whether the filthy hovels, the stinking gutters, and the holes in the eight-hundred-year-old fortifications of the original city in which the poorest inhabitants now made their homes and their playgrounds attained the uniformity, the comparatively mild degradation, that the name implies. It was impossible, as Vera had pointed out, to proceed through such places as these; but I had a look at them, and at the people fated to live there. This was the part of his heritage that Nikki had tried to change. I understood now why he had chosen to run away rather than to contemplate, helplessly, this festering sore on the body of his kingdom. I remembered his mother's careless "Our people have to be kept down," and the dazzling luxury of her idle, useless existence.

One or two ragged creatures crept out of their lairs to stare at us, and there was even an attempt at a cheer; but I was glad that I didn't know enough to understand their comments and exclamations. On the whole, I was received with the indifference of hopeless misery.

"We shouldn't have gone there," said Vera, as we turned into the residential quarter once more, and the carriage was followed by a mob of cheering, stalwart young people, mostly of the bourgeois class. "Queen Elena will have something to say about it, I'm sure. And Vanescu."

"I shall tell them—tomorrow," I said, with a sudden lift of the heart.

Tomorrow—by then Nikki would know that I was on his side

over this tragedy, as over all the others. I seemed to see the days that were to come in a radiant haze. Tomorrow! Tonight! Both words were magical. As I ran up the great staircase to my private apartments, they rang in my ears like a peal of bells. How busy— and tired and disappointed, sometimes—Nikki and I were going to be!

Then I forgot everything as I came into the boudoir and found on the centre table an immense bouquet of pale pink roses, a shade deeper than the ball dress that was laid out for me in the room beyond. Attached to the flowers was a small round golden box. In this lay the betrothal ring.

It wasn't ugly at all. It wasn't even archaic or heavy—just a broad, thick gold band with a huge ruby in the centre. On this some words were engraved. But I couldn't read them, and neither could Vera.

"Shall I send for Countess Varsov?" said Vera at last. "She's waiting in the anteroom to know if the flowers——"

"Yes, ask her. She came to Murania with Queen Elena—she'll know."

Countess Varsov, a majestic, plump lady, came in, curtsied, and bent over the ring.

"The inscription is in Greek, Your Highness. The ring was taken from the dead hand of the Princess Athelmé after the victorious siege of Retmos, in 1492. The reigning Orosvar—King Paul II——"

"Please tell me what the inscription is, Countess. I know the story."

"Yes, Ma'am. *Everything Leads Me to Thee.* It was the Princess Athelmé's wedding ring. Her husband was killed in the siege by King Paul himself."

"Thank you, Countess. How appropriate that it should be a ruby."

"Your Highness?"

"Oh—and the flowers are perfect. Will you tell Her Majesty how grateful I am?"

When she had gone out, Vera and I stood looking at the ring. "Well, they have some funny ways here," said Vera finally. "He should put it on your hand himself, surely? An engagement ring?"

"It isn't their custom," I said dreamily; I was hardly listening.

"Well, it's very handsome, I must say. I meant to tell you—the Prime Minister asked me what flowers I would like for my bouquet, and I chose white roses."

"White roses?"

"You see, I'm wearing my lilac dress, and I thought . . ."

"It doesn't matter." I was still looking at the ring.

"Christiane . . ."

"What?"

"I keep thinking—about last night. Should I have told you? Will it—has it—made you dread this evening?"

"No, my dearest, kindest Vera. Nothing can do that. I'm not even thinking of Madame Karillos—now." And I suppressed a smile. "Please believe me."

"You're a wonderful girl, Christiane—a good girl. Your father would have been proud of you today." And, with a tremulous embrace, she left me to dress for the ball.

Two hours later, dressed in pink and silver, and wearing the tiara that had been the gift of the City of Bledz, I stood waiting. I heard the music die away as my name was called. Vera was trembling. I found myself strangely self-possessed—lifted, as it were, above agitation and doubt, into the empyrean. Now the moment in which I was to bring joy and reassurance to the one I loved best in all the world was before me.

The curtains were drawn back. "Her Royal Highness Princess Christiane!"

I stepped forward into a blaze of light, and walked to the centre of a dais. I was looking down onto a mass of brilliant and variegated colour. Uniforms, jewels, lights, gold and silver tissue, satin and velvet, smiling, expectant faces, the sooty blackness of Court dress, the gleam of women's hair, the glitter of their feathers and trains, the chalky pink and white of their arms and bosoms—all this made a pathway to one figure in a dark, plain uniform, standing beyond the rest, alone.

That was how I imagined he would be—motionless, haughty, not smiling, barely interested. For another few seconds I was still to be the enemy, the stranger.

The trumpets blared. There was a rustle, and a gentle creaking and clinking, as those bands and circle of colour and light bent before me. Over the top of his courtiers' heads I looked at him. I walked slowly down from the dais and came towards him. He did not move. I went on, until I was within the prescribed three feet, and then sank away from him in a long, billowing curtsey.

As one released by a spring, he came smoothly forward and raised me. He kissed my hand. We were looking at one another. It was as if we were alone. All those myriads of watching faces faded away . . .

Everything Leads Me to Thee.

CHAPTER FIVE

How I Learnt My Lesson

IT SOMETIMES HAPPENS that in a moment of great excitement the power of observation is not heightened but enfeebled. So it was with me, as I stood facing Nikki in the centre of the throne-room. By some reversion of thought that I cannot attempt to define, I had before me the images of my little cousins, Hulda and Kirsten. I kept wondering what they would have said: how they would have behaved. I suppose the fact was that I had reached a state of tension where it was no longer possible for me to be aware of what was happening to me, or to Nikki; I was looking at him through a mist, and had passed the stage where anything he did or said could surprise me.

It was therefore with a curious dead feeling of acquiescence that I heard him say, in a low, contemptuous tone, "Exquisitely done!" Sarcasm, bitterness, rage, disgust—all were there: but I could not take them in. I was still gripped by the mood of triumph and happiness in which I had anticipated this climax. I stood there with the smile that training had engendered pinned to my face. I must have looked pretty silly, and thus appeared all the more infuriating to a man who had been fooled. Complacent—that was how I must have seemed to Nikki. I can't, now, conceive of a less propitious meeting.

He pulled himself together almost immediately, and continued, in a formal, icily courteous manner, "I regret that my illness has prevented my meeting you before, Princess."

Those nearest us—some dozen or more people, among whom

were Queen Elena, Prince and Princess Cyril, Vera, and Vanescu—were now listening with the same bland geniality of expression with which I had greeted his first words. I realized later that this general assumption that everything was going off spendidly must have enraged Nikki still further. He added, in a louder voice, "Or may I call you—Astrid?"

It was then that I began to feel frightened, and to have a dim awareness of some ghastly blunder. I replied, however, with a fatal attempt at pleasantry, "As you wish, Sir—but, as my name is Christiane, I may not hear."

As soon as the words were out of my mouth I saw myself as a saucy, *gauche* schoolgirl, trying to assert herself. And the worst of it all was that I had never seen Nikki looking so handsome. His beauty—and, as beauty in a man is rarer than in a woman, so it is more startling and unforgettable—pierced me to the soul. His attitude made me feel as if a mine had blown up beneath my feet.

He turned a little away from me, and said, "Strange—I could have sworn that your name was Astrid."

"Christiane, Sir." I was incapable now of anything but a faint repetition.

"How odd," he went on, after a short pause, contemplating me with controlled hostility, "that we should meet in public for the first time."

I didn't take in the implication. The reply, "Not at all; it's generally so with people in our position," was in my mind; but I could not utter it. I saw that he was now so angry that he could only speak at random, as a man whistles a tune when he is engrossed with some difficult task.

Nikki was occupied in preventing himself from striking me across the face, or turning on his heel and leaving the ballroom. He went on, in the same harsh, mechanical tone, "We must be unique in history."

I tried to say something. No words came. I knew that it was impossible now to hope for a gleam of amusement, of tolerance even. I felt as if I had been thrown back against a wall. Then I perceived Vera's rigorously controlled alarm.

Apparently determined to drive home every single aspect of my impertinence, my degraded folly, Nikki continued, on a note of rising disdain and bitter mockery, "Have you brought no *entourage*—no charming maids-in-waiting?"

"Only one, sir," I said, in an extinguished voice. "Countess Le-menken—may I present her?"

"But of course," he said, as Vera came forward. "And she has come all the way from Norseland with you? What devotion! Welcome to Murania, Countess. We hope you will stay long with us."

"Your Majesty is too gracious."

"Sir——" I began.

He turned on me. His hands were shaking so violently that he had to clasp them behind him. All this time the murmur of those who had arrived, full of loyalty and devotion, for a party of pleasure, encircled us.

He said, in a much louder voice: "Why so formal? Surely you know my name?"

"Oh, yes," I said faintly. "As well as you know mine."

There was a frozen silence. If only he would stop smiling, I thought, I could bear it; I could try to establish some kind of understanding, however momentary and hollow. But that vulpine smile of disdain, that caricature of courteous attention to everything I said, that mocking bend of the head, were gradually sapping my resistance. In another moment I should have dropped my fan and bouquet and screamed or fainted. He made me feel as if I were naked.

Suddenly Queen Elena was beside us. I could see that she was agitated. Her glance fell on my bouquet, and she shrank back with a gasp. Mechanically I looked down. In the rush from our apartments to the anterooms I had picked up Vera's bouquet of white roses. She was holding mine. It was the last straw, the last incongruous stupidity.

Queen Elena said, in a distracted manner, "My dear child, you look quite ravishing—doesn't she, Nikki?"

"Oh, yes," said Nikki coolly. "But then I never knew a Princess that didn't—officially." He bowed and smiled, as if he were teasing me, being gay and charming, but I felt the anger behind the words, and a lump came into my throat. I said nothing; I think I managed to smile.

Then suddenly I remembered that I had a defence—one that might perhaps be turned into some sort of a bond between me and this furious, dangerous creature. During the next few minutes the thought of it helped me to be calm: outwardly, at least. Some days before, I had made a plan to get Nikki's sympathy and liking, and my spirits rose again as I realized that this scheme was now on the point of fruition.

With a desperate effort, I made a movement towards Count Vanescu, who was hovering about our group. Prince and Princess Cyril had left it, and were the centre of another. Vanescu, looking, for him, extremely perturbed, made me some compliment—I think it was about the number of public engagements I had managed to get through during the last two days, and how I had acquitted myself—and we began to converse.

Nikki and Queen Elena were just behind us. In the distance music began, softly, rather as an accompaniment to sociability than as an invitation to dance. As Vanescu and I went on talking, in a subdued yet artificial manner, I was able, by means of a pause here and there, to hear most of what Nikki and his mother were saying. She was so upset, and he was so indifferent, that they did not pitch their voices very low. They spoke rapidly, interrupting one another, as people do in the midst of an argument in which bad temper is conquering discretion. During this interlude all four of us smiled and bowed and murmured a word here and there, as we received the greetings of the guests, who had begun to circulate from one royal group to another. My conversation with Vanescu became an undercurrent to Nikki's with Queen Elena.

2

"Mamma, you are looking incredibly beautiful."

"Then I must have iron self-control. My face should be distorted with rage."

"*And, as I was saying, Ma'am, to His Highness Prince Cyril, a new face, and, if I may add, a beautiful one . . .*"

"*My father wouldn't approve of all these compliments, Count Vanescu. I was very strictly brought up, you know.*"

"Hasn't everything gone as you planned it, Mamma? I might not have turned up at all."

"What can you have against Christiane that you should so humiliate her?"

"*It is common knowledge, Ma'am, after a week's stay, that your upbringing must have been very exceptional.*"

"*You're very kind.*"

"What could I have against her?"

"Have you no consideration? Your first meeting—and, I should think, your last."

"My last?"

"*Yes, His Royal Highness Prince Michael suffers perhaps from being an only child . . .*"

"Oh, Nikki, you're impossible—worse than your father."

"Old swine."

"I will not have your father called old——"

"*Indeed, it's all delightful, but rather bewildering. You remember, Count Vanescu, what a very simple little affair our ball at the Summer Palace——*"

"Listen to me, Nikki, I command you! How could Christiane stay if she found out——"

"Found out what?"

"This appalling insult. That creature might have had the decency——"

"Who? What are you talking about?"

"She could have pleaded illness——"

"*In my country the music—I mean, for an occasion of this kind——*"

"Stop pretending, Nikki! I shall go mad! Do you deny asking Marta Karillos to the Palace tonight?"

"Marta? Here? I never ask Marta to official receptions; they bore her almost as much as they bore me."

"Are you speaking the truth?"

"*We shall look forward to seeing you open the ball with His Majesty—an historic moment.*"

"I always speak the truth; it saves time."

"Nikki!"

I could bear no more. I went up to Nikki and began, in a rush, "Sir—I—took the liberty"—he raised his eyebrows, but desperation had driven me beyond terror—"of sending an invitation to a very old friend of yours—someone I don't know, but someone I feel I should know."

"Well?"

"Christiane——"

"Oh, Ma'am"—I turned from one to the other—"I didn't want her to be left out—Madame Karillos."

"It was you—*you* sent her an invitation?"

"One moment, Mamma," interrupted Nikki, in an unnaturally calm tone. He motioned me to stand a little aside, and went on, speaking very low, "What did you say?"

"Madame Karillos, I hear—I mean, I know, that she is an old and devoted friend . . ."

His smile became perfectly dazzling. "And you asked her here—tonight?"

"Did I do wrong?"

"How could that be? I feel quite sure that you've never done anything wrong in your life."

"Oh, please—I would like to think that—that any friend of yours would be a friend of mine."

He stood back and looked at me, and again I had the feeling that all my clothes had been torn off and that I was standing in the teeth of an east wind. "Really? I'm afraid that you and Madame Karillos would have very little in common."

I was by now perfectly reckless with misery. "If she is a friend," I stammered, "I shall be happy. If she is an enemy——"

"Are we suddenly acting some kind of melodrama? Why should she be an enemy?"

"If she is—I shall at least know whom I am fighting."

He laughed. The diamond star of the single order that he wore quivered and glittered, as if reflecting his cold and merciless amusement. "I warn you—it would be a losing fight."

"For whom?"

"For you."

"Then I hope——"

"Oh, you hope, do you?"

"—that I shall learn to take my defeat gracefully."

For the first time, he seemed a little taken aback. "You are very direct," he said at last, in a negligent manner, as if I were a tiresome child that had been thrust upon him.

Queen Elena was beside me again. Once more I became aware of the music and the lights, of the throng of curious, elegant guests moving about us. I realized with a gasp of relief that Nikki and I appeared to be talking constrainedly but amiably, and became conscious of warm glances, sympathetic smiles, admiration, congratulation—in fact, of all the elements that should have been carrying us along together. For one terrible moment I looked back at yesterday night—and it was as if I were peering down at some hideous travesty of our two figures, locked in one another's arms, writhing in a death-struggle. . . .

Queen Elena was speaking.

". . . and there are several people who would like to be presented."

"The Princess," said Nikki, speaking deliberately and incisively, "is very anxious to meet one of my oldest and most devoted friends—Madame Karillos."

A figure moved forward from a group near by, and stood before me; then it sank to the floor. Mechanically I put out my hand.

Nikki's voice rang out, as if to make certain that everybody's attention was on us. "Princess! May I present—Madame Marta Karillos."

"Your Royal Highness . . ."

I drew myself up, and handed that unfortunate bouquet to Vera. The heavy scent of the roses was beginning to make me feel sick. Then I looked at Marta Karillos—and knew that I was defeated.

3

She was dressed in white and silver, and her silvery-golden hair was like a crown; perhaps that was why she wore no jewels but a diamond-and-turquoise necklet and earrings—such hair as that would have looked absurd under a tiara. This comparative simplicity made her conspicuous enough; but what struck me first was the gentle composure of her manner, her low, caressing voice, the kind smile she gave me as our eyes met. Ten years ago her beauty might have been more dazzling, but it could not have had the nobility, the distinction, that I now saw. I knew—I could see—her steadfastness, her quality, from that first moment, and I became defiant and cold, because I also knew that I couldn't hope to compete with her.

But it was, after all, to please Nikki that I had engineered her invitation: so I spoke warmly—and I don't think the warmth was entirely assumed.

"Countess, I am so happy that you were able to come. I feared that my invitation might have got to you too late."

The sweetness of her look was like a dagger in my heart. Ah, if only she had been my friend, and not Nikki's mistress!

She said: "I was charmed to receive it, though a little puzzled. I didn't know Your Highness knew of my existence."

"But of course," I said, feeling a good deal easier. "Even in Norseland. In my country we are always delighted to receive beautiful artists—they're so much more clever and amusing than we are. Perhaps if you could find time to visit me again, we might have some music?"

There was a little gasp from Queen Elena.

Nikki struck in, in what I can only describe as a very nasty manner, "I have heard that you sing."

"But only as an amateur," I said, smiling at him. "I'm sure Madame Karillos could teach me so much."

In the pause that followed, I realized that I was no longer speaking naturally, or even pleasantly. I turned to Madame Karillos. She was looking at me with a wondering expression. Then for the first time I realized that she might have been jealous of me.

She said, very gently indeed, "I think, Your Royal Highness, that I could teach you—nothing."

Now I knew that I was surrounded by enemies. I said desperately: "Couldn't you? Not even—endurance?" and turned away from her.

Then Nikki was beside me. I saw that he was still very angry. "Are you by any chance proposing to manage my life?" he said evenly.

I resolved to make one last appeal. "Oh, no—no—but——"

"Well?"

"I should like to make it—easier."

"You have already made it intolerable."

I stood there, silent and abashed. Vera came up to me, and, on a pretext of giving me back my bouquet, touched my hand.

Then I heard Queen Elena say to Madame Karillos, "You have just arrived?"

"A few weeks ago, Ma'am."

"Are you staying with us for long?" said Queen Elena, very coldly. "Or are you settling your affairs before returning to Paris?"

I turned, and saw that the victim was quite unruffled. "I settled my affairs in Paris before returning to Bledz," she said calmly.

"And won't you find it very quiet here?" went on Elena, in a bullying tone.

"I have my own circle of friends, Ma'am."

"Which you have deserted for tonight. How sad they must be."

"If I receive a royal command, Ma'am, I can only obey."

"You've been obeying royal commands for far too long," said Queen Elena, in an outburst of pettishness, but even this did not shake Marta's poise—if only she could have spared some of it for me!

"Ma'am, may I assure you that I was deeply touched at being asked tonight—and extremely surprised?"

"Then you should have had the good manners to refuse," said Queen Elena viciously.

Marta paused; then she said, with a slight tremor in her voice, "I think, Ma'am, I am not the only person in this room tonight who suffers from lack of manners."

"Vanescu," said Elena, "escort Madame Karillos to the ball-room." And she swept over to me and murmured, "My child, you were mad to invite her—but you behaved with great dignity."

During the course of the next few minutes I perceived that Vanescu had returned to the throne-room; I wondered vaguely what he and Marta talked about when they met, which couldn't, after all, be often. I noticed also that he seldom left Queen Elena's side; then I heard her say to him in a low voice, "Who is that extremely good-looking young man in the Royal Guard uniform?" I didn't hear Vanescu's answer; but a moment later Queen Elena and the young officer were standing together. It was evident that he knew what to say to her; she looked quite radiant, and was flirting her fan, in the manner of her generation.

"Who is he? Do I know him?" I said to Vera.

"Count Egon Stanieff—no. But he was in attendance two days ago—do you remember?"

"He is good-looking, isn't he?" I said, with an effort.

"I heard the Queen telling Vanescu to find him some more duties in the Palace," Vera replied, and I laughed. Already I was feeling a certain relief from the strain of forcing back my tears.

The music swelled suddenly into a waltz. Vanescu came up to Nikki, who was standing in the middle of a group of young officers, and said, in his most sonorous, formal manner, "I think, Sir, they are waiting for you to lead the dancing."

I was aware that Marta Karillos had returned from the ball-room. Instinctively I handed my bouquet to Vera. Nikki looked across the room and saw me do so. Then he said, without taking his eyes from my face, "Madame Karillos!"

"Sir?"

"Will you honour me?"

Then at last I saw her gentle calm broken and destroyed. She shook her head and whispered something. He took her hand and said, very clearly and deliberately: "The Princess is on duty. She has to be gracious to a hundred people. I am sure she will forgive me if I am gracious to one."

Still she seemed to be resisting. "Please," said Nikki, in the same cold, deliberate tone. Then, without waiting for her consent, he swept her hand under his arm and walked away with her. I looked after them. Everybody was staring at me.

Before I could quite take in what had happened, Queen Elena had presented Count Stanieff to me. I looked at him dully, and thought what a nice-looking boy he was, and wondered what I should say to him.

Rather red in the face, he blurted out, "If Your Highness is dancing—may I have the honour?"

Still feeling as if I had been knocked on the head, I gazed at him dumbly. I tried to speak. I was afraid that when my voice did come out, it would crack. After several blundering beginnings, I said something about his being very kind.

He began to speak, and then stopped himself. The people standing near us had fallen back, all except Vera, who whispered anxiously, "My poor child, you're as white as a sheet—can't Count Stanieff get you anything?"

"I'm all right," I said, speaking as if we were alone. "It's just that I meant to do the right thing. I thought he would have seen that. But he didn't."

Poor Count Stanieff—I heard afterwards that he was only a year older than I, and that it was his first Court Ball too; he was looking almost as miserable as I felt. Vera went off on somebody's arm, and we were left alone.

I looked up at him helplessly. "You're very kind," I said, as if I were repeating a lesson.

"Not kind!" he burst out vehemently. "Blind with fury. I——"

"Please!" I said, with a slightly hysterical laugh. "This isn't—I mean, emotions are out of place here."

"How can I help you? What can I do for you?" he said, in a low voice.

"Talk to me," I said, in the same tone. "If you talk and smile, and I smile—oh dear—it's all gone wrong! What was I saying?"

"We are talking," he said, with a blush. "Everything's all right. If Your Highness were to sit down, I could stand between you and ——"

I sat down, and looked up at him. Yes, he was kind.

"You can't stand between me and my destiny," I said, with a faint smile. "Never mind. I shan't cry now. I dare say everyone's saying how—how gay I am. Or how insensitive."

"They'll never say that," he declared. "Never."

I opened my fan, and looked at him over it. Again the incongruous recollection of Hulda and Kirsten was in my mind; surely they would have envied me if they could have seen me trying to flirt with this handsome young man?

"Oh," I said, wishing my hands wouldn't tremble so, "I have a champion. I never thought I'd need one."

He clapped his hand on his sword-hilt. "There's not a man in this room that wouldn't run him through the heart for that insult to you."

There was a long silence. Suddenly I began to despise myself for that attack of self-pity. I stood up.

"Count Stanieff," I said, attempting a smile, "you're talking to your future Queen."

He didn't seem very much abashed. I think at that moment we both forgot our respective positions and suddenly became friends, as one does sometimes in unhappy situations. He looked at me consideringly.

"So it's true—what people say," he said slowly. "You are in love with him."

"Is that what they say? Already?"

"Oh, well—it's just that one hears—I mean——"

"If they ask you, you can tell them the truth."

"Your Highness?"

"Will you take me into the ballroom? You asked me to dance just now," I said, getting up and taking his arm.

We progressed slowly through lines of curtseying and bowing courtiers. In the centre of the great archway, decorated with lilies and roses, I turned and looked at him; then I said, "Yes—I am in love with him. Tell them so, if they ask you."

4

As we danced, Stanieff and I, I saw Nikki and Marta standing in the embrasure of a window. She seemed to be trying to reason with him; his anger had evidently cooled, but he was, as I afterwards discovered, in one of his most recalcitrant moods. Then he looked across the ballroom, and our eyes met. His face darkened. He took Marta by the arm, and they walked out onto the balcony.

Agonizing though my situation was, it might have been worse. Nikki might have been indifferent, uninterested; that would have killed such hope as I had left. His anger at being, as he thought, trapped, and by a chit of eighteen, was preferable to a total lack of feeling.

And it was fortunate that I had not been left alone with him. That would have been unendurable. If he disliked me so much that he couldn't even stay in the same room with me—well, it was at least something that I had been able to make him aware of me.

So I consoled myself; but it was a wretched business altogether. I danced with Cyril, with Vanescu, with one or two other elderly and, I suppose, pitying, wondering courtiers. Later on I was escorted back to the dais in the throne-room, and a number of slightly less important guests were presented to me. Then it was time for supper.

Was I now to receive the final, the crowning insult? I was prepared for it. But Nikki, who had been, as far as I knew, alone on the balcony with Marta for nearly an hour, came forward with an impassive face, and offered me his arm.

As the trumpets sounded he led me to the canopied dais on which our table stood. It commanded a view of the whole room, and of the E-shaped design of the other tables, that were set out with gold plate, decorated with crystal bowls of orchids and lilies, and backed by walls covered with brilliantly coloured mosaics, of which the designs, as far as I could see, were Byzantine in origin and feeling.

Queen Elena, Prince and Princess Cyril, Vanescu, and Vera were seated facing the rest of the room on either side of Nikki and me. Shortly after the first course had been served, my conversation with Cyril died away. I turned, and saw that Nikki was looking at me, with a relentless, inimical stare.

"I wanted to thank you——" I began, forcing myself to speak naturally.

"What for? What can I possibly have done to deserve such a thing?"

I moved my left hand, so that he could see the outline of the betrothal ring underneath my glove. "For this."

"Ah, yes!" he said coolly. "My mother, I remember, always used to complain that it was too heavy. I imagine you won't find it so."

"It's very curious—and beautiful too," I faltered.

For quite a long time he said nothing. His expression was remote and severe. Then I saw that the pulse just above his temple was throbbing. I knew that he was still very angry; but I hoped that his anger might have been touched by compassion.

"I haven't looked at that ring since I was a child—and I haven't the least desire to do so now," he said at last.

After that I did not dare speak again. It seemed to me that we sat there, horribly conspicuous, ostentatiously silent, for a long time. Nikki had been staring at the tablecloth. Suddenly he turned on me and said, with the hard, dreadful smile that he seemed able to assume when he liked, "Please don't imagine—will you?—because I'm engaging you in what passes for conversation, that I want to do so. We're on show. We must talk, and with apparent amiability, if it can be managed. Are you fond of music?"

Nothing could have been harder to bear than this—or so I thought at the time. I didn't know what was to come. I could not answer for a minute or two. Then I muttered, "I used to be."

"I understand you are extremely accomplished. What do you enjoy? Perhaps private theatricals are more to your taste?"

"I know," I began, after another painful silence, "that I've made a terrible mistake. But I meant—it wasn't——"

"Please don't look so serious. This is a festive occasion. Have you forgotten?"

"If you think," I said, turning to him with a smile that was a pale reflection of his own, "that you're going to make me break down and cry, you're mistaken. I'm past that."

He laughed. Those sitting at the table just below looked up at us, and interchanged sympathetic smiles. Queen Elena, who must by now have become aware that everything was not as it should be, interposed with a question, and the conversation became general.

For the first few moments I heard nothing that was said. Then I realized that Princess Cyril was asking me something.

I leaned forward, and she repeated, "Do you know Mornavitza?"

"No. Is it far from here?"

"Far enough to make your honeymoon a real rest. It's on the coast, nearly thirty miles from Bledz. The castle has been restored, but it's still very fine."

"I look forward to seeing it," I said.

"So do I—with you . . ." Nikki struck in, and a look of approbation ran round the table. His tone was such that I couldn't make any comment; but I suppose my downcast eyes and burning face looked quite bridal, from the point of view of the outsider. He went on, turning to his mother: "How did you find it, Mamma, all those years ago? You've not been there since your own honeymoon, have you?"

"Oh, it was charming—charming——" Queen Elena began.

"My father was taken ill there, just before he died," said Nikki to me. "He found Mornavitza a pleasant change from the rush and bustle of the capital. But he had to come back here to die, of course."

"Nikki!" put in Queen Elena, in a low, protesting tone.

He looked across at her, and said something in Italian. She turned her head away, and answered him very shortly; then a smile crept over her face, and they both laughed.

This secret interchange was yet one more sign of hostility. Long afterwards I asked Vanescu what those brief, rapidly spoken phrases meant, and he told me, although unwillingly. Nikki had said, "By the way, did my father die a natural death?" and his mother answered, "Why, of course—my own doctors attended him." To this he had replied with a laugh, in which she could not prevent herself from joining.

They were an odd pair, Nikki and his mother; and the oddest thing about them was that they seemed to enjoy drawing attention to the half-embittered, half-affectionate understanding that existed between them. Nothing they said to one another—whether evasive, satirical, or tender—was completely sincere. I had the feeling, long after that first terrible evening, that they were merely going through the motions of an intimate relationship, and that neither trusted the other. The mingling of the Orosvar and Bourbon-Parma strains had resulted, in this case, in an acid and scalding brew, from which the fumes of angry derision, half-forgotten hatred, dead love, old dependence, and long-standing irritation inevitably arose.

The banquet went on, with the heavy and implacable succession of courses that was the custom of the day. After some three hours of it I was just beginning to get used to the sound of Nikki's arid banter and jerky attempts at general conversation, and to feel that I might begin to hold my own, when the signal for the toasts was given. A huge golden loving-cup was set between Nikki and me. He drank, and handed it to me; our fingers touched as I grasped the handle and raised it to my lips. I didn't look at him. I had ceased to be able to do so. I just sat there, motionless and shining—like a doll in a shop-window. "Royal and Radiant"—that was how the newspapers described me on that occasion. Another editorial was headed "The Melting of the Snow Princess," I remember, with the sub-title "Love Conquers All." Well, I suppose it did, but not quite in the way they meant. As Nikki rose to answer the congratulatory speech made by Vanescu, he fixed his eyes on Marta. She was sitting opposite him, in the middle of the table facing the dais.

During the whole of his speech Nikki never once removed his glance from that silvery-golden figure. He spoke of the honour that had been done him and his countrymen by an alliance sealed, as he believed, with my tenderest love, and his lasting devotion. He spoke of the long and weary exile from his home, of his unexpected return, and of the wonderful happiness that awaited him. He spoke of his plans for the future government of the kingdom, touching momentarily and lightly on reforms of which no single member of his audience could possibly approve, in a faintly ironical tone. He spoke of the welcome already given to the young Princess from the Far North, and of the admiration that he now shared with his people for his bride. He spoke—and this was, I think, the worst moment in all that fearful evening—of my youth, my beauty, and of the sacrifices I had made in coming almost unattended to be his wife. And all the time he never once ceased to look at Marta Karillos.

Then the whole company rose and drank to us. There was a deafening, splintering crash as some five hundred glasses were thrown back against the wall. The wine was red, I remember; and here and there the women's dresses and the men's uniforms were dashed with a crimson stain.

As the cries of "Vivat! Vivat!" rang out, Nikki turned and looked at me. His eyes shone with triumph and revenge. I sounded then all the depths of his hatred and his rage. But there was something else in that blinding, terrible look, something stranger and more frightening than his anger. I know now that it was desire.

CHAPTER SIX

How I Became a Queen

You SEE HOW IT IS, Christiane," said Queen Elena two days later. "No one listens to me. I've argued this point for more than forty years—haven't I, Vanescu?"

"Yes, Madame."

"Economy!" she went on, throwing up her jewelled hands. "If I so much as mention another tiny estate, or a diamond necklace—the Orosvar diamonds are negligible, quite negligible, and they go to the Princess, anyway—I get a scolding. But when I suggest to the King that he should stop this idiotic custom of breaking some five hundred crystal goblets for a single toast—and it's bound to have an effect on those mosaics in the banqueting-hall in the long run——"

"If I might suggest——" Vanescu began.

"You can suggest anything you like. My son will take no notice."

Vanescu stood up, and, shading his eyes with his hand, looked across the gleaming stretch of the water-garden that separated us from the Palace. "Here is His Majesty," he said, in a tone of relief. "Shall I inform him that Her Highness is with you?"

"Is he alone?"

"Count Stanieff is with him."

Queen Elena leant back with a smile. She and I, with Vera and Countess Varsov, had been walking about the gardens, and were now sitting in a marble summer-house—a sort of Parthenon in miniature—set at the top of a slope. Just below a stream, bordered by forget-me-nots and kingcups and bridged by a rustic arch in honey-

coloured stone, followed a deviating course towards the great artificial lake at the foot of the gardens.

It was almost impossible to believe that we were in the midst of
the capital. The breeze that had sprung up as the shadows length-
ened and the long, hot afternoon faded into dusk was gently shaking
the flowers and the topmost branches of the trees that backed the
temple. That faint rustling, the sound of the brook, and the distant
murmur of Vera's and Madame Varsov's talk—they were sitting
some yards away at the foot of the slope—were beginning to soothe
me into an exhausted acquiescence; but the spell broke as soon as I
knew that Nikki was near. I had been sleeping very badly again, and
I could not help starting whenever I was taken by surprise.

I did not do so now, partly because I was always on the watch
in Queen Elena's company—for her mockery, or her kindness.

"Be so good as to tell him where we are," she said languidly. "I
have no doubt that he is looking for the Princess."

Vanescu glanced at her for a moment without speaking.

"Shall I inform Count Stanieff that you wish to see him also?"
he said coldly.

"Stanieff? Oh, yes—that boy whose father I used to know. If you
like."

"It is as Your Majesty likes."

Queen Elena sat up. "Don't you approve of him?" she said, in a
provocative tone.

"I hardly know the young man."

"Well, you soon will. He is to be attached to the Princess's household."

It was the first I had heard of it; but I was chiefly interested at
that moment in the spectacle of Vanescu's ill-concealed jealousy,
and in Queen Elena's deliberate encouragement of it. Had Vanescu
once been—was he still—her lover? I didn't know, and I didn't much
care; but the realization that I was considering such a possibility
made me feel as if I had left my home ten years, rather than nearly
ten weeks, ago.

Vanescu and Queen Elena went on talking; I did not listen.
Nikki was coming nearer. I could hear the sound of his voice, then
his laugh, then an exclamation of "My dear fellow, I assure you——"
and Count Stanieff's "No, Sir, indeed——" as they walked across
the lawn and paused on the far side of the stream.

Nikki was about to cross the bridge. Then he saw us, sitting in the shadow. He turned, leant back against the parapet, and began to talk to Stanieff in a low, rapid tone. Stanieff, who had spoken of him so bitterly but forty-eight hours since, was now plainly entranced by his informality, his assumption that they were both men of the world, his rather caustic gaiety. As Nikki finished his story, he joined in the young man's laughter.

As soon as they had crossed the bridge, I got up. Nikki stopped me halfway through my curtsey, in the approved manner. He was looking at his mother.

"Did you want to speak to me, Mamma?"

"Yes."

"Alone?"

"I think—perhaps——"

Vanescu bowed, and, with Stanieff, walked down the slope and along the stream. I moved towards Vera and Madame Varsov.

"Christiane, this concerns you. Sit down, child."

"You look deeply serious," said Nikki. He leant back against a colonnade, pushing his hand through his hair. "I hope you're not going to break some terrible news to me."

"No, no——"

"Such as," he went on, looking over our heads and rattling off the words, "the failure of M. Worth over your toilette for the wedding——"

"Of course not——"

"Or the collapse of your hairdresser under the strain of designing a new——"

"Nikki, don't be——"

"Or of your masseur. By the way, he's new, isn't he? One of our people, by the look of him."

"He's a Swede," she interrupted impatiently. "If you would just——"

"Rather a good-looking fellow, I thought."

"Nikki! Do stop——"

"Well?"

"I want to speak to you about tomorrow. About the presentations in the City Hall."

"I know about them. They're going to be endless. I think I shall make one of those boyish speeches, this time. I'm rather tired of the majestic vein."

"Please, please be serious. Christiane will get such a bad impression . . ."

"I hope not. That would be disastrous, at this stage," he said insolently.

His eyes flickered over my face. I thought he seemed a little ashamed of himself, nevertheless; but he was now more of an enigma than he had ever been.

The arrangements for the next day were discussed for some time. I spoke when I was spoken to, which wasn't often. Queen Elena was now fully aware of Nikki's treatment of me; she had decided to ignore it, and rightly—what else could she have done?

In the midst of a rather plaintive speech from her about the broken goblets, he struck in with "By the way, Mamma, don't interfere with my allocation of those three hundred seats in the North Gallery, will you?"

"What are you talking about?"

"The wedding. The Cathedral."

"The Chancellor's Secretary said something about your inviting some peasants—but of course he gets everything wrong."

"Well, he's right for once. Each village is sending a representative——"

"Are you mad?"

"Don't be rhetorical, dearest. It's too hot."

"Nikki! How can you? Do you want to be assassinated on your wedding-day?"

"Not particularly. Why?"

Queen Elena burst into a stream of protest. Then for the first time he looked at me and said—quite simply, without the shadow of a sneer, "What do you think?"

2

I lost my head in my anxiety to say the right thing. "I think it's an excellent plan. In Norseland we always——"

He turned away. "Ah! in Norseland everything's perfect. By the time you have been here ten years or so, perhaps Murania will have got within a stone's throw of the ideal."

Queen Elena began to smooth things over—rather too markedly. He interrupted her by saying, with a return of his taut, icy smile:

"Everything will go off perfectly, Mamma, don't worry. But let us get one thing clear." He paused.

"Of course, dear. Go on."

"I mean, odd though it may seem, to be master, not only in my kingdom, but in my home. Is that understood?"

"Naturally——"

"If you"—he paused again, and glanced at me—"if you interfere in any of my schemes—I shall have you killed."

"Ah, that's my boy talking!" she replied, without a moment's hesitation and smiling radiantly. "You're so like your father sometimes."

They both burst out laughing; this characteristic parry and riposte was one of their forms of relaxation. To me the whole episode was detestable, not so much because it savoured of swagger and bad taste as because it rang so false—at least, that was what I thought then. No two people whose relationship had ever been happy could have spoken to one another as Nikki and his mother sometimes did. A few moments later I left them together. They were still laughing as Vera and I walked across the water-garden towards the Palace.

During the next ten days Nikki and I attended many public functions. At all of them he behaved with a modicum of correctness, only speaking to me when everybody was looking at us, and then in the most distant and uninterested manner. I was so miserable that I should have been glad if, at the end of any one of those days, I had been told that I should not live to see another. But I never thought of going home, or of making a scene—my training had made either action impossible. I did find it necessary at last to tell Vera everything; she was getting so worried about me that her health was affected. Her reception of my news was less horrified than it might have been.

"Any knowledge—however dreadful—is better than being kept in the dark," she said. "But oh, Christiane—how could you? Brought up as you have been——" And she prepared to dissolve into tears.

"Don't, Vera, darling. It's done now."

"My own little girl—I can't bear to think——"

"You aren't going to tell my father?"

"My dear child, it would be the end of him," said Vera, reverting to her practical manner. "He'd think we'd both gone off our heads."

"Sometimes I feel as if I had."

"But, Christiane—how *could* you? How can he, whatever he may have done, respect you after——"

"At least, he can't discount me."

"I can see that he doesn't do that. Sometimes he looks at you in such a very odd way; so——"

"How?"

"I can't explain. I never met a man quite like him. Oh, dear! Perhaps the honeymoon will bring you together."

"I can't imagine it—either the honeymoon, or the being brought together."

"Christiane—you've changed so terribly!"

"You mean, I'm no longer——"

"Don't dear—don't speak like that. You're not a child any more—that's all I meant. I must try not to treat you as one."

There was a long silence. Then I said, in a stifled voice: "He makes me feel as if I didn't exist, except as a figurehead. Perhaps that's all I was meant to be."

"I still think—in spite of everything that's happened—that you're fitted to be a queen. And I can't forget that it was I who in the first place persuaded your father——"

"Never mind about that. It's being a wife, not a queen, that I worry about, Vera. What's going to happen? In three days from now we shall be married."

"I shall always be with you."

"Yes—you and Astrid. You're coming to Mornavitza."

"Who is he taking?"

"One equerry, and his old body-servant, Giulio."

"That Sicilian creature?"

"Yes. Have you seen him?"

"Once."

"What's he like?" I said, after a pause.

"Devoted—much too familiar—limps, and waves his arms about all the time he's talking. I think he drinks, too."

"You saw him with Nikki?"

"Only for a few minutes. I should have been rather touched if I hadn't felt that everything was going wrong for you."

"Giulio's the only person who has any real influence over Nikki," I said, after a moment's reflection. "The Queen told me so. Even Marta Karillos can't get round him as Giulio can, I believe."

The next day I was able to verify the truth of this rumour during

the course of an extremely painful half-hour. The royal apartments
—Nikki's and mine—had been tastefully redecorated for our marriage. Now we had to make a formal tour of the rooms together,
accompanied by the Steward of the Household, two other Court
dignitaries, the Palace architect, his chief decorators and upholster-
ers, and—inevitably—Giulio, who considered this sort of thing to be
within his province.

He was much as Vera had described him—tall, stooping, voluble,
paunchy. He had been with Nikki for more than thirty years. He
was, of course, an old villain—I knew, for instance, that he stuck at
no lie when his or his master's convenience was in question; but he
was friendly—and that, in those days, meant a good deal to me. He
knew Nikki's situation with regard to me, as he knew everything;
long afterwards I discovered that he had taken up a protective attitude towards me, partly because he had always been jealous of
Marta. Nikki indulged him to an extraordinary degree; they always spoke to one another in Italian, using the *tu*, gesticulating,
sometimes shouting like a couple of peasants. And the only thing
that seemed to disturb Nikki's sardonic calm during the last days
before the wedding was his servant's disapproval of the disposition
of his rooms. I understood Giulio to be complaining that there was
no place near enough to the State bedroom in which he could sleep.

"The valet's bedroom is here—I have shown Your Majesty just
how——" the architect began offendedly.

Giulio interrupted with a flood of complaints in his own tongue;
he understood several languages, although he was obdurate about
speaking anything but Italian.

Nikki began to explain, in what seemed to me a strangely mild,
almost self-exculpatory tone. Giulio shrugged his shoulders and
walked away. Nikki turned to the architect and said abruptly, "You
must make a rearrangement of some kind."

A violent and slightly absurd discussion ensued, in which I took no
share, although Giulio was gazing at me hopefully from beneath his
wrinkled eyelids.

"Thank Heaven Mamma isn't here!" said Nikki, in an undertone
to me; as I smiled and murmured something sympathetic, he looked
coldly away.

During the last phase of the argument both Giulio and the architect turned to me. I shook my head, and referred them to Nikki. He
took Giulio by the arm, led him aside, and seemed to be calming him

with the reassurances he needed. As they came back I heard Nikki say something about *"la Principessa,"* with an almost friendly glance in my direction.

Giulio threw up his hands. "Ah! *poverina!*" he exclaimed. There followed a phrase I didn't understand, and then he repeated, *"Poverina, davvéro!"* shaking his head at me with a smile.

The attendant officials were shocked and disgusted; but my heart warmed towards Giulio. For one thing, I couldn't but agree with him; and it was rather comforting to feel that someone who loved Nikki could also be a little sorry for me.

3

By the time the question of Giulio's room had been settled, the worst of the tour was over. It had one advantage, in that it showed me a side of Nikki's character of which I had not hitherto conceived—his interest in the arts, and his taste in literature.

During our progress through the apartments it became clear to me that the father's collection of pictures had already been sifted by the son, and that the crude and amateurish products of the local artists and portrait-painters were to be superseded by the Canalettos and the Bouchers of which the elder Nicholas had made a specialty. Ignorant as I was, I found the Canalettos a trifle uninteresting; but the lush exuberance of the huge Boucher canvases appealed to me, and I ventured to say so.

Nikki paused in his inspection and looked at me, his eyes half closed. "You're rather like a Fragonard yourself," he said abruptly.

"I'm afraid I never saw——"

"There are none in any of the private collections here, or in the galleries," he said, in his most impenetrable manner.

A little later, when he was engaged in discussion with one of the plasterers—a Neapolitan, who with half a dozen others had been brought to Murania for this work—I wandered back to Nikki's own sitting-room, and began to look round the bookshelves that lined the walls. Most of the contents were in French—history, memoirs, a few novels, a little poetry; there was also an English section that included a number of volumes of old plays. I took one out at random and turned over the pages. It looked rather stiff and dry, and I didn't much care for the relentless beat of the rhyming couplets or the un-

couth names of the characters. Abdelmelech—Ozmyn—Almahide—
Lyndaraxa—what sort of archaic personages were these?

A door shut behind me. I turned, and saw Nikki standing at the
other end of the room.

"I'm sorry," I faltered, "I was just looking——"

"Do you approve of what you see?" he said, with an ironical
glance.

"I didn't know——"

"That I ever opened a serious book?" he said, as my voice died
away. "Odd, isn't it? But there you are."

His tone was puzzling—not friendly, nor even very approachable,
but contemplative, faintly amused. "What have you got there?" he
continued.

Speechlessly, I held out the book, as if to keep him off. He took
it, and opened it in the middle.

"Yes," he said, after a pause, "there's something rather applicable
here."

"Applicable?"

"This scene, where the false Lyndaraxa—you've heard of her?"

"No—of none of them. I found it all rather mystifying."

"Did you?" he said indifferently. "This bit is quite clear." And,
leaning back against the shelf, he read, in a low voice:

> "No, Lyndaraxa; 'tis at last too late:
> Our loves have mingled with too much of fate.
> I would: but cannot now myself deceive:
> O that you still could cheat, and I believe!"

There was a long silence. At last I ventured to look at him. He
was staring at me with raised eyebrows and a bitter smile.

"I'm no Lyndaraxa—I haven't the experience," I began, in a shaking voice. "But if I ever cheated——"

"If!"

"It was because I—because . . ."

"Well?"

"Because I wanted to—to please you."

He laughed shortly. "You're like all the other women I ever met—
except one."

"What do you mean?"

"You may, as you say, have wanted to make some sort of an impression. Well, you did, so you can be easy in your mind about that.

But you also wanted, like all your kind—the respectable, well-brought-up kind—to tie me down."

I had no answer to this; I was trying to assimilate his thought, and it was hard for me.

He shut the book with a snap, and went on fiercely: "All my life women have tried to get hold of me, to worm themselves into my privacy, my freedom, to claw out everything I had to give—money, power, admiration, flattery. My mother began it when I was six years old. God! how I——" He stopped short, and turned away.

"None of this—nothing that you say—has anything to do with me."

"Certainly it has. You're not content with being a queen—oh, no, you must have my life to play with as well! You cheated me—made a fool of me. Possession—that's all your sort have ever cared for. Well—you'll never possess me. I'm an old hand at this game, let me tell you. I know all the turnings."

"It wasn't a game."

"No? And yet I thought you played it so well—for a beginner."

"Don't speak to me like that!" I burst out, between rage and despair. "I've got nothing to do with the mess you made of your life. It happened before I was born."

"Yes—but you came in on your cue, with all the same notions that the others had. I'm to give up my life with Marta Karillos, settle down between you and my mother, and be a model king—the kind that floats along on the surface of the kingdom. This country—however, that's certainly nothing to do with you."

"But it has! I've seen a little of what's going on—the inequality, the injustice. I want——"

"You're amazing, really! You're just eighteen. And yet you believe in nothing but yourself."

"That's not true."

He was walking up and down the room, glancing at me furiously from time to time. "And how dared you have the impertinence to ask Madame Karillos to that ball? Do you think she had the least desire to be there?"

"I did it to please you."

"Go on! Go on! I see you're undefeatable."

I stood silent and trembling, my eyes on his drawn face. Even then, preoccupied though I was with my own torments, I was aware of his unhappiness, his desperation.

"Well—Lyndaraxa?" he said, in a low voice.

"Don't—I can't bear it!"

"What you can't bear is the realization that you've failed. Annoying—isn't it?—when one's plans go wrong?"

"I had no plans."

"Except to collect me, and keep me."

"No—no! I wouldn't have interfered between you and her . . ."

"Ah! 'Would that you still could cheat, and I believe!' I tell you again"—he stopped in the middle of the room and pointed his finger at me—"I know your sort. You're so predatory, so ruthlessly determined, that you'll stick at nothing. I've been fighting you all my life!"

4

I did not see Nikki again until the day of the wedding. The increasing pressure and complication of the arrangements preoccupied me, I suppose—because I don't remember sleeping quite so badly as before, or indeed, feeling quite so miserable.

At least he had declared himself; and though the misunderstanding between us could not now be cleared up, I might, in a quieter period, try to make him see that I had been mistaken rather than malicious. I hoped for something from the honeymoon; not his love— that, I knew, was all for Marta Karillos—but for comprehension, the beginning, perhaps, of friendship.

The wedding was to be combined with my coronation as Queen Consort. Both ceremonies were long, elaborate, and further complicated by shreds of the antique ritual that had survived through many centuries. Rehearsals were necessary. Nikki, rather to my relief, went through the movements required of him under the guidance of the Cathedral authorities, sending one of his equerries to take his part when it was time for me to be instructed in what I should do.

When the time came we played our parts well enough. In those days, and in that country, the bearing of royal brides tended rather towards stiffness and solemnity than radiant happiness. I moved as if under a spell throughout the creaking, involute ceremonial—kneeling, standing, sitting, turning from one side to the other, repeating my portion of the marriage service in a clear, steady voice. (That was what they told me afterwards.) Nikki, rather to my surprise, seemed more agitated than I; when he came to the penultimate, supremely ironic phrase, "With my body I thee worship," his voice was shaking. His hands too were unsteady. I wondered drearily where Marta Karillos was, and what she was feeling.

Then came the moment of my installation as his Queen. I knelt. He placed the golden circlet on my head, and, raising me, presented me to the people—to the privileged few, that is, in the Cathedral. I then knelt again, and, putting my hands under his, swore allegiance.

I would have given anything in the world during those few minutes to convince him of what I really felt, of what I had failed to say at that last dreadful interview. It was, of course, impossible to do so. Weighed down by my heavy robes, loaded with barbaric jewels, conscious that I was and must ever be the fated victim of political scheming, I did all that was required of me mechanically, and almost without feeling. As we came out onto the steps of the Cathedral, and the cannon thundered a welcome, I looked down, and saw, first the State coach; then the crowds of shouting, gaily dressed people; then, between them, the long, straight road that led from the Cathedral Square through the gates of the Old Town to the Palace. And, for a moment, I saw beyond those also; to the winding, uphill track along the coast, to the cliffs, to the castle where, after all these scenes of contrivance and artifice and display, we should be alone together, my husband and I. I was not yet broken, not yet utterly discouraged. There, at Mornavitza, we should surely come to an understanding; at the very least, be able to agree to differ.

Bowing and smiling, swaying forward with the movement of the coach, I felt my spirits rise yet a little more as the drive began.

Halfway through a salute, Nikki glanced at me, and said dryly, "More than a quarter of an hour of this is guaranteed to upset the strongest stomach."

"I don't mind it," I said hastily. "Do you?"

"I was trained to it. When I was a child my father was always making State progresses through the capital."

"Shall you?"

"Good Heavens, no." He was smiling quite charmingly as he spoke—but not at me. The cheers and shouts had become deafening.

After another thunderous interval, he went on, still apparently absorbed in acknowledging his people's tributes: "By the way—it was arranged, as you know, that we set out at four this afternoon for Mornavitza. We are expected there in time for supper."

"I know."

"That arrangement has been altered."

"By you?"

"By me."

For a long time he said no more. I went on waving my hand, and found myself contemplating it with frozen amazement, as if it were attached to someone else's arm.

"What have you arranged—about the honeymoon?" I said at last, in a voice I hardly knew as my own.

He did not answer immediately. I glanced at him sideways. His face might have been carved out of marble. Then he said, "I will tell you later on—when we leave the Palace."

CHAPTER SEVEN

How One Agrees to Differ

A WEEK after my wedding-day I was walking with Vera through the woods of Dhrevin, some twenty miles inland from the castle of Mornavitza. Behind us stood a small hunting-lodge, backed by stables, and surrounded by a vegetable garden. There was no other house within many miles. The events that led up to our installation in this deserted spot can be briefly told.

When the old-fashioned berline in which Nikki and I (accompanied by Vera and Nikki's equerry) were seated had taken us about a dozen miles beyond the capital, there was a halt. I looked out, expecting a change of horses: but we had stopped at a crossroads. During the whole drive we had sat, all four of us, in silence. Now Nikki descended from the berline and said to me: "Will you get out for a moment? I have something to tell you."

He then led me to the other side of the crossroads, where a slightly larger closed carriage was waiting. In a low voice he told me that it was best to part here and now, until the time came for us to return to the capital. Before I could open my mouth, he went on to explain that all precautions had been taken to ensure absolute secrecy. It would shortly be given out that he himself, insisting on complete privacy for his honeymoon, had carried me off to an unofficial residence of his own in the depths of the country; his people—those who could read the newspapers, and were in other ways in touch with what was going on—would be implored to respect his desire for peace and quiet and—he said this with a characteristically satirical inflection—the romantic aspect of our flight towards an unknown destination. In fact, he concluded, the carriage I now saw was waiting to take me to the hunting-lodge at Dhrevin, in the Great Forest. Here I should be surrounded by every comfort, and when a month had gone by we should meet in this same spot, and enter the capital as if we had spent our honeymoon in rapturous isolation.

I was sufficiently angry and disgusted by these arbitrary methods to walk to the second carriage without making a single comment, or giving Nikki the fraction of a glance. As Vera got in, I whispered to her to say nothing until we were on our way. When we arrived at the lodge, I found Astrid and those Muranians who had already been attached to my personal service awaiting me.

That night I slept as I had not slept for weeks. I awoke in a more vigorous, and as it were a harder, frame of mind. He did not want me —he never would. Very well. I could not cease to love him, but I must do without him. So I reasoned, not without many bitter pangs and paroxysms of grief and anger; yet I had enough strength of mind to adjust myself to my decisions.

So I came to Dhrevin. After one exhaustive discussion, Nikki's name was not mentioned by Vera or me. I was thankful to feel quiet and unmolested.

It was therefore with resentment and dread that on this walk with Vera, I heard Astrid's footsteps behind me, and her breathless "Madame! There is a message for you."

She was now beside me. I have not yet described Astrid. She was —she still is—so much a part of my life that I find it difficult to do more than enumerate her best features, which were then a pair of large dark eyes, a neat figure, and a brilliantly rosy complexion.

"Who is it?"

"Madame, it's Count Stanieff. He asks if he may wait upon Your Majesty."

"Where is he?"

"At the lodge, Ma'am. He asked if he might remain until you returned."

I looked at Vera. "Shall I see him?"

She hesitated. "He may have come from——"

"What difference does that make? I'll see him. Let us go back." I walked so fast that Vera had to run to keep up with me.

Count Stanieff was standing in the porch. As he kissed my hand I saw that he was very much agitated.

"Would Your Majesty have the goodness to see me alone?" he said, as soon as I had greeted him.

I nodded, and went before him into the little parlour. I sat down. He stood by the mantelpiece, looking at the ground. I saw then that he must have ridden fast and far, and was now at a loss as to how to begin.

"Well, Count Stanieff?" I said at last. "Have you come with a message that you're afraid to deliver?"

He looked at me for a moment in silence. "I don't know what to say to Your Majesty, and that's the truth."

"Whatever it is, I shall not blame you——" I began.

"Good God, Madame! Can you believe that I would take any message that would—that you might——"

"Please go on. Have you come by the King's order?"

"Partly—yes, Ma'am."

"What does he require of me?"

He flushed painfully. "Nothing. That is—he sent me to—to inquire after Your Majesty."

I laughed. "As you see, I'm in good health."

"Not only that; I can see that Your Majesty is more—more——"

"Well?"

"More beautiful—and perhaps a little less——"

"Unhappy?"

"Madame, I should not say these things . . ."

"You were very kind to me not long ago," I said gently. "I should like to think of you as a friend."

"And so I am—I am! If only I could——"

"You can do nothing in this matter," I said, as he broke off in distress. "Except, perhaps, to tell me how I stand. I mean, with regard to the people of this country. How many of them know, or guess at, my situation?"

"None, Madame. The few servants here are to be trusted."

"I can hardly believe——"

"Ma'am, they will hold their tongues. They know the punishment if they fail."

"I see. And the others? There must be some near here—villagers, woodcutters—who know who I am?"

"No, Your Majesty. None of the peasants about here has ever been near the capital. If they were to see you they would not know who you were."

There was a short silence.

"Well," I said at last, "that at least is something of a relief. But I still don't see why you were sent here."

"His Majesty was concerned——"

"Ah, no, Count Stanieff! I may have been a dupe, but I'm not an idiot."

"He wished—I am ordered to inquire as to Your Majesty's comfort."

"Thank you; I am well served. The lodge isn't damp, or draughty. There's plenty to eat."

"Your Majesty! If only——"

"Don't distress yourself," I interrupted, speaking in a less embittered tone. "It is not your fault; I am aware of that. You did not ask to be sent on this—mission."

"But, Madame, I did! Forgive me—but it was I who—I begged His Majesty to let me come."

"He told you I was here?"

"I—you see"—his embarrassment was pitiable, and rather touching—"I suspected—I saw—what was happening. I sought him out, and asked him if I might visit you, wherever you were."

"I don't suppose you had much difficulty in finding him," I said, in a low voice. "But why have you come? You can do nothing for me. Believe me, I am not ungrateful—but you have travelled a long way to no purpose. In a fortnight's time we shall meet again, in the capital."

He twisted his hands together.

"I had no right——" he began at last, in a hesitating voice.

"No right, perhaps, but a great deal of kindness," I said, forcing a smile.

"For God's sake, don't talk of my kindness! I'm in love with you! Can't you see that?" he burst out. He turned, and, leaning against the mantelpiece, buried his face in his arms.

Strongly moved, I got up and walked over to the window. Wounded myself—stricken, as I had thought at one time, to death— I felt a good deal of tenderness for one who was in almost as hopeless a position as myself. I turned, to see him looking desperately at me.

"I should not have said it. Forgive me—but I'm so very unhappy," he stammered.

I walked up to him, and put my hand on his shoulder. "So am I," I said, very low. "We are companions in misfortune, you and I."

He seized both my hands and kissed them. "Oh! God bless you for your heavenly sweetness! Just to be with you—to look at you . . ."

"Wait. You know, don't you, how I stand?"

He looked at me, and then away. "You love him still—after all he's done?"

"Yes," I said, "I love him still. I shall always love him."

2

A few minutes later, when we had both forced ourselves to speak of other things, I persuaded Egon Stanieff to rest and eat; he stayed with me for an hour, and then rode back to one of his father's castles, situated on the edge of the forest. Before he left he begged leave to visit me again. "I should like—if it is not too much to ask— to come here every two or three days," he said, avoiding my eye. "I promise to say nothing that might offend Your Majesty."

"You'll kill yourself—and your horses," I said, with a smile. "How far is it?"

"A mere matter of fifteen miles. I——"

"Please visit me again, Count Stanieff," I said, as he paused. "I should like to see you."

"And—if I might suggest——"

"Yes?"

"You are looking a little pale. Could I persuade you to ride with me in the forest sometimes?"

"Yes, I should like that," I said, after a moment's hesitation. "I have wanted to ride. But Countess Lemenken doesn't care for it, so we have spent rather too much time indoors."

Then followed a strangely peaceful interlude. Every two days Egon Stanieff appeared, and stayed to luncheon; then we would ride in the forest, talking of many things, but tacitly avoiding the circumstances in which we were placed. He told me a good deal about himself and his family—his married sisters, his eccentric old father, his invalid mother; we talked about politics (rather guard- edly), music, and the theatre, for which he had a passion. He was a good, simple, not very interesting young man, with whom I could have been happy, if—if—but I dared not now let myself dwell on what lay ahead of me. I was glad to be a little peaceful; resigned, at last, to my husband's neglect, to his occasional outbursts of irritation and dislike—for I had an idea that nothing was likely to change between Nikki and me. I was no Patient Griselda. Sometimes I hated him so much that it made me physically sick to recall the night before the ball; and often I was so disgusted at the thought of my own inadequacy that I could not bear to be alone.

In both these moods Egon Stanieff was a support. I was grateful for his boyish adoration, his silent loyalty to Nikki, of whom he disapproved but could not quite condemn. We spoke of him once more after that first conversation. Egon Stanieff said, "I don't know much about what happened when he was a young man—but I know that he was desperately unhappy."

I said something resentful about his making up for it now; I had been trying to put aside the picture of Nikki in Marta's arms.

Egon said abruptly: "He is not with Madame Karillos, Ma'am. They have not seen one another since the—since you parted at the crossroads."

"Are you sure?"

"Quite sure. I was with him all the time until I came here. I am also in communication with him."

"You surprise me."

We had been riding along the stream that ran through the lower part of the forest. He glanced at me rather timidly.

He must have guessed that I was too proud to ask for any more information, for he went on, in a conversational tone, "Yes—the King is in the Eastern Province, travelling about with no one but his body-servant, *incognito*."

"I was told that once before."

"It is true this time, Ma'am. I can prove it to you."

"I believe you. But how—I don't understand how anyone can think that we are together, if that is what he is doing."

"No Orosvar has set foot in that part of the country—the industrial part—for more than a hundred years. It is governed by a Minister who is responsible to Count Vanescu. The Eastern Province is neither picturesque"—he glanced down at the sparkling water—"nor very loyal. His Majesty has gone there to find out if anything can be done."

"In disguise?"

He ignored the mockery in my voice. "There's no need of that," he said simply. "To the people there he is no more than a legend."

"A disagreeable one?"

"I fear so."

"And you are in touch with him?"

"Yes, Ma'am. I can show you——"

"I believe you. It would be hard to believe anyone else."

He flushed with pleasure. We said no more until we reached a clearing, where the stream widened suddenly.

"Look—who are those people?" I exclaimed, reining in my horse.

Stanieff had been occupied in holding back the branches for me. Now he stopped, and raised himself in the saddle. "It's the gipsies. They are generally here at this time of the year. I'd forgotten—shall we turn back?"

"Would they know who I am?"

"Oh, no, Ma'am. They never go near the towns, and none of them can read."

"Let us go on then."

"They're—they might presume. They're very odd people."

"It might be amusing."

Still he hesitated; then he murmured something about thieves and beggars.

"We can ride away if they threaten us. Are you afraid?"

"For you—naturally," said Egon, with one of his shy glances.

"Let us go on." And I rode forward.

Immediately we were surrounded. Haggard, bold faces, gesticulating bare arms, filthy rags, here and there the gleam of a gold earring, the flash of white teeth between wings of matted black hair—it was like an adventure in a romance.

"I can't understand a word," I said, laughing. "Give them some money."

"Very well. But don't get off your horse, whatever you do."

There was a yell and a scramble as he threw a handful of coins into the circle. From the dozen or more that had come out of their tents and caravans to whine and beg, one stood apart, glowering at us from a distance—an old, old woman, white-haired, upright, contemptuous. She stood in the sunlight on the other side of the clearing, smoking a short clay pipe and shading her eyes with her hand.

"Do you think any of them speak Muranian?" I asked, as they crowded round us and our horses began to fret and pull at the reins.

"I'll try them," said Stanieff, now entering into the spirit of the adventure. A man came forward and answered his question.

"None but this fellow," said Stanieff, with a smile.

"Would that old woman over there tell my fortune? He could translate."

"Really, I think it's most inadvisable——"

"Let him ask her."

To Egon's question the man replied with a nod, adding a further explanation.

"He says," Egon went on, looking rather worried, "that she will. Then they want to dance for you."

"What music do they dance to? Guitars?"

"Drums and flutes."

"I should like that. Let's go over to the old woman."

"But, Ma'am——"

"How can they hurt us? They seem good-humoured enough."

"Very well," said Egon resignedly. "But you must not get down from your horse."

"I needn't. Look, she's smiling at us. Let him"—I beckoned to the man who spoke Muranian—"translate to you, and you can interpret to me."

Before taking off my glove, I gave the old woman a gold piece, that she spat on and put away without any thanks. Then the fortune-telling began—a slow process, owing to the translation from Romany to Muranian and then into French.

"She sees a crown behind your head, Madame—not on it——" Egon began.

"Well?"

"And a—a big building, with many windows."

"That's a pretty safe guess."

There was some more muttering; then the younger gipsy roared with laughter. As he translated, Egon blushed scarlet.

"Go on—tell me."

"Oh, I—it's nothing—some rubbish . . ."

"Count Stanieff, I command you! Are you going to disobey the first order I've ever given?"

"Well—it's—she says you've not long been married."

"Ah! and she thinks you're my husband, I suppose."

"No. She says he's far from here, and that he carries a great load on his shoulders."

"Tell her he's a master-builder," I suggested. "What else?"

"She says—not to be afraid—because——"

"Go on."

"Because your—son—will help your husband to carry his burden. And then—then she said something about a dark river."

I spared Egon's blushes, and looked at the old woman with a smile. She gave me a grim nod, and dropped my hand.

"Give her this ring," I said hastily. "She's earned it."

"It's all nonsense, Ma'am, of course . . ."

"Never mind. It's cheerful nonsense, at least. Shall they dance now?"

"If Your Majesty pleases," said Egon, with disapproving formality.

So the gipsies danced. I had never seen anything like it. And their music! Nowadays gipsy music, or watered-down editions of it, is heard everywhere. Then those throbbing rhythms, those wild melodies, were as unusual as they were unforgettable.

I listened; I gazed; I was entranced. Dirty and ragged beyond belief, these people seemed to revel in their earthy squalor, to take a violent pride in their bounding freedom. They danced like inspired furies, knives shining, hair tossing, red lips drawn back from pointed teeth, until, in the centre of a whirling ring, one hollow-cheeked boy made a gash on the arm of another, and smeared the drops of dark blood on his forehead; then they all uttered a cry and sank panting to the ground. I almost expected them to disappear through it, like the trolls in the legend. They turned towards me, pointing and laughing.

Egon Stanieff flung some more coins into the centre of the circle, and as they rushed at them we rode away. Then we wheeled our horses round and looked back. The sun was setting. The gipsies were standing together in a line, waving after us. Their hoarse voices combined in one last wailing cry of derisive gratitude and haunting farewell. The dying light turned their dark faces into gold and their rags into splendour. They seemed now to be a part of the earth and the water. We put our horses over the stream, and entered the sanctuary of the forest.

3

Since the moment of my arrival in Murania, I had been writing regularly to my father; it is hardly necessary to add that my letters left out a great deal, and amounted, on the whole, to a distortion of the truth. Until this moment my father's replies had been those of a man whose fondest hopes have been realized; now the single gentle-man-in-waiting he had sent with me was back in Norseland, and had given a very different account of what was happening. The result was that I received a series of agitated notes, followed by a telegraphic message, suggesting that my father should now pay his long-promised visit to Bledz. With Vera's help, I managed to persuade him to postpone this expedition. Poor Vera! This was, I think, the hardest thing I ever asked of her; but she did realize how essential it was that I should further adapt myself to the circumstances in which I was placed before facing my father. The fact of having to deceive him made her very unhappy. So it was in a mood of gloom and anxiety that she made ready to leave Dhrevin.

My own frame of mind was less melancholy. Though I dreaded the meeting with Nikki, I felt extraordinarily well, rested and ener-getic, as if I had been undergoing a cure. So I had; and Egon Stani-eff's share in it had been even more effectual than the quiet and comparative freedom of Dhrevin. He was, after all, the first man who had ever openly declared himself to be in love with me. He was a charming companion; he had made me feel that I was neither fool-ish nor disagreeable—and, with one exception, all my interviews with Nikki had given me the impression that I was both.

Furthermore, Nikki's last piece of cruelty—for so I saw it—had braced, instead of disintegrating, my resistance. I set out for the rendezvous at the crossroads determined to show him that I was a person of character and independence. I had already prepared a statement in which I hoped to make it clear that our relationship must be set on a more convenient basis. I therefore asked him to let us drive into Bledz alone, as I had something of importance to say to him. I saw his look of surprise as, without waiting for his permission, I asked Vera and his equerry to take their places in the second carriage.

Nikki looked extremely forbidding that afternoon. His mouth was set in its grimmest lines, his eyes were half shut; but I preferred this aspect to one that produced false smiles and artificial gallantry of manner.

"Can't it wait till we've reached the Palace?" he said sulkily.

"No, I'm afraid it can't," I replied in a tart voice, and again he looked a little taken aback.

Then I told him—but, alas! my resistance began to sink as I be-came aware of the grace and gaiety with which he was acknowledging the cheers of the people—that I proposed henceforth to lead as independent a life as was compatible with the circumstances. In public, we should of course appear a great deal together; privately, I expected to spend no time with him at all. I faltered a little as I said the last words.

Nikki said dryly, "You seem to have made all your plans."

"You must be glad not to be included in them," I said, trying to speak in a detached manner.

"These things can't be arranged in a minute," he said, after a short silence. "I shall have a great deal of work to do that will take me away from Bledz. Every now and then it will be necessary that you accompany me."

"I will do so whenever you wish."

He muttered something about agreeing to differ, and we said no more during the rest of the drive.

During the following six weeks, Nikki and I fell into what would now be called a routine. We evolved a technique of appearing on excellent terms in public and ignoring one another on all semi-private occasions. Obviously, Nikki must have made an appeal to his mother, for she did all that she could to make things easier for us. The others—Cyril, Anna, Vanescu, and the higher Court officials—seemed to take it for granted that this was a loveless marriage. Egon Stanieff, whom I saw constantly, but never alone, was unobtrusively helpful; I knew that he was unhappy.

I was miserable: increasingly so, as the weeks went by. It would have been much easier for me if Nikki had gone away altogether; as it was, while spending a great deal of time with Marta Karillos, he was far too often at my side for me to be able to attempt to forget him, or to avoid the recollection of our few hours of intimacy. And he had a way, too, of looking at me and talking to me that was painfully hostile. He made me feel that he was drawn towards me, in a sense that I could not define—and disgusted with himself for being so. Double-edged compliments; mocking asides; embittered comments on my duplicity—I had to endure them all. By degrees my newly found confidence was totally undermined.

Then, some two months after our return to Bledz, I became aware that that first, fatal *démarche* of mine was not, could not, be forgotten: that there might be consequences, in fact, a baby.

I was appalled. I had never thought—in spite of the slight tremor caused by the gipsy's prophecy—that such a thing could happen.

I had always desired it, in theory; but I didn't want to bear the child of a man who hated the sight of me.

After consulting with Vera, I decided to take Queen Elena into my confidence. She was very sympathetic and, naturally, delighted. Shortly afterwards two of the Palace physicians were summoned—secretly. My suspicions were verified. As soon as we were alone, my mother-in-law embraced me, and shed a few scented tears.

"Oh, my dear child! I'm so thankful, so relieved. It's what we've all hoped for——" she broke off as she caught my eye, and then resumed, leaning forward and speaking in a low, confidential tone. "Now, Christiane, I can feel you're really my daughter."

"Thank you."

"And I'm going to help you. Yes, really. I know what you're thinking."

We were sitting in my boudoir, where she had come to interview the doctors. I had been slightly distressed by the examination, and was lying on the sofa; her hand was on mine, and she was looking at me with a tearful smile. I was feeling very lonely, and rather frightened.

I turned towards her and said, "Do you—do you think you can help me?"

"Indeed I can. I wouldn't do it for everybody, I can tell you. Just think of my being a grandmother!" (She looked round for a mirror, but there wasn't one handy.) "I'll do everything I can. I know what you dread most, you see."

"It isn't exactly——"

"Ah, Christiane, I was young once! I remember all I went through before Nikki was born. Now I'm going to promise you something—and it's a promise that will be kept. After the child is born—as soon as you like, and the doctors permit—I'll lend you Mr. Svenson."

I sat up and stared at her. "Mr. ——".

"My masseur. I wouldn't do it for everyone—poor dear Anna has asked me again and again. But you're my dear little daughter, and I want to do everything I can for you."

There was a long silence. Then she said affectionately, "It's for Nikki's sake too—you must keep your figure for him, mustn't you?"

"Yes. You're very kind."

"Nonsense, dear." She got up, and leaned over the head of the sofa. "Are you quite all right now? Not frightened?"

"A little."

"Oh, I do understand. But you've no idea what a genius Mr. Svenson is—he can do miracles, I assure you."

"Yes."

"Now you'll be wanting to tell Nikki. Shall I send for him?"

I felt the blood rush over my face. "No—no . . ."

"What's the matter?"

"I can't tell him—I can't."

"My dear!"

"Must I?"

"Well, it is usual."

"He and I—he's not——"

"Now, Christiane," she interrupted, with a nervous look, "don't be silly. He must be told immediately."

There was a short silence. Her change of tone had had its effect, and already I was pulling myself together.

"Just a minute," I said confusedly. "You must think me very stupid—but there's something I can't remember."

"What?"

"Do you—do you have the Salic Law in Murania?"

"Oh—I see. Yes. So of course we shall be praying for a boy. But don't let that begin to obsess you. I should like a granddaughter. Why, child, you're not nineteen yet. There's plenty of time."

"Yes."

"Now, do let me send for Nikki."

I got up from the sofa and gripped her arm. "I can't—I can't be the one to tell him."

"You're not shy?"

"Yes," I said feverishly. "I—we haven't known each other very long, and he's so much older than I, and I—I don't feel up to it."

"I hope you're not going to be nervy," she said, in a tone of mild disapproval.

"Not about having the baby, I promise. It's only—oh, please—couldn't you tell him?"

"You really wish it?"

"Yes—really."

She drew back, looked at me curiously. "Very well. I'll go now."

"Is he in the Palace?"

"He was with his secretaries half an hour ago. I'll go to my own rooms, and send for him."

I fell back on the sofa. "I am so very grateful."

"Don't fret yourself, Christiane. Shall I ring for Countess Lemenken?"

"I'd like to be by myself for a little."

"Very well." At the door she turned, and said, with a reassumption of her maternal manner: "If I were you, I'd have a little sleep. It's an hour before you need think of dressing for dinner."

4

I got up and went over to the window. It was close, thundery weather, and I felt stifled. I went out onto the balcony, and then, suddenly restless, came in again. The room seemed different somehow—why? I noticed that all the flowers were drooping. Then I remembered that I had intended to look at myself in the mirror. I went to the one over the mantelpiece, and received no impression whatever. I must have stood there for some time, gazing vaguely at the pale face and rumpled hair of a stranger.

I heard footsteps coming along the corridor—footsteps that I recognized, and dreaded. I turned round, drawing the long folds of my tea-gown about me.

Our eyes met as he came in. He stood still a moment, leaning back against the door. So he had stood once before.

His eyes were brilliant and fixed; he was deathly pale. I was terrified of his laughter, of his derisive inquiries. I put out my hand, as if to keep him away from me. I felt a hideous, rising nausea. Then I fell forward.

I came out of a swaying cloud of darkness to find myself sitting on the sofa. He was standing above me. Someone—not Nikki—was saying, "Christiane—Christiane—it's all right—put your head down." I knew it wasn't Nikki, because the voice was kind, almost tender. Dimly wondering whom he had summoned to look after me, and feeling as if I had been unconscious for several hours, I did as I was told. A few moments later I looked up. He took his arm away from my shoulders. We were alone.

"Are you all right?" he said, in a low voice.

I leaned back and drew a long breath. "Could you get me some water?"

I shut my eyes as he disappeared into the mist that still hung about me. When he came back with the glass, I took it quickly, edging away as I drank. There was a long silence. I felt nothing but an enveloping exhaustion.

I sat up and put the glass down on a little table that had appeared, mysteriously, at my elbow.

"I suppose I fainted," I said vaguely.

"Would you like me—shall I send for anyone?"

I looked up. His voice had startled me. Then I saw that his eyes were full of tears. His hands were trembling. But I couldn't connect what I saw with anything that had happened.

"Who was here just now?" I said at last.

"No one."

"Yes, there was. Someone who told me to put my head down. Why did you—was it Vera?"

"Countess Lemenken hasn't been here. Do you want her?" he said abruptly.

"No—I don't want anyone."

He walked over to the window and undid the shutter. Then he turned.

With an immense effort, I reassembled my memories, and said, "You've been told—your mother told you?"

"Yes."

"I'm quite all right, you know," I began suddenly, in a bright, would-be conversational tone.

To this there was no answer. He was standing with his back to the light. If I hadn't been prepared for something quite different, I should have said that he was trying—and failing—to speak. Then he moved out of the shadow and came nearer. I must have shrunk back again, for he stopped in the middle of the room.

Now I could see him clearly. The mists had lifted, and I was quite sure of what I saw. The tears that had made his eyes so bright were running down his cheeks. He put up his hand and brushed them away.

He saw me looking at him, and turned aside.

After a short silence, he said, in that odd, jerky manner, "You must—take care of yourself. Shouldn't you be lying down?"

I laughed faintly. "I can't lie down for months on end."

He took a step forward. We looked at one another without speaking. In his face I saw remorse, hope, doubt—an appeal.

In most women, however young and untried, there is, at the basis of their power for love, another instinct—that of revenge for love denied. I didn't recognize what it was that rose within me now, making me feel hard and triumphant. I only knew that I was speaking under the influence of an excitement that was pleasurable in its embittered ferocity.

"Yes!" I said loudly. "I'll be careful. I know. I've become valuable."

He said nothing. He went on looking at me.

"I—possess—what you want," I continued, feeling stronger and more resilient with every syllable. "Nothing will be too good for me now—after all, I might have a miscarriage. But don't concern yourself. I won't disappoint you."

"I deserved that," he said, after a pause; then, clasping his hands in front of him (this was a characteristic gesture, one that I was later to associate with moments of strong emotion), he went on, "I know—everything went wrong."

"But it's all right now!" I exclaimed, with rising exhilaration. "I'm the shrine—aren't I?—in which your treasure lies."

"You hate me—don't you?" he said, after another silence.

"I don't hate you. I know how you feel—that's all."

"Do you?" he said, with an echo of his sardonic tone. "I wish I did."

"You want a son, of course. You told me so once . . ."

"Christiane . . ."

There was another echo in the word. But I was not going to let myself believe for an instant that he had been tender toward me, or careful of me. I clapped my hands over my ears. Now the excitement was turning into hysteria.

"Don't speak to me—don't tell me anything!" I said, speaking low and fast. "I know what my duty is. I learned those lessons before I had anything to do with you. I'll do all that's expected of me—because this will be the only child that we shall ever have, you and I."

Still he said nothing.

"I shall pray every day," I said, in a whisper, "that it may be a girl. Then, perhaps, I shall have something of my own."

He walked up to me as if he were going to silence me by force. I stood glaring at him (I must have looked rather ridiculous), trying to ignore the cold, empty feeling in my heart. I had destroyed, now and for always, whatever kindly emotion he might have begun to feel for me. I was savagely glad of it—and agonizingly, desperately miserable.

"Our loves were brief—weren't they?" he said at last.

"Yes—thank God. Now we need have no more to do with one another."

He gave me one long, strange look. I know now that even then, if I had been able to tear myself away from the claws of my own vicious, tigerish passion, I might have won him back. But I was beyond that. I said no more. I did not move. I turned my eyes away.

"There's nothing, then," he said hoarsely, "nothing more that you have to say to me?"

"Nothing."

He jerked up his head, as if he were shaking himself free. When he got to the door he waited. I stood there, speechless, arrogant, wretched. Then the door shut behind him, and I heard his footsteps die away along the corridor.

I stood for a long time as he had left me. Presently I heard myself saying over and over again, in a dull, heavy voice, "Alone—alone—alone . . ."

CHAPTER EIGHT

How I Became a Popular Figure

I HAVE ALWAYS had a good deal of sympathy for grass widows, partly because I was one during the months of my pregnancy. Nobody seemed to think that this was peculiar; the news that Nikki had left, first the Palace, and then the capital, was accepted with equanimity by all those who knew him best. This attitude saved my pride, but tried my patience. Only one person made any comment on my husband's behaviour, and that was the unfortunate Princess Cyril. She hurried to reassure me with the news that Nikki was spending very little time with Marta Karillos, who yet remained attendant on his caprice in the villa.

Poor dear Anna, as the Queen-Mother always called her, was very kind to me at this time; in her clumsy way she made it clear that she bore no malice. She expected my child to be the first of a large and healthy family, and had long ago resigned herself to taking her place in the background. This was not the case with her husband, who wreaked his disappointment on her, and was often brutally unkind. She had to entertain his mistresses, put up with his drunkenness, and let him destroy all her attempts to train Prince Michael, who became, so Queen Elena told me, more impossible every time she saw him. Anna was frankly envious of me because Nikki let me alone.

"You can do what you like—within limits," she said, with a sigh. "You don't know how lucky you are."

When I told Vera about this conversation, she exploded. "They're all dreadful!" she declared. "No standards, no morals . . ."

"We must try to adapt ourselves," I put in. "But I don't know what Anna means when she says I can do what I like, do you?"

"Well—you have no public engagements——"

"But the waiting will seem endless without any duties at all. And in a month's time I go into complete retirement."

"I'm rather looking forward to that," said Vera, and, after a moment's consideration, I agreed with her.

According to the custom of the country, I took up my residence at La Gloriette, an exotic version of the Grand Trianon, standing at the end of the great artificial lake and directly opposite the Palace, with which it communicated by an underground tunnel. It had been built during the latter half of the eighteenth century for the invalid Queen of Alexis II; he was a Francophile, and one of the most eccentric of the Orosvar kings. La Gloriette was an exquisite structure of honey-coloured stone; eight pillars of orange marble divided the façade, which was topped by a crystal dome. The interior was built round a circular hall, carried up through all the floors. The rooms were decorated in the style of the French Regency by a pupil of Got; the general effect was one of extreme delicacy and elegance. In the grand saloon, the dining-room, and the library, gilt mirrors and *trompe-l'œil* wall-paintings gave one the feeling of having stepped into a picture by Watteau. Indeed, the decoration of the card-room and of my boudoir frankly reproduced the background and some of the figures of *l'Embarquement pour Cythère*.

It was impossible, when the moment came for my retirement to this charming pleasure-dome, to feel altogether neglected and unhappy. For one thing, everybody—my mother-in-law, the Court ladies, and even the unbending Vanescu—did all they could to distract me. A tiny theatre was attached to La Gloriette, and to this both amateurs and professionals were summoned. Concerts, plays, and ballets succeeded one another. These were followed by little suppers, and preceded by picnics on the lake. Everything that could be done to amuse me was done. My gratitude for all this kindness helped to fill the emptiness in my heart.

Of course, I thought far too much about Nikki—and, with secret tears, blamed myself for rejecting what I realized to have been an advance: an inarticulate, but spontaneous and genuine advance. As the weeks went by and the languorous autumn mists crystallized into the frosts and snows of winter, I began to think more continuously about the baby. How I longed for it to be a girl! I felt very well all the time. A strange peace, an indifference to the past and the future, came over me. I was almost happy.

Then my newfound tranquillity was shaken. Astrid came to me in tears, and announced that she wanted to be married.

Before I could speak, Vera exclaimed: "You wicked girl! You've forgotten your promise!"

We were sitting in the little salon on the first floor. The curtains were drawn, and the porcelain stove was glowing redly. Vera and I had been playing piquet; it was the first evening we had been alone together for some time.

"Come, Vera, isn't that rather hard?" I expostulated. "Why shouldn't she get married if she wants to? I suppose," I continued, turning to my sobbing foster-sister, "that it's some one in the Palace?"

"No, Madame—no——"

"Well, don't cry. Tell me about it."

"She had no business——" Vera began.

"Vera, darling, please—tell me who it is, Astrid."

"His name is Rudy Selkar," said Astrid, sniffing.

"Do I know him?"

"No, Ma'am. He doesn't—he isn't——" She broke off in great distress.

"You mean he isn't on the staff here at all? He lives in the city, perhaps?"

"I met him in a café in the Old Town," said Astrid, glancing at Vera. "My purse had been stolen, and he looked after me, and saw me home."

"It sounds quite respectable. Is he a nice young man?"

"Very—yes——"

"Why are you so upset, then?"

"Because—because—— Oh dear!—I shouldn't have said yes, I know I shouldn't," said Astrid, hiding her face in her hands.

"Do you mean," I said, getting up slowly and carefully, and putting my hand on her shoulder, "that you're going to have a baby?"

"Oh, *no!*—how could you think——"

"It has been known," I said, with a faint smile. "Is he poor? Can't he afford——"

"No—he's got a good place."

"A good place, indeed!" Vera muttered.

"What is the difficulty, then? I'll help you; you know that."

"Oh, Ma'am—he's—I didn't know till we'd met several times. He's steward to Madame Karillos."

There was a long silence. Vera glanced from one to the other of us, made a despairing gesture, and went out of the room.

I put my hand to my head and tried to take in what I had been told. I saw two white-frocked little girls, racing down the long corridors of the Summer Palace in Kraken, tobogganing along the slopes by the frozen lake, running about the gardens, climbing trees, playing with their dolls. . . . In the years before Kirsten and Hulda came to live with us, Astrid and I had been everything to one another. I had always known that she would marry, and had solaced many lonely hours since my arrival in Murania with making plans for her.

This was a blow, a slap in the face that I hadn't expected; it left me speechless and bewildered. I said, in a stifled voice: "Leave me for a little while. I can't say anything more till I've had time to think."

In the end I sent her away with the appearance, at least, of good will. But it was hard. Astrid was a part of the happy life that I seemed to have said good-bye to forever.

2

Astrid's departure made me feel as if I were being isolated. I see now how unreasonable this was; then, I could do no more than let her go, and secretly resent her absence. Vera, in whom she had at first confided, described her behaviour as treacherous—but could I, so fatally struck myself, agree with this harsh view?

The alternative to losing Astrid would have been to offer her young man a post in my own household; but that would be even more distasteful than forbidding the marriage. Finally, I sent for Rudy Selkar, who impressed me favourably, and suggested (rather coldly) that the marriage should take place at once, and that Astrid should divide her time between looking after him at the lodge, helping with the work in the villa, and spending a few hours a week with me, until the baby was born.

Vera protested. "She'll be running backwards and forwards with all sorts of horrible gossip," she said. "If you're going to allow the marriage, she should leave you altogether."

"But that would break her heart."

"Hearts aren't so easily broken, Christiane," said Vera, with a significant look.

"If you mean mine——"

"Well?"

"Having a baby will make up for a lot of things."

There was a short silence, in which Vera, who had been sitting on the end of my bed, got up and moved away.

"Are you still in love with him?" she said, in a low voice.

"I shall never love anyone else. You mustn't blame him entirely," I went on, as she muttered something about brutes. "Something went wrong—terribly wrong—after we came back from Dhrevin." And I gave her a brief account of my last interview with Nikki.

"Does the Queen-Mother know what happened?"

"I don't know. I can't talk to her about him. That doesn't mean," I added, leaning back with a smile, "that I can't listen to her when she tells me what he's like. She knows his worst side, you see."

It was difficult to prevent myself from encouraging Astrid to talk. For some weeks now there had been a conspiracy of silence about Nikki's movements, and the only news I had of him came through her. He spent very little time at the villa; when he did he was gloomy and silent. It was believed that Marta Karillos, feeling herself estranged from him, was very unhappy—but she never complained.

A couple of months after Astrid's marriage, I heard from Queen Elena that Nikki was behaving "outrageously," and that she and Vanescu were worried.

"I suppose there's another woman," I said, in as indifferent a tone as I could manage.

"If only there were!" was the answer, followed by an account of Nikki's activities, collected from the reports of Vanescu's secret police.

It appeared that Nikki had recalled Vanescu's rival and enemy, Stefan Rell, who had for a short time been in the Cabinet; shortly after Nikki's elopement with Marta, his father and Vanescu between them had managed to oust Rell from power. Nikki had now summoned him from Switzerland, and was touring the country with him; they had made several expeditions to the Eastern Province together. Finally, Rell had been installed in a little house on the Mornavitza estate, and, with the help of a small staff of liberally minded enthusiasts—revolutionaries, Vanescu called them—was working out a reconstruction of the country's economic arrangements. The details of this scheme had not yet been acquired by Vanescu's spies; but both he and the Queen-Mother anticipated dangerous and possibly fatal results from these machinations.

"And the worst of it all is," Queen Elena concluded, "that Nikki's making himself so unpopular. He's never on show, never at the Palace, and it looks so—well, not right, not right at all."

"I know you think he ought to be with me," I said, after a pause, "but you may as well know that we had a serious disagreement. You must have guessed——"

"I did think—he seemed so pleased about the baby, when I told him. What happened?"

"It was partly my fault. I'd rather not discuss it, if you don't mind."

She gave me one of her sharp looks, and then said, very sweetly indeed: "Dear child—you're so good and patient. Everyone admires you for it. But if only you'd taken your opportunity when it came——"

"I don't know what you mean," I said, rather coldly.

"Well, my dear, it seems that Nikki and Marta—he doesn't spend much time with her, you know."

"So I understand. But in the past he often used to desert her. And she used to wait for him, as she's waiting now."

"This is different. Our agents tell us that he's—that he doesn't —he spends one to two evenings a week at the villa, and then goes back to Mornavitza, or to his apartments in the Palace, for the night."

Astrid's reports—which I listened to with mingled feelings of guilt and amazement—had borne out this news. I so much disliked hearing it from Queen Elena that I made an effort to change the subject. I was beginning to fear her—partly because I saw that she was lying when she professed herself unhappy at her son's behaviour. She was determined to combat his political schemes; and the less he appeared in public, the better she was pleased, because she hoped to regain the power she had lost on the death of his father. At the time this was not clear to me; I became aware of it later.

A month or so after this conversation, I was sitting on the balcony of my bedroom, wrapped in furs, thinking, rather nervously, of what lay ahead of me. I had already gone through the morbid stage, that of envisaging my own death, planning the funeral, and so on, and was trying to stifle an instinctive dislike of the nurses and doctors who were beginning to hover in the background of my life.

Suddenly a tall, bulky figure appeared astride on the end of the balcony. It was Giulio. He smiled, made a reassuring gesture, and came up to me. In reply to my agitated question, he told me, in strongly accented French, that he had entered the grounds by a secret way.

"Why have you come?"

"It was necessary that His Majesty should know——" He broke off with a smile.

"I have no message for the King," I said coldly. "I'm in excellent health, as he may see from the newspapers."

Giulio shrugged his shoulders. Then he remarked casually that he had not in fact been ordered by his master to come and see me.

"I knew," he said, with a rather engaging intimacy of manner, "that he was thinking about you. Now I can tell him that I have seen Your Majesty with my own eyes."

"How did you know that he was thinking about me?"

He spread out his hands. "I know. How should I not know?"

"If they find out how you got in here, you'll get into trouble," I said, smiling in spite of myself.

"Perhaps Her Gracious Majesty will protect——" began Giulio, with a wheedling expression.

"You had better go now, by the way you came."

He bowed. Then he added something in Italian that sounded like a blessing, or a wish—I couldn't understand the words, but his expression and manner conveyed some part of his meaning—climbed over the balcony, and disappeared.

I leaned back, still rather breathless from the shock, and oddly exhilarated. I wasn't frightened any longer.

3

A few days before the baby was born, I was taken across the lake to the Palace, where a suite of rooms had been set aside for me. When I asked, rather nervously, why I couldn't have stayed there all the time, instead of being moved back and forth, I was told that my retirement to La Gloriette was part of a tradition that dated from the fifteenth century, when the Queen-Consorts of Murania withdrew altogether from the capital for the births of their children, and were shut up in a gloomy fortress that had long since fallen into decay.

It was the "unconventional" Alexis II who had instituted the custom of retirement to La Gloriette; and Nikki's father had made it a rule that all the royal children should be born in the Palace. So both methods of procedure were now combined, with the result that I set forth one cold and snowy morning in a covered barge, oared by masked rowers in eighteenth-century dress, and thus reached the east wing of the Palace, in which I had never set foot until this moment.

I was tried and alarmed by the pomp and formality of this journey, brief though it was. The rooms which had been made ready for me seemed frighteningly large and gloomy after the cheerful elegance of La Gloriette. Doctors, nurses, and attendants appeared so portentous and *affairés* that by the time I had settled in I was thoroughly scared. It was just as well that I had no notion of what I was to undergo.

I have no intention of dwelling on the length and severity of the ordeal that followed my reinstallation at the Palace. I was told afterwards that I had been very brave. I had need to be. No anaesthetics were used in Murania at that time.

As soon as it was known that I was in labour, proclamations were issued, and the Palace was surrounded by crowds of people, who settled down to wait for Nikki's appearance on the balcony with his child in his arms. When the news of the proclamations reached Astrid, she set off for the Palace. She found it impossible to approach any of the entries, and returned, in great distress, to the villa. This was in the early morning. During the evening of the same day she made another attempt, and was again frustrated.

Her second return to the villa coincided with that of Nikki; he had already been sent for from the Palace. A supper-party was in progress. Astrid was on duty during the whole course of the evening. Some weeks afterwards she quarrelled irrevocably with her husband (chiefly over their disparate loyalties), and returned to my service. She subsequently gave me a full account of what happened at the villa on the night my child was born. Her misery and anxiety were great, and, it seemed, unforgettable. Long afterwards, when she was a very old woman, she could recall much of the conversation and many details of Nikki's aspect and behaviour; indeed, they had been burnt into her memory. To Astrid's version there was added, soon afterwards, another, whose source I shall reveal in its proper place.

From these two widely varying descriptions it has been possible to re-construct the scene.

As soon as Nikki arrived, the guests—some twenty people—pre-pared to withdraw. Marta Karillos, undisguisedly relieved, got up to bid them good-bye. Nikki called out, in a peremptory and defiant manner: "What nonsense! Everybody must stay, Marta! What are you thinking of? Make them sit down."

With embarrassed looks and manufactured amiability, he was obeyed. Marta, also attempting a complaisance she could not have felt, took her place beside Nikki at the centre of the long table. He called for wine, and drank thirstily; complaining of hunger, he heaped his plate, and then appeared to forget all about eating. He gave his mistress one tortured look, and sank into silence.

Somehow Marta got the conversation going. She exercised all her charm, all her gaiety.

Suddenly Nikki looked down the length of the table, and, grasp-ing her hand, said, in a hoarse, uneven voice, "What entertainment have you planned for us after supper?"

"Some dancers from the Opera——"

"Good! Young? Pretty?"

"I think so, Sir. We shall see."

"Are they here?"

"Yes. As soon as supper is over——"

"Well, it is, isn't it?" he said, looking round with his blank, brilliant smile. "Let us go upstairs." And he got up, taking her by the wrist.

She appeared to accept this strange behaviour calmly, and led the way to the salon on the first floor of the villa. Here the musicians and dancers were waiting; the servants followed with liqueurs and coffee. Marta installed her guests with remarkable *sang-froid,* and the entertainment began.

Nikki stared at the moving patterns of half-naked girls as if he were seeing beyond them some vision of his own. As they sank, panting, to the floor, he applauded vociferously, glancing from one guest to another, with a look of suspicion. Then he noticed Conrad Volkov, a young officer in the Royal Guard, and beckoned to him. They spoke together for a moment in undertones. Nikki turned to Marta, who was trying not to watch him.

"They dance well," he said, in a rapid, mechanical tone. "That's unusual in the State Opera. You should let them appear with you in Paris."

She laughed quite naturally, and put her hand on his arm. "No, Sir—those young things! I couldn't afford to. The audience already have an idea of my age. I don't want them to be certain."

"Ah," he said, eyeing her, "some women never age."

"A man never says that to a woman until she has."

He stared, then laughed. "I must think that out," he said, and walked away from her.

For a few minutes she sat alone, looking at the ground. Then she roused herself, and began to move from one group to another.

So an hour went by. Nikki seemed unable to let Marta out of his sight; but as soon as she said anything to him his manner became artificial and strained. When she ventured to rally him he answered at random.

He suddenly turned from her to Captain Volkov, and said, his voice shaking, "Is there any news?"

"Sir?"

"From the Palace."

Everyone stopped talking at the sound of the last word. Nikki seemed unaware of the silence.

Captain Volkov said quickly: "Not yet, Sir. There are six messengers with fast horses waiting on the road. They will pass the message on to each other, as to—as to——" He mumbled, and broke off, then added, "You should hear within twenty minutes."

"I shall hear before that," said Nikki impatiently, turning on his heel. He thrust his hands in his pockets and looked at the ceiling. "How many guns for a boy?"

"Twenty-one," said someone, after a pause.

"And for a girl?"

"Eighteen, Sir," from Volkov.

"How very unfair!" said Nikki, with a laugh. "But eventually girls get even—they always do." In the dead silence that followed, he looked at Marta and said, with a perceptible effort at gaiety: "What a delightful way of approaching fatherhood. I believe the husband usually walks up and down and has a raging toothache, doesn't he?"

"In the novels——" she began.

"I prefer wine, women, and song"—he spoke as if he were repeating a lesson—"and, talking of song, Marta, sing to us."

"What shall I sing, Sir?" she said, still smiling, but very pale.

There was a brief discussion. Then Marta sang a French song very popular in Bledz at that time, *Le Maire de Perpignan,* which contained, some believed, one or two disloyal references to Nikki. He hardly seemed to hear it; but he applauded as wildly as a schoolboy. By this time it was plain that Marta was on the verge of breaking down. When he asked her to sing again, she shook her head without speaking. Then, rolling through the chatter and the music and the clink of glasses, came the sound of the guns.

4

Volkov looked nervously at Nikki, who was standing in the middle of the room. Marta gazed at him imploringly; but he seemed to have forgotten her and the others, and appeared equally indifferent to their curiosity and her distress. Then he said, with an unsuccessful attempt at a casual tone, "Will someone count for me?"

Volkov began to do so. Nikki muttered something about finding it impossible to count up to more than ten; he glanced at Marta, and she smiled faintly. He continued, as if speaking to himself, "Five—they must be using two guns."

As the next reverberation thrilled through the silence, he went on, "Strange—that silly booming noise is telling us our future."

"Eight, Sir——"

"They'll like a boy," said Nikki, looking round the ring of perturbed and embarrassed faces. "They'll only tolerate a girl. Why?" No one said anything. He added, in an extremely bitter tone, "Women are so much stronger than men."

"Ten."

He glanced at Marta, who was gripping her fan so tightly that it was shaking. "The weaker vessel—nonsense!"

"Twelve."

Nikki walked up to Volkov, and said, with a hard stare, "I suppose they think of me at the bedside, where officially I am."

Marta interposed, with a temulous smile: "I should hate them to know where you really are. My life wouldn't be worth a kopeck."

"Fifteen."

"Yes!" he said, in a loud, harsh voice. "The Queen has a great following. As her stock goes up, mine goes down. But then she always does the right thing—she's doing it now—I always do the wrong."

"Eighteen."

There was a second's wait. Although no one but Nikki and Volkov had uttered a word, Nikki raised his hand, as if for silence. Then the guns spoke again.

"Twenty-one—a boy——" said Volkov, in a breathless whisper.

Nikki stood still, gazing in front of him; then he smiled—a strange smile.

Volkov, after an interchange of glances with his comrades, came up to him, and said, in his clear, boyish voice, "May I be the first to congratulate you, Sir?"

Now the other young men crowded round him, and he shook hands with them. All this time Marta had not ceased to look at him. I often wonder if at that moment she was afraid of him, as I had been afraid.

At last he jerked himself out of that baleful silence and said, looking from one to another: "More music! We must celebrate. Perhaps the National Anthem—wouldn't that be appropriate?"

Marta moved towards him, as if to protest. He turned away from her, and went on, "Does anyone know it?"

Bursts of laughter, and cries of "Yes, of course," greeted this piece of bad manners.

"Go on, then," said Nikki, in the same level, mirthless tone, "sing it."

By this time the professional musicians and entertainers had been dismissed. At a sign from Volkov, one of the younger officers sat down at the piano and banged out the opening chords.

A look of horror and disgust came over Nikki's face, as everyone stood up and began to sing. He may have thought that it would be amusing, piquant, to lounge about and listen to those too familiar sounds; he may have expected some of the wilder young men to caricature the words, or the music. When they did neither, he ceased to listen, and walked over to the window. Pulling at the collar of his uniform as if it stifled him, he leaned against the wall, half smiling, half contemptuous.

Then, slowly, as the grave melody and the simple words penetrated his tormented mind, Nikki became composed and serious; he stood as the others were standing, at attention. Finally, his attempts at indifference and ease, his false and cruel gaiety, fell away. He looked at Marta as if he needed her. She came up to him and took his hand.

He said, in a low voice, "I find myself strangely moved—for the first time," he added, looking away.

"I think it's not really for the first time—is it?"

He made an impatient movement of his hand. "I don't remember."

Suddenly her eyes filled with tears. Nikki moved in front of her, and called out, "Something gayer! Sing!"

There was a moment's hesitation. Then the young man at the piano rattled off a popular tune, in which everybody, except Marta, who was gradually recovering, joined; with a sly glance at Nikki, he drifted into *Le Maire de Perpignan*.

Marta, rousing herself to speak with a semblance of gaiety, said to Nikki, "Do you like that particular song so much, then?"

He did not hear her, and she had to repeat the question.

"Oh," he said then, with one of his flashing, meaningless smiles, "I used to hear it everywhere, you know. I was curious. When I came near, people used to stop singing. Is it so applicable?"

"I don't think so," she said, putting her hand on his arm.

He looked down at her absently. "It's odd—isn't it?—what such songs can do to a dynasty. *Lilliburlero*—the *Marseillaise*—and this one——"

"There's no resemblance," she said quickly.

"No? I wonder." He turned to the pianist. "Go on—it's delightful. Why don't you all join in the chorus?"

There was a great deal of laughter, and a medley of voices took up the song. Nikki walked away from the window and sat down on the other side of the room, as if he were completely exhausted.

The double doors were suddenly flung open. Queen Elena, dressed in a long, glittering cloak of black and silver, stood on the threshold.

As the voices died away, Nikki turned with an angry look. Then he saw his mother, and started forward; his pallor now became livid. They stood staring at one another in silence.

"What an honour!" he said at last, forcing out the words. "But why? What has happened?" There was a pause, and then he added, more composedly, "Oh! I see—you've come to fetch me home."

She drew herself up. "Dismiss these—your friends. I must speak to you."

Everyone went out. Astrid, lingering in the hope of news of me, withdrew behind a long table at the far end of the room, and sat down, screened by a huge bowl of flowers. She saw and heard everything that happened.

Marta curtsied, and, with an impassive look, turned to follow her guests.

Elena stopped her with a gesture. "No, Marta, stay and hear what I have to say."

For a moment or two there was silence. The two women were looking at one another. Nikki, his head between his hands, was staring at the carpet.

Queen Elena said, in a low, pleading voice: "I thought you were an influence—in some ways quite a good one. And yet the night his child is born——"

"It is not by my wish that the King is here, Ma'am," said Marta, with gentle dignity.

Nikki stood up. "No, Mamma," he said, "I came by my own wish. I utterly refuse to play in this charade."

"How dare you!"

"I feel nothing—nothing!" he interrupted vehemently. "Why should I?"

"You're striking an attitude, Nikki. It doesn't deceive me in the least."

He came towards her; then he stopped, shrugging his shoulders. "Very well. Have it your own way. What do you feel?"

"Tremendous relief."

He stared at her, and burst out laughing. "Yes, I see what you mean! You can devote yourself to your grandson, instead of concentrating on your son's" —he paused, and glanced from one woman to the other—"your son's nocturnal activities."

Marta shrank back at this derisive reminder of the gap between them.

Queen Elena looked at her curiously. Then she said, in a gentler tone: "You make me very unhappy. Why are you so bitter?"

He turned on her and said fiercely: "Because I've been used! Everything has led up to today!"

"Used—what rubbish——"

"I tell you it has! How dare you stand there and look at me with that expression on your face and pretend you don't know what you've done?" In the pause that followed, he seemed to be controlling another outburst; then he added, in a low, contemptuous voice, "Yes! There's an heir now—and God help poor Nikki!"

"My dear, don't——"

"I can't be fooled any more. Do you think I don't know what's in your mind?"

"You're not yourself . . ."

"Don't underestimate Christiane, though," he went on, as if she had not spoken. "She's made of cold steel—and she's like one of her own snow-fields, into the bargain. Yes! 'The ice-brook's temper . . .'"

"Nikki——"

"I shan't fight you; I'm too tired—but she's not; she's young, and strong, and the people adore her, for what she's given them. *You* were adored once, for the very same reason—do you remember?"

Queen Elena covered her face with her hands. "How can you— how can you!"

"I'm warning you—don't you see? You're out of date at last, Mamma, in spite of all your trouble. They're tired of us, with our lovers"—he waited to see the effect of this shot, but there was none "—our lovers, and our mistresses. We're old-fashioned. But she— she's new. The latest thing—a good woman!"

Elena glanced at Marta, whose eyes were on Nikki. Then she said, in a low voice, "What do you want?"

He hesitated, and shook his head, as if it were impossible to explain anything to such a woman. Then he turned away, and said, in a calmer tone, "At the moment I have a strong desire to see my son— I know he's been designed to push his father off the throne, but still . . ."

"You should have been in the Palace——" Elena began.

"I wonder which it will be this time," he continued. "Exile or assassination? Have you and Vanescu decided yet?"

Elena turned to Marta with a despairing gesture. "Can't you speak to him?"

Marta came up to Nikki and took his hand; then she said, in her sweetest, most persuasive manner: "I think, Sir, you should go immediately to the Palace, whatever you feel. After all, it can do no harm to show yourself on the balcony with the little Prince, and——"

"Yes," he interrupted, with a return to his gloomy humour. "And if I had any sense I'd drop him over."

"Nikki!"

"I said, *if* I had any sense, but I haven't." He got up, and took his mother's hand. "Come, Mamma—one last bid for popularity." At the door he turned, and his eyes met Marta's; he said gently: "Good-night, Marta, my dear. As always, you've given me a delightful evening."

Queen Elena gave them a long, intent look, and went out.

Marta said, with a slight tremor in her voice, "And shall I see you?"

He smiled. "Constantly. Nothing has changed."

"I wish I could be sure of that," she said, with a wistful look. "Good-night."

He turned back and took her face between his hands. "How long is it? Over twenty years. Twenty years on a precipice." She shook her head, her eyes filling again. "Yes," he went on, speaking very low, "women are wonderful creatures." Then he followed his mother.

When Nikki reached the Palace, he came straight to my room. I had just come out of a stupor of exhaustion when they told me he was there. I felt nothing, not even triumph. Then, as if it had been conjured up to haunt my dreams, I saw his face, bending over mine. With an immense effort, I roused myself to speak.

"It's done," I muttered. "Take him. It's what you wanted."

"A fine, healthy boy, Your Majesty," said an obsequious voice, from what was apparently a long way off.

Nikki seemed to disappear. Then—was it soon afterwards?—I saw him take the white bundle in his arms.

"He's a very large baby," I said, shutting my eyes.

"Christiane—for God's sake . . ."

Was that Nikki's voice? It was near and yet confused, a part of the dream into which I was sinking again.

"Yes," I said, "for God's sake—and for our loves——" but it was too much trouble to finish the sentence, or even to think of what I had meant to say to him.

Then I heard him whisper, "Here, take the child—I can't——" and there was a murmur and a rustle above me.

"Wait," I said feebly, "I want to see you holding him," but the murmuring and rustling went on, and I was afraid that no one had heard me. Perhaps the baby was dead . . .

"Open your eyes, darling," said Vera's warm, loving voice in my ear.

I did so; there was Nikki, holding the child. He put his free hand into the middle of the bundle, and leaned forward so that I could see. A minute, purple fist was twined round his finger. Well, it's alive, anyway, I thought; they told me afterwards that I had said the words aloud. But I couldn't understand why Nikki didn't say anything. I had to force myself to look once more, because I was getting drowsy— and then I saw that he was gazing at me with a desperate, miserable expression. How odd—because everything was all right, they'd told me so; and I could hear, dimly and far off, the cheering and the guns.

I shut my eyes; but I could still see the faces, one pale and ravaged, in a ring round my bed. The voices swelled and died away. A great wave of darkness rolled over everything, and I sank beneath it, floating down and down . . . but I had to get back, somehow, because of the baby. Then I remembered that Nikki was holding him, and gave myself up to oblivion.

CHAPTER NINE

How to Deal with a Crisis

IT WAS NOT THE CUSTOM of the Queen-Consorts of Murania to attend the christenings of their children; these were celebrated some ten days after the announcement of birth. My baby was christened Paul Alexander Nicholas Rodrigo. The last name, that of his maternal grandfather, seemed to me one of ill omen; for Queen Elena's father had been murdered in peculiarly horrible circumstances soon after she came to Murania.

I had long ago decided to accept the decisions of others over the question of names. They were of no importance compared to the establishment of my authority over my son's training. I was determined that his grandmother should have as little to do with that as possible.

Paul was an extremely well-behaved and placid baby; even when he was teething he remained healthy and serene. When he was very tiny he reminded me of my father (of course, I knew better than to make any comment on this to my mother-in-law), but very soon after he was born this resemblance disappeared, and he looked like no one but himself. I didn't want him to be like the Orosvar portraits, and I dreaded any signs of the Bourbon-Parma strain; I secretly hoped that he would look exactly like Nikki.

My convalescence was a long one. It would have been shorter, I suppose, if I had consented to leave the capital and recuperate at one of the castles on the coast. This I refused to do. I had a feeling that very soon Nikki would come to see me (he did visit the nurseries, but never when I was there), and I still hoped that we might come to some sort of an understanding.

Without telling me, Queen Elena had decided to keep us apart. She told Nikki that I had refused to see him, while to me she continued to deplore his neglect and bad behaviour. Long afterwards the whole extent of her plan was revealed to me. It was quite a simple one: to get control of her grandchild, and, with Vanescu's help, to make herself unofficial Regent of Murania, while Nikki relapsed into Marta's arms, and eventually into a second exile; to prime me with tales of Nikki's degeneration, and disgust me with my own position, thus forcing me to return to my father; finally, to establish herself and Vanescu as dictators of a tyrannical and outdated régime, while training Paul to follow in their footsteps as an absolute monarch. This could only be effected by eliminating me—for Elena suspected, and rightly, that I should be the first to support and encourage Nikki's ideas for reforming the country.

Queen Elena and Vanescu set to work immediately after the christening. They began by instigating the murder of Stefan Rell, to whom Nikki was deeply attached; without Rell, his schemes for a better Government were bound to be delayed, perhaps altogether frustrated. Rell was found in a ditch, his throat cut from ear to ear, some two miles from his house on the Mornavitza estate.

My mother-in-law informed me of this disaster (for so it proved ultimately to be) with the utmost nonchalance, and a little mild deprecation of Muranian savagery. To my horrified exclamations and inquiries she replied by such phrases as: "I told Nikki he was running this sort of risk in getting Rell back, but of course no one listens to what *I* say," "My dear, naturally they'll trace the murderer in the end, but what good will that do?" "I don't want to appear harsh, but really, he was a most tiresome creature"—and so on.

Stefan Rell's murder threw Nikki into an abysmal and violent depression. He knew perfectly well who was responsible; he also knew that he could do nothing to avenge his friend and counsellor. This realization, combined with the belief that I had refused to have anything to do with him, caused him to abandon all his plans. He said to his mother, "You've played your cards almost too well—you need fear nothing from me for the moment"—and forthwith retired to the villa on the Hervat Road.

This withdrawal, and the fact that I had become, to use a journalistic phrase, the people's favourite, sent Nikki's popularity (lately rather shaky) down with a rush. He was spoken of as a cynic and an adulterer, who rejected his innocent wife for a predatory and selfish mistress. Two months after the christening, leaflets were secretly printed and distributed describing his conduct on the night of his son's birth; one of these fell into my hands. I found it on my desk on my return from a visit to the nurseries. As soon as I had read it, I sent for Vera. When she had read it, we looked at one another with horrified faces. (It must be remembered that at this time neither of us knew who was at the bottom of these misunderstandings and disturbances.)

"It's disgusting—horrible," said Vera. She added, in an uncertain voice, "It would be best to take no notice of it, surely?"

"I don't know," I said slowly. "Sometimes I think one can be too careful of dignity, and not careful enough of—more important things."

"What things?"

"As I see it, this leaflet—which must by now have been read by every literate person in Bledz—is a warning."

"To the monarchy?"

"Yes, and more than that—a menace to Paul's future. It's the kind of thing that, if it's neglected, can lose you a kingdom. My father used to warn me never to ignore——" I broke off, shivering a little.

"But what can you do, Christiane?"

"I haven't thought. Something must be done." I took up the leaflet and read it again. Then I said, "In the last sentence, you see, there's a threat——"

"It's all threats."

"I mean, to her."

"To Madame Karillos?"

"Yes."

Vera took the paper and read it through once more. "I don't see that that matters," she said at last. "It's partly her fault, after all."

"But suppose they acted on it? Suppose the people behind this organization bribed some roughs to break into her house?"

"It would teach her a lesson."

"Vera, don't you see? It might make him—I don't know—desperate. He might go away, if anything happened to her."

"What can you do to prevent that?" said Vera, after a pause. "He never—I mean—well——"

"You mean, I've lost him anyway? I won't believe that."

She looked at me with a despairing expression. "You always were an obstinate little thing," she said, trying to smile.

"I know."

"But, Christiane—there is something else. Have you seen the papers this morning?" As I shook my head, she went on, "It's been discovered—how, I can't make out—that Madame Karillos has got five million roubles out of this country."

"Show me."

She handed me the paper. I read this new attack with a sickening twist of the heart. Five million roubles!—how could Nikki have allowed such a thing? Did he care for nothing but Marta? Yet the shock of the discovery gave me an idea.

"Vera," I said, getting up, "what time is it?"

"Half-past four."

"Tell them to order a carriage, please—a closed one. And see that Count Stanieff is in attendance—no one else."

"Christiane—what are you going to do?"

I looked at her triumphantly. I was young enough to be stimulated by the drama of the situation, and by the consciousness of my own share in its development.

"You mustn't try to stop me—because it wouldn't be the faintest use," I said, smiling. "We're going to Madame Karillos's villa."

2

Egon Stanieff insisted on riding beside the carriage, although I would have preferred him to sit with us. He seemed to think that we were embarking on a very dangerous expedition, and supported Vera as far as he dared in her reiterated criticisms of my rashness.

Vera said that to visit Marta Karillos was not only inadvisable but idiotic. "Besides," she added, "there was a rumour that she was leaving the country. If this is so, you will have wasted your time."

"I don't care," I said recklessly. "My intentions are honourable."

"Well, *I* don't think it's a thing to joke about, but of course . . ."

"We have Count Stanieff to protect us," I said, pinching her hand. "He's armed to the teeth, I'm quite sure."

No more was said until we reached the villa. Rudy Selkar, who received us, looked perfectly flabbergasted. He hardly seemed to hear my inquiries for Astrid, and muttered something about it all being most unfortunate. By this time we were standing in the hall. As I looked round me, I began to feel extraordinarily light-hearted.

"Madame is not receiving?"

"If Your Majesty would care to wait—Madame assured me that she would be home by five."

"Very well."

He led us to the music-room on the first floor. It was here that Nikki had spent the evening of Paul's birth; I tried to visualize the scene, and failed.

Yes—it was a charming, one might even say a sympathetic, room, decorated in a manner that had nothing to do with the French influence, which prevailed in the palaces and castles that belonged to Nikki and me. The wall-paintings were of the native variety—primitive, brilliant, arresting. The chestnut velvet curtains, the single huge baroque mirror, the Russian needlework carpet, the gilded lamps, the pair of chased silver *torchères* that stood on either side of the open hearth, where a log fire was blazing—all these combined to make a gay yet intimate atmosphere: a home.

There were very few ornaments. On a small ormolu table by the fire I saw a mother-of-pearl work-basket and a miniature of Nikki, framed in turquoises and brilliants. I stood looking about me, as if in idle curiosity, my heart beating very fast, while Rudy Selkar hovered in the background.

"May I offer Your Majesty some refreshment?" he said nervously. "I fear the household is a little upset."

"Of course it is," I said, looking at him coolly. "Nothing upsets a household more than impending departure."

He blinked, his poise momentarily disturbed. "Madame's decision was so sudden, Your Majesty. I will inform her that Your Majesty is here the moment she returns."

"Please do so," I said carelessly.

As he stood there, a little doubtful—he was a typical Muranian, tall, harsh-featured, handsome, in the rough-cut, sombre manner of his kind—I began to feel uneasy. I thanked and dismissed him. As soon as we were alone, I went over to the mirror. It was a long time since I had been so concerned about my appearance. That concern was, I think, the last remnant of rivalry. I wanted Marta Karillos to see me at my best.

I was wearing a new gown that Madame Kasha had just designed for me. I have it still; about ten years ago, I so far lost my sense of humour as to express the desire to be buried in it. It was of palest lilac crêpe, very tight-fitting, caught in round the knees, with a short train. My hat and muff were of Parma violets, my gloves and shoes of pale grey kid. I knew, as I looked at myself, that I had regained my looks, and my figure; and, at this distance of time, I can add that they did not displease me.

"This house has charm," I began, turning away from the glass. "Yes, it's gay, after the Palace. I see why he liked to come here." There was no answer from either of my companions, and I added, "Count Stanieff, don't look so gloomy."

"Ma'am, I *am* gloomy. This was a very dangerous thing to do."

"Why dangerous? We go for a little drive in the country—I see a charming villa. What could be more natural than that I should want to see the inside?"

"But——"

"And if Madame Karillos has callers—unwelcome callers who arrive unexpectedly——"

"With knives and guns," Vera put in crossly.

"It isn't," I went on gaily, "as if the King was likely to come in. He's gone to Mornavitza."

"Suppose they break in, as they've threatened to do?" exclaimed Vera.

"They would hardly dare——" I began.

"Madame," cried Egon Stanieff, "you don't understand."

"Well?"

"These people are fanatics. If they wish to dispose of her, they won't care who stands in their way."

"I thought that they—whoever 'they' may be—were supposed to be attached to me. That's what the newspapers say." He groaned, and made a despairing gesture. I went on: "It's quite simple. Madame Karillos decides to leave. I pay a formal, farewell call. A charming scene! The Queen comes to say good-bye to an old and faithful friend."

"Absurd," Vera muttered, and Egon Stanieff looked at her approvingly.

"What shall we do while we're waiting?" I persisted. "Look at photograph albums or is that too banal? A little music, perhaps? Music has always played a big part in this house. Yes—that's a splendid idea, it might soothe the feelings of any—passers-by."

"You should have put a guard round the house," said Vera.

"Yes, indeed, Your Majesty——"

"Wouldn't that hurry on a crisis? No, I think my way is best."

I went over to the piano. Now the eyes of the miniature seemed to be following me about the room. Standing there, uncomfortably conscious of my companions' disapproval, I began to turn over the music in the rack.

It was then that I suddenly saw myself as impertinent and foolish. Suppose Marta Karillos were to come in before she was expected, and find me coolly scrutinizing her possessions? There was something extremely personal about the music that lay under my hand. Many of the songs were dedicated to her by the composers. Others—I pushed them hastily to one side—had messages and comments in a hand that I had seen only on official documents.

It was horrible to feel so unwanted—that brief thrill of exhilaration sank and died. I stared vaguely at a song entitled *Qu'as-tu fait de mon cœur?* (what indeed?) and felt a lump rise in my throat.

But I was determined to hide my disappointment, and said, with an attempt at a laugh, "Let's all sing this one—*The Gates of Paradise.*"

"Christiane, I don't think——"

"Don't spoil my first private outing, Vera, darling, please. I'll play it, and we'll all sing." As they drew near and looked at the music over my shoulder, I added defiantly, "It will sound delightfully peaceful and domestic."

Egon Stanieff had a pleasant tenor voice. During his visits to Dhrevin he and Vera and I had often sung together. We had reached the second verse when I heard the sound of a door being shut, and footsteps running up the stairs. Both noises were muffled and distant; I guessed that Marta's steward was on his way to warn us of her arrival. I looked at the others, and realized that they had heard nothing. By this time I was much too nervous to stop, so I went on playing, like an automaton, wondering what could have induced me to behave so senselessly. She would come in, and find us installed. I should give her my warning and promise of protection, and she would thank me, coldly and suspiciously, knowing that they were already out of date. It was an impossible situation—and I alone was to blame.

The doors at the end of the room opened quietly. I pretended to hear nothing, and went on playing. Then the voices behind me faltered, and faded away.

Nikki was standing there, looking at us. His expression was not to be read by me, in that moment of alarm and confusion. He was dressed in one of his plain dark uniforms, with no orders. He remained where he was, without speaking, for a few moments.

Then he said, in a withdrawn, frigid tone, "Count Stanieff, will you escort Countess Lemenken to the other room?"

As they hurried out, I turned my eyes away. I fumbled for the keys with the intention of starting to play again. But I couldn't manage it; my hands dropped, and I sat looking down at them.

Nikki walked up to the piano and stood opposite me. I wondered with passionate resentment why it was that I always did the wrong thing, and was never spared the consequences.

3

"And what does this gesture mean?" he said at last.

I looked up at him. Against that background of soft and brilliant colour he was like a statue carved in ebony and ivory.

Now, recalling that moment, I might more fitly compare him to Erebus, the deity whose parents were Chaos and Darkness, and whose name was given to the world of the dead—so fatal did he seem to me, so strange, so menacing. Then I saw, with heightened perception, the physical details, the characteristics that seem unique in the person one loves—the way his eyebrows grew, the curve of the nostril, the sweep of the black, silky hair from the high forehead, the long fingers that were now loosening his cloak.

I muttered, "Gesture?" hardly aware of what I was saying.

He paused, as if he were forcing himself to speak calmly. "I don't seem to remember meeting you here before—and on today, of all days."

"Shall we call it a formal visit of farewell?" I said, in a high-pitched, artificial tone.

He laughed shortly. "My God, you're clever! You engineered the whole thing—made her position here intolerable——"

"I haven't—I didn't——"

"And then you put yourself completely in the right by calling on her."

I felt my anger rising. That was a relief. It was pleasanter to be angry than frightened.

"I have engineered nothing," I said coldly. "Madame Karillos has realized, a little late, that her presence in Murania is no longer to be tolerated."

As I uttered the pompous phrases I disliked them; but it was not the moment for qualifications.

He had been walking up and down. Now he turned, and said, very low, "And why? Because of you."

"That's not fair——"

"Fair! The word comes charmingly from you, I must say. I've disappointed them—so, very naturally, they turn to you." He glanced at me from beneath his long lashes, and continued, on a note of contemptuous enumeration, "The saint—the people's friend—the mother——"

"Of your son!" I broke in, clenching my hands. It was easier to be angry, better to rise to his insults, than to sink beneath them. "I see that you're quite uninterested," I went on, wishing that he would look at me again instead of fixing his eyes on the ground.

There was a long silence. Then he began to speak in an icy, gentle tone. "My interests are more varied than you might suppose——"

"And if I am the people's friend," I interrupted, "don't you think they need one? During the last year Madame Karillos has sent five million roubles out of the country. She will live in the utmost luxury—and who will pay?"

"Spare me your rhetoric, please."

"You know it's true," I said stubbornly.

"Are you giving me any news?" he said, looking me up and down. "Do you think I don't know? Let me tell you something, as you're so interested in public affairs. She's not making provision for herself. That five million roubles will be all that we shall have to live on, she and I."

There was a short silence. "You and she," I repeated, in an extinguished voice. "Oh, no—no!"

"Certainly. She will be leaving almost at once, and in a few weeks"—he drew himself up, his eyes fixed on my face—"I shall slip out of the country—and that will be the end."

"The end?" I stammered.

"Of course," he said sharply. "What else did you expect? My plans have been destroyed—my only friend murdered . . ."

"That was dreadful——"

"It's so kind of you to sympathize. I'm all gratitude."

"Don't—don't sneer at me!" I cried out. "I came here to see her, not to pester you. It was announced that you were at Mornavitza. How could I know you would be here?"

"Well? What difference does that make? Here we are, abusing one another as usual."

"We didn't always——" I began, and broke off as I saw the look on his face. I added hastily, "You've made it very plain that I'm not wanted——"

"You're amazing!" he interrupted, with an angry laugh. "You seem to forget that I got all your messages from my mother."

"I sent no messages."

He stared at me suspiciously. "She said you had begged her to keep me away from you."

"I did no such thing. I was waiting for you."

I thought that this revelation might soften him. But all he did was to gaze absently in front of him; then he nodded, as if he had made up his mind.

"It seems that Mamma's been up to her tricks again," he said, with a faint smile. "Well, well! I wonder what the object of that was?"

"Please—don't let's consider that now——" I began.

"I don't, I assure you."

"I—it's very hard for me to ask you anything——"

"Really?"

"Don't do this—don't go away. Don't let the past kill the future——"

"I'm sorry—but your reasoning is beyond me."

"You've had your life, you and she—stay here. Oh"—as he made a contemptuous sound—"not for my sake, but for your son's. You pretend not to be wise—but you are. As long as you're alive——"

"I'm not going to get myself killed, even for you and your party."

"I've got no party! I'm talking about Paul. You can guide him. Think of his life—a little boy, surrounded by a cruel, ruthless——"

"Are you speaking of my mother? It's not a bad description."

I wrung my hands together. I tried to go on with what I had planned to say during all those long, lonely months. But I had begun to cry, and I couldn't stop. Between my sobs I heard myself saying, "Oh! please—please . . ."

I don't know how long it was that I stood there. As soon as I could command myself, I muttered an apology, and moved towards the door.

He said, in a low voice, "Is it possible that you are, after all, human?"

I turned. He was standing by the window. Now at last the hard, bold stare was gone, and his eyes were kind.

"Have you ever tried to find out?" I said brokenly.

He shook his head. "I don't know. I thought——" He stopped, with a helpless, bewildered gesture.

"What could you have thought? Tell me."

"That you were ambitious—scheming——"

"I never schemed."

"You trapped me once," he said quickly.

"I had to—I had to!"

"Why?"

I walked towards him. My knees were shaking; I was cold and sick. This was the last throw of all. I was desperate.

"You fool!" I whispered at last. "Can't you guess?"

He came nearer. "Tell me," he said, slowly and heavily, as if the words were being dragged out of him.

I shook my head, I was defeated, hopeless. "It's no good—it's all finished," I said, putting my hands over my eyes.

There was a long silence. Then I heard his voice, low and gentle and clear. "Christiane—tell me——"

We both turned, and saw Marta Karillos, standing in the open doorway. Selkar was beside her, supporting her. She was trembling, and very white.

4

Marta came towards Nikki with outstretched hands. He told Selkar to bring some brandy, and, putting his arms round her, led her to a chair. It was very odd; but the jealousy that I had expected to feel the moment she came into the room was lost in my anxiety, not only for her, but for myself. Had I done the right thing in coming to her? As she described, with gasps and sobs, the attack made on her carriage, the wounding of her coachman and footmen, and her panic-stricken flight to the shelter of her home, I began to wonder whether I had arrived too late.

Marta was too much agitated to be surprised at the sight of me. It was now nearly a year since I had seen her, and it seemed to me that she had aged a little. She was as nobly beautiful as ever. The turn of her head, the movements of her hands, were still exquisite; the shadows under her eyes and the increased fragility and slenderness of her figure gave her a romantic, almost a tragic, appeal. I could see that she had been very unhappy, that her nerves were in tatters; finally, as she became calmer, it was evident that her quick glance from Nikki to me had told her more, perhaps, than I knew myself. If at that moment I had been asked to say at what stage our relationship was, I should have found it impossible to answer.

As she concluded, "I'm afraid! Such hatred—I never realized——" and turned her shuddering gaze towards the window, I looked at Nikki.

By this time he had summoned Stanieff, who, like a hero in a melodrama, was fingering his revolver (I expect he would have preferred it to be a sword), and was all on fire to be of service.

Nikki said gently: "In a few days' time you will be safely away. But you must leave this house immediately. Stanieff——"

He drew the young man aside, and began to talk to him in a low voice.

Marta, with a glance at me, got up, but I wouldn't allow this, and we sat down on the sofa together. She looked round and said, with a sad smile: "I loved my little house. I have been happy here."

Nikki caught the last words, and came towards her, dismissing Stanieff with a gesture. "And you will be happy again," he said quietly, speaking as if they were alone. "Think of Paris, and all your friends."

She looked again from him to me. Then she said steadily, "How long shall I be alone?"

I was surprised at the frankness of the question; but there was a certain dignity in the manner in which it was asked.

He hesitated, cleared his throat, and began, "How do you mean?" She repeated the question in a more urgent tone.

He replied with a smile, "You could never be alone for long."

She stood up. Then she said, in a low voice, "Are you wilfully misunderstanding me?"

As he began to answer, Egon Stanieff burst into the room, exclaiming: "Sir! They've broken into the grounds of the villa—

they've killed two of the guards. You should leave immediately. I am responsible for Her Majesty's safety."

There was a moment's silence.

Then Nikki said, "No, Stanieff—I am responsible for Her Majesty's safety." He spoke lightly, almost as if he were teasing the agitated young man.

"But, Sir—they're threatening to burn the place down, and everyone in it!"

Nikki went over to the window. Marta and I were standing by the fireplace. We could hear—we could have heard some minutes ago if we had had time to listen—the murmur of a crowd of people in the courtyard below. This low, creeping noise was much more frightening than the angry shouts described by Marta.

Stanieff continued breathlessly: "I implore you, Sir—in two minutes it will be too late! They're surrounding the house."

Nikki smiled. "What a charming story that would make—can't you see it? 'The King and Queen slink away from hysterical peasants.' Pull yourself together, Stanieff," he added briskly.

Now the sounds were becoming louder. I was thankful that I couldn't understand what they were saying.

Poor Egon Stanieff, his revolver in his hand, again implored Nikki to leave with me, "by the cellars." His touching assumption that Nikki would fall in with this scheme was almost funny.

For some minutes it had become plain that Nikki was working out a plan of his own.

He turned to me, and said, in a low, rapid voice, "I want you to do exactly as I say—go into the next room, and wait there."

"And you——" I began.

"I shall stay here."

"But you can't——" Marta expostulated.

"Please do as I say. Go with the Queen into the next room. Stanieff, you'll stay with me."

Marta and I withdrew. Vera had disappeared. I heard afterwards that Egon Stanieff, almost as anxious for her safety as for my own, had taken her down to the cellars, in spite of her protestations; he had persuaded her to do this by assuring her that I was already on my way back to the Palace. It can be imagined what a scene she made when she discovered the truth.

Alone in the antechamber—it was little more than a closet—leading out of the music-room, Marta and I glanced at one another, and smiled. The door was covered by a portière that Nikki had drawn behind us. Marta opened the door and placed a stool for me beside it. She stood behind me, looking over my shoulder.

Stanieff was bustling about, as if preparing the music-room for a siege. His arrangements were so businesslike, and so inept, that I had some difficulty in restraining myself from laughing out loud. I looked up at Marta, and she put her finger on her lip. I realize now that I was too much absorbed with my own problems to be frightened by an attempted irruption.

Nikki watched Egon Stanieff for a moment, and then said, "And now—won't you relax?"

Stanieff, who had been ramming an armchair against the double doors, gave him an exasperated glance. "Sir!"

"I assure you, it is essential."

"But how can I?"

"I don't know, but please do," said Nikki, sitting down on the sofa, and spreading out his hands to the fire. He added, in a tone of mild derision: "And take that chair away—it looks perfectly ridiculous. Those doors open the other way, in any case."

Stanieff, distraught, but still heroic, removed the chair. Now the noise had reached the balcony. There was some muttering, and the scraping of boots against the stone.

Nikki went on: "They may think better of it. If they do come, don't be provoked by anything they say."

In the silence that followed—and the crowd in the courtyard was now strangely, ominously quiet—Nikki continued, in a louder voice: "And where are you thinking of spending your leave? With your father?"

"My leave?" repeated Stanieff vaguely.

"Yes——" said Nikki, turning round as if to pursue the conversation, and then breaking off.

Two men—a third—then four or five more—had climbed onto the balcony, and were now standing just inside the room. They were all young, dirty, and ragged. And yet—this was perhaps rather reassuring than otherwise—they were not, I could see, of the lowest and most wretched type, the type that I had seen creeping out of the hovels in the fortifications of the Old City.

They all stopped as soon as they were inside, and stood in a half-circle, looking at Nikki with impassive faces. There was one with a beard, one dark, good-looking and slender, one with red hair, and two fair, plump fellows who might have been brothers. I could not differentiate between the rest; they were nondescript. Somehow, all of them gave the impression of being slightly disguised.

Nikki said nothing for a moment or two. Then he got up from the sofa and strolled over to the door. He stood there, surveying them from a distance with an expressionless face.

He said something in Muranian; then, appearing to change his mind, he went on in French, with a glance at Stanieff, "We seem to have an audience."

No one said anything. It was clear that all the men, ill-clad and impoverished though they looked, understood what he was saying.

He turned to the one nearest him, and went on, in the same language: "Do you usually enter private houses by climbing balconies? This is a private house, you know."

"Yes, we know," interrupted the dark-haired boy, in a surprisingly educated voice. "The harlot's house."

Nikki's lips tightened a little. Then he said casually: "Is it? and I've been coming here for years—someone might have told me." He paused, adding, in a lower voice, "Why aren't you kneeling?"

"We've done with kneeling," said the man with the beard.

"I think not," said Nikki coldly, restraining Stanieff with a movement of his hand. "You ought to kneel in chains for the rest of your lives for this outrage—or perhaps it isn't an outrage, just a friendly call. If so, why these glowering looks?"

There was no answer.

He glanced round, and added, in a harsh yet rallying tone: "Have you a grievance? Some petition you wish to present? Tell me—don't be tongue-tied."

After another pause, the red-haired young man, in strongly accented but perfectly grammatical French, announced, "We've come here to do a job."

There was a murmur of approbation from the others, and another added, "A job that should have been done long ago."

"Aren't you rather young for this sort of thing?" said Nikki, turning to him with a smile. "Or does the University of Bledz encourage a little treason during the vacation?"

"Don't answer him!" said a tall, fair man, who had not yet spoken. "He's talking like this to gain time."

"We mean no harm to you," the dark-haired boy added, in an awkward manner.

"I'm relieved to hear it," said Nikki icily.

I saw that he was now restraining his anger with great difficulty. As for poor Egon Stanieff, he was in a state of bursting fury; but he kept his temper admirably, never taking his eyes from Nikki's face.

"Whom are you threatening, then?" continued Nikki, his eyes on the dark young man.

There was a moment's pause. Then someone said, "An enemy of the Queen," in a loud, angry voice.

"Has she an enemy?" said Nikki, leaning forward a little, as if to look more closely at the speaker.

"She's got an enemy, and we know her name!" said the man with the beard, stepping out of the half-circle. "Karillos! Hand her over— we'll deal with her. Karillos! We spit on her!" And he spat on the floor. "Isn't the Queen good enough for you?"

Nikki's hands had been clasped behind him. Now they seemed to spring forward of their own volition. But he gripped them together with such a violent effort that his whole body shook, and he shifted his weight from one foot to another.

There was a long silence. Then Nikki said, in a breathless, almost inaudible voice, "Far too good, my friend—far too good."

No one said anything. The men were watching him keenly, a little puzzled.

Nikki walked slowly down the pair of shallow steps that led from the door into the centre of the room, and went over to the man with the beard.

"Do you know what it is like to be fed with lies?" he said, very low. "It's an upsetting diet. Hadn't you better——"

"We know lies when we hear them," interrupted a very young man, with melodramatic bitterness.

"But do you know the truth?" said Nikki, who seemed now to have recovered a little of his composure. "Do your professors——"

"That's enough about them—we stand for the people," interrupted a voice from the centre.

"I wonder."

"We know one truth," said the man with the beard, who had begun to look a little doubtful. "You and your Karillos are breaking the Queen's heart."

Again there was a murmur of approval.

"Oh—I see," said Nikki slowly. He was now very white. The effort of keeping his temper had once more become difficult. As he locked his hands together, I saw the sweat break out on his forehead. After a moment's silence he went on, more smoothly, "What a nauseating phrase—breaking the Queen's heart." He turned away, and glanced up at the ceiling. "Odd," he went on, as if communing with himself, "she never told me her heart was breaking. I must ask her about it."

Then he walked to the door of the antechamber, so quickly that Marta and I had barely time to stand back, looking rather guiltily at one another.

"My dear," Nikki went on, in an artificially breezy manner, "have you a moment?"

I whispered to Marta, "Let us pretend we've been gossiping—and—and——" She nodded. I walked into the music-room, my arm in hers. Gazing at her with that exaggerated yet meaningless look of animation used in amateur theatricals, I said eagerly, "I was just making a list of things I've asked Marta to send me from Paris—you see——" I broke off, as if suddenly aware of the others. "Oh—you're busy. Another time."

The men drew back a little, staring at me, and then at one another.

Nikki went on, in a clear, metallic voice: "My dear—would you mind answering a very simple question? Is your heart breaking?"

I gazed at him. Then I said slowly, with memories of my elocution lessons at home: "My heart breaking? What is this—some joke?"

"I should have thought so," said Nikki, breathing rather fast. "But these—*my friends*—here, think not. Is it true? Is your heart breaking?"

"Well—that's a strong word," I said, with a smile. "I'm sad, naturally—one is always sad when a good friend goes away. And she's sad too, aren't you, Marta?"

There was another and louder murmur, another interchange of glances, this time frankly perplexed.

I glanced at the audience, gave them a gracious smile, and said, in the peevish tone of a spoilt child: "Oh, please—what does all this mean? Surely our last evening all together could have been private?"

There followed a very long silence indeed. Nikki turned from me to the revolutionaries.

One said to another, "We've been fooled," in a low voice.

Nikki caught the speaker's eye, and said, with a cool, bold smile: "No—not now. But I think you've been very much fooled in the

past. I shall have to come to some of the lectures they give you—
incognito. You must have been reading—what? Saint-Simon? Ba-
kunin? Or have your instructors bored you so much that you've had
to find your own political theories?" There was an unwilling smile at
this. He went on, in a more serious tone: "Don't think I don't know
the malicious lies that have been spread about me. I even know
who spread them."

The man with the beard stepped forward, and said pompously,
"We came here with the intention——"

"Of doing a job—I know. But are you quite sure that it needs to be
done?"

"We meant——"

"Be silent!" said Nikki, suddenly exploding. In the pause that
followed he mastered himself, and added, in a quieter voice, "Why
don't you go home and wash that very obvious dirt off your faces?"

The words were extremely provocative; but they were spoken in
the tone of one man of the world sharing an absurd joke with another.

"You have my word," I struck in, "that, as far as I am concerned,
Madame Karillos is a valued and faithful friend. If I could persuade
her to stay in Murania, I should do so."

At this point the dark-haired boy—he could not have been more
than twenty—took off his cap. Two others bowed, and began to back
away. Then all of them retreated, in some confusion, to the windows.

"Please," I went on, "go to your homes. The King and I will try to
forget that this ever happened. I shall even forget your faces," I
added. "And I am sure the King will too."

"I shall try," said Nikki acidly. "But I shall find it extremely difficult." As they withdrew, he raised his hand and said peremptorily,
"Don't go by the balcony—you might break your necks, and you
know how I should hate that to happen." There was a faint sound
that might have been an appreciative titter, and he went on: "The
front door this time. Count Stanieff will be so kind as to show you
the way."

They went out. We stood in silence until we heard their voices
raised; they were speaking to the crowd outside in Muranian, telling them, as I guessed, to disperse.

As we heard the clatter of feet, Nikki drew a long breath. He said,
in a low voice: "Thank you, Christiane. That was very well done."

It was the first time he had ever spoken to me in that natural, cordial way. As I looked at him, I hardly heard Marta's murmured exclamation.

Nikki walked quickly over to the window, and, standing behind the curtain, looked out into the courtyard.

"They're going," he said, after a pause. "Those boys have them under control, it seems. They appear satisfied—but for how long?"

After another glance, he turned to Marta, and said, in the same practical, friendly voice that he had used to me: "I will send a carriage for you, from the Palace. You must hide yourself until you can get away. I've arranged it with Stanieff. He will escort you."

"Very well," she said calmly. "I know that I must go—and the sooner the better."

He seemed unable to meet her glance. He turned again to the window.

Marta continued, in a lower voice, "Ma'am—could I have a few moments with you alone?"

I said, "Yes, of course," looking at Nikki.

He walked away from the window, stopped, and contemplated us both for a moment or two. Then he said, in an abstracted voice: "I have to go back to the Palace. I will leave the Queen here with you."

"Is it safe for her——" Marta began.

"Can't we go together?" I said, before I could stop myself.

He shook his head. "I'll take your carriage, and send one back for you. I have a Ministers' conference at half-past six, and it's nearly that now."

"I can't help feeling anxious for the Queen——" Marta said.

"Wherever she is she will be safe, I think," said Nikki, with a return to his satirical manner. "And you will be safe with her. I must leave you." And, with a slight, unsmiling bow, he turned away.

"Oh, wait a minute!" I exclaimed. "Those men who were killed? Shouldn't we——"

"Stanieff is seeing to that. The bodies have been carried to the cellars."

"But the people who did it——"

"I promised to forget, didn't I?"

"You can't!" I exclaimed. "They're murderers . . ."

"We're all savages in this country, I'm afraid. But even savages must keep their word, if they're kings as well," said Nikki, rather wearily.

I was silenced.

As Nikki reached the door, he turned again, and said, in his sardonic manner, "Oh, Marta, by the way—don't betray me entirely, will you?"

"Betray——"

"The Queen thinks I'm a bad character, you see," he said, with a faint smile. "Don't disillusion her."

Then he went out, leaving us staring at one another.

CHAPTER TEN

How I Found a Friend and Lost an Enemy

MARTA and I sat down on either side of the fire. She looked into it for a moment or two, and then began: "Ma'am—I want to try to tell you in a few minutes what would ordinarily take a lifetime. It's about him and me."

"I had hoped that you would," I said. "But I have done all the wrong things—I know that. When I asked you to the ball, for instance."

"Ah, yes," she said absently. "That was a dreadful evening."

"It wasn't because I wanted to assert myself in any way. I knew what you and Nikki were to each other. I was trying to overcome my own jealousy."

"I could feel that," she said, after a pause.

"If it hadn't been for you," I went on, "what would have happened to him? What was he like, when you first knew him?"

She looked down, and then put her hand over her eyes. "So different . . ." she said, in a low voice. "He'd had a miserable life. But he wasn't embittered, or cruel. He'd never been loved. I was the first person who loved him for himself, not for what he could give. That made him dependent on me, I suppose."

"You know, I think, that I'm in love with him—that I always have been?"

She smiled. "Forgive me, Ma'am—but you're so young. To you a year seems, I know, a very long time——"

"I loved him in my mind before I came to this country," I interrupted; and, with some hesitations and blunderings, I told her of my childish daydreams and of my first sight of her and Nikki, in the South of France.

She looked at me wonderingly. "If he had known you then—but he was a young man, and you were a child."

"Tell me some more about those early days."

"I think that his upbringing was just about as bad as it could possibly be," she said, in a more detached and reminiscent tone. "It made him—all that he wasn't meant to be. He was idealistic, gentle, and kind. His mother's treatment of him (it's best not to go into that, for I know that, in spite of her good nature and her charm, she's very unscrupulous) made him distrustful of women. His father's jealousy oppressed and bewildered him. The courtiers—the young men who were chosen to be his companions—flattered and spoilt him. And he was clever enough to see through them, and that made him cynical. Well—then there were the women. They wanted him to make love to them, of course, and he did." She smiled. "But they also wanted presents and favours. When he realized that he was being made use of, he became disillusioned. It's a commonplace story, in many ways. One's read it in the history books, often enough."

"But for a long time he took his job very seriously," I said, as she fell into silence.

"Yes—yes," she began, rousing herself. "But his father made it quite clear that he wasn't to be anything but a figurehead, until he succeeded. He was impatient, like most young men. He couldn't bear to wait; he didn't like wasting his time. He saw his father living on and on, and himself as a middle-aged man, coming to the throne when it was too late. So he threw up all his ideals and schemes, and set his heart on one thing—freedom. Then he met me."

"Did he tell you all that he'd been through?"

"Not at once. It came out by degrees. King Nicholas was a violent, cruel man. At the time Nikki and I met, there were rumours going about that frightened me very much—for Nikki. It was believed that the King hated him so much that he was going to disinherit him, and make Prince Cyril the heir."

"But how could he have done that?" I exclaimed.

"His plan was—and he had begun, I think, to carry it out—so to treat Nikki as to make him" —she paused, and I saw her hands tremble as she stretched them out to the fire—"unfit—completely unfit, to reign."

"I don't quite understand."

"Well—to persecute him, and—and then shut him up, so that he should become an invalid, a mental case. The Kings of Murania have absolute power over their heirs, as you know. King Nicholas began by imprisoning, and eventually exiling, a friend, an older man—one of the Ministers—whom Nikki trusted and looked up to ——"

"Stefan Rell?"

"Yes. He was a wonderful man. I wish you could have known him." She paused, and then went on: "Whether rightly or not—I've never got to the bottom of the whole horrible story—Nikki was in fear of his life when he met me. And not only that. He was afraid of being 'disciplined'—that was his father's euphemism—to the point of madness. There had been insanity in the Orosvar family. Not much—not nearly as much as in the Habsburg or Bourbon rulers—but enough. Enough, at any rate, to make Nikki afraid of what might happen."

"I see," I said, trying to speak calmly. "But it seems to me that Nikki's father must have been—a bit odd—himself."

"He was a clever old man," said Marta thoughtfully. She added, in an expressionless voice, "I have been told that he changed considerably after his marriage."

There was a long silence. Then she continued: "Well—Nikki and I fell in love. I don't think his father really objected to that—it was quite in the Orosvar tradition to have a mistress both before and after marriage. But he instinctively thwarted Nikki in everything that he wanted to do—and Nikki used me, as I realize now, to gain his freedom. He came to me one night after a terrible scene with his father, and said, 'It's exile with you—or disintegration here.' We sat up all night talking. I was trying to soothe him. I didn't think, then, that he really meant to run away."

"He was lucky to have found someone like you," I interjected.

"Yes," said Marta, in the same calm, unemphatic tone, "I think he was. That was all I meant to him then—freedom. Not, of course, freedom as people like myself understand the word, but as kings and queens meant it—freedom to keep yourself from the abyss. That was all Nikki could hope for—and I helped him."

"He loved you with all his heart and soul—he told me so once," I said, in a burst of resentment.

She looked at me, and smiled. It was the smile of one who is beyond hope or despair. "He may have thought so," she said quietly, "but for a long time now——" She broke off, and looked away. "You're the mother of his son," she added, after a pause.

I said nothing, and a moment later she resumed, in an even, narrative tone: "I'm his youth. The youth he never had."

Suddenly my eyes filled with tears. "I'm glad you were able to give it him," I said confusedly. "I've been able to give him nothing but an heir—and he doesn't seem to care——"

"Forgive me, but you're wrong. He does."

I shook my head. She put her hand on my arm. "It will come right," she said, in the gentle, loving voice that made me long to bury my head in her lap and pour out all my miseries. "Who should know that better than I?" And she laughed softly.

"It isn't fair!" I said violently. "He's made you so unhappy. And he doesn't think, or care——"

"We were happy, all those years," she said, looking into the fire again. "Very happy. It's odd—such silly, incongruous things come back to one. I was thinking, when I got up this morning—but perhaps it's not——"

"Please tell me."

"When he was very young—when we first met, here, in Bledz— he used to come to my house for supper. I never knew whether he was coming or not, of course. We'd talk; and sometimes I'd sing." She added simply, looking at me, "It was before I became his mistress. I didn't really know him then."

"Go on."

"Well—we had a ridiculous joke—about the time. I'd say, 'It's past twelve—oughtn't you to be going?' and he'd say, 'I never could count up to more than ten—eleven, if given a chocolate.' And then I'd hand him a box of chocolates. I don't know why—but it's those pointless, absurd things that stay with one when everything else has gone."

"You're still happy together?" I said tentatively.

"When he decided to come back, he clung to the shreds of happiness that remained—that was all."

"But——"

"He wanted to be King. When his mother came to his hotel in Paris—I found them together—he was as excited, as hopeful, as if he were a young man. That was a strange moment—like the fall of a curtain. I'd seen it coming for twenty years—sometimes clearly, sometimes dimly; but it had always been there. I said to him later,

'Why aren't I crying, making a scene?' And he said, 'It's going to make no difference. This time I shall have absolute power, absolute freedom.' Freedom, for a king! I wanted to laugh. But I spared him my laughter—and my tears."

"You're wonderful," I said, drawing a long breath.

She looked at me vaguely. Then she went on, as if I had not spoken: "Yes—he wanted to be King—he also wanted me. He thought it would work. And then he fell in love—for the first time."

"You can't expect me to believe——"

"You see, I had been a symbol. I was a companion. There were times, in those twenty years, when I lost him. He came back. Now he won't come back—ever."

The words gave me a strange and bitter ecstasy. I had no answer, no comment.

She went on, in the same unemotional, gentle voice: "I knew it—instantly. But I had everything to lose—and I wouldn't recognize it. That's what they call being feminine, isn't it?" she added, smiling. "Well—I've recognized it, now."

"How do you know he's fallen in love with me?"

She looked at me. Then she got up and turned away. "Not because of anything he's said—or done."

"Then——"

"But because of what he hasn't said—and hasn't done."

"I wish I could believe it."

"You will, Ma'am," she said, dropping the intimate manner, and speaking rather dryly. "This has been my—explanation—also my apology. I know that this year has been unhappy for you—desperately so. I'm sorry."

"I've nothing to forgive," I said quickly. Then I added: "I don't know why it is—I've only been jealous of you at odd moments. I suppose it's because for many years you were part of a romance, in which I sometimes took your place—in my imagination. It would have been like being jealous of myself," I went on confusedly. "I can't explain these things."

"No—no one can," she said, in a low voice. "But one can understand them, even so. I've often blamed myself for letting him come here," she went on, resting her hand on the mantelpiece and looking down. "But—he's all my life. I've robbed you of a whole year of happiness—not without qualms, not without scruples, believe me."

"I realize that," I said, putting my hand on hers. "And I've learnt a lot in this year. I wasn't ready. Perhaps I am now."

She glanced down at my hand—and at the betrothal ring of the Orosvars. I walked over to the window. Then I turned, and looked back at her.

She was middle-aged—I was barely nineteen. She had yielded—I was, so she would have me believe, triumphant. She was going away—I was installed. And yet, as we looked at one another, I knew that I stood for an ancient tie, a tie that could be irksome and odious—that of an arranged marriage; while she, still beautiful, still alluring, stood, now and forever, for the youth and freedom that she had given to my husband, twenty years before. In this game—of which I had barely learnt the rules—wives were at a disadvantage, and mistresses were undefeatable.

I came out of this reverie to hear Marta saying: "I think you are ready, Ma'am. You have learnt not to expect too much, at any rate," she added, in a lighter tone.

"That's true enough," I said, and we both laughed.

2

I wouldn't allow myself to hope that Marta was right about Nikki and me. He had ceased to hate me; I was sure of that. But if he had fallen in love with me, he wouldn't have left me at the villa; he would have sent a message to put off the Ministers' conference, and we should have returned to the Palace together.

During the drive home I prepared a reassuring version of the attack on the villa for Vera. Dreading the sight of her anxious face and the sound of her protests and lamentations, I came into the Palace with a bright, false smile on my face.

She and I were to spend the evening together in the rooms that I had occupied since my arrival in Murania, and which I had returned to as soon as I was well again, because they were near the nurseries. I had not set foot in those prepared for Nikki and me since that painful scene in his library, just before the wedding.

As I came in, the footmen were standing there as usual to open the doors for me. But there was no one in the antechamber, no maid waiting about in the corridor, and I began to feel rather uneasy, as I recalled the events of the afternoon. I walked through three deserted rooms to the boudoir. At first I saw no one. Then Nikki got up from the sofa. The doors closed behind me. We were alone.

It occurred to me that something terrible might have happened to Vera, and that he was going to break the news to me. As I stood in the middle of the room staring at him, completely at a loss, I noticed that he was now wearing an order—the eight-pointed, jewelled star of Saint Jerome, that he put on for official occasions. Then I remembered the conference; he would have had to wear it for that. He must have come from the Knights' Hall straight to my rooms. It was curious—but I could not stop myself from dwelling on this triviality, to the exclusion of everything else.

"And now," he said, after what appeared to me an interminable silence, "may we resume our conversation?"

He looked very grave. His tone was courteous; it held none of the inflections I had learned to dread. *But it was too late.* I stood there, helpless, intimidated, bewildered.

At last I repeated, "What conversation?" like a dull child.

He gave me a long, considering look, and then walked over to the window. He stared out, his hands clasped behind him, and said, in the same serious, subdued voice, "I asked you why you tricked me—and you called me a fool."

"I was angry," I said, in a low voice. "I didn't mean—what I should have said was, you were blind."

He neither turned round nor answered. It was easier to speak to him when he wasn't looking at me.

I went on, in a more confident tone: "I had to do it. Love makes one do strange things—wrong things. I know now that I——"

I stopped as he turned round, fixing his eyes on my face. "Love?"

Now his voice was as I had heard it all too often—harsh, severe, alarming. Yet there was something in his expression that gave me courage to go on.

"Yes," I said, trying to speak collectedly; "did it ever occur to you that I might have been in love with you?"

"How could it? We'd never met."

This was not the moment for lengthy revelations. I must speak briefly or not at all.

"I fell in love with you seven years ago," I said, in an even voice.

In the silence that followed, I began to wonder why I felt so calm.

And as we stood there, gazing at one another, I saw again the balcony looking out over the Mediterranean, a wondering child, and a man and a woman sitting apart, self-sufficing, oblivious, legendary. That was a scene that I could not venture to describe; but it did lead up to something that must speak for me. I went to a chest and took out of it the album, rather shabby and battered now, that I had shown—as it might have been in another age—to my father, on the morning of my eighteenth birthday. I opened it, and handed it to Nikki.

He took it, with a puzzled, suspicious glance. "What's this?"

I walked away from him. Then I heard him turning over the pages. He said something that I could not hear: it sounded like an exclamation. By now, such powers of endurance as I had left were worn down to the socket.

Then at last he spoke again.

"I thought I'd put the past behind me. Why have you conjured it up for me like this?"

I turned and looked at him. I saw he was deeply moved, whether by the spectacle of his lost youth or by the fact that I had the record of it in my keeping, I could not tell.

I forced myself to speak quietly, as I answered: "I didn't mean to remind you of anything you wished to forget. But that book is the only proof I have."

"I don't understand."

"I collected those photographs and cuttings when I was a little girl. They prove, as no words or looks of mine can do, what you were —what you are—to me."

"And what is that," he said, in a low voice, taking a step towards me.

"Romance."

"We're married. There's nothing romantic about our situation. Unless——" He stopped; his voice had sunk to a whisper.

"Perhaps not—to you. But I saw you once, long ago, with Marta. I was eleven. I fell in love with you. I know how foolish, how ludicrous, that must seem. Then I loved you as one loves the hero in a play, or a story. Now—"

"Go on."

"Now, I love you because I belong to you. I don't pretend to know what you're really like—I can't guess what you feel. I only know that I have always—always—felt the same."

He looked from the book to me. Then he put it down.

"That's not possible!" he said, in a queer, breathless voice.

I said nothing, I did not move.

"You've got everything," he went on, staring at me. "Beauty: power: youth: a child——"

I shook my head. "I love you," I said, after a pause, trying to speak deliberately. "And I wanted you to love me."

There was a long, dreadful silence.

At last he said, in a hard, dry tone, "I do love you—God help me!"

"Is it true? Is it?"

"Christiane——"

I could not look at him any more. I hid my face from those blazing eyes. He put his arms round me, and drew my head down to his shoulder. Then he kissed me.

And as he did so I felt the star pressing against my heart, through the heavy silk and the delicate lawn, pressing into my breast. He held me away from him; he looked at me, and smiled.

And still I felt the pain of the bruised flesh, as if the star were within me, freezing, burning, turning my blood from ice to fire. Later, in the reeling darkness of his long embrace, I became gradually, dimly, aware that he had bridged all the gulfs, stripped off all the reserves and defences. Bound and locked together, we gave ourselves up to the rhythmic ebb and flow of a tide that was carrying us on to speechless oblivion.

Just before I sank away, I wondered vaguely how long we were likely to be left alone.

I murmured, "Suppose someone comes in?"

"No one will, my darling—my sweet angel—my love," he whispered, curling his fingers in my hair. "I told them they were all to go, as soon as you came back."

"Were you so sure of me, then?"

"Sure—no. Hopeful—waiting—longing . . ."

3

I awoke from a deep and dreamless sleep to find myself tucked up on the sofa in a shawl. Nikki was standing over me; I could just see his face in the grey light that was beginning to creep through the shutters. I looked vaguely from him to the shawl, and remembered

—as one remembers something seen many years ago—that it had been draped over the sofa when I last set eyes on it.

Nikki touched my shoulder, and whispered to me to stay where I was till he came back.

I caught at his hand. "Tell me one thing, just one—what are you going to do?"

"I'm going to love you all the rest of my life. But first—"

"I mean about going away. This afternoon——"

"Yesterday."

"You said you were going away—with——"

He bent down and kissed my forehead. "That was yesterday. I'll come back for you in a few minutes." And he was gone.

I must have fallen asleep again, for I woke with a start as he came softly in, wearing a dressing-gown and carrying what appeared to be a bundle of grey velvet over his arm. As I sat up, holding the shawl against me, he dropped it into my lap.

"Will this do?" he said, with a smile. "I dragged it out after going through half a dozen cupboards."

I gazed at it. "It's an opera cloak," I said, in a bewildered voice.

"It looked warmer than most of the other things. Won't it do?"

"Am I to put it on? What do you——"

"I want you to come with me. But you mustn't catch cold," he said, and walked over to the stove, where a few embers were still glowing dimly.

Still rather sleepy, and very dazed, I swathed the folds of velvet and chinchilla round me. They wouldn't hold together, so I stripped the sash from my lilac dress, and made it into a belt. Then I thrust my bare feet into the grey kid slippers and said, rather doubtfully, that I was ready.

Nikki had thrown open the door of the stove, and was warming his hands. He turned, and held out his arms; in the faint pink light he looked very tall, and as dark as a gipsy.

"I wonder what you're feeling," he said, as I leaned against him. "You look about twelve, and it makes me feel horribly guilty. Are you frozen? Tell me"—enclosing my hand in both his own.

"I'm not a bit cold. But I'm rather hungry," I said, after a moment's consideration.

He burst out laughing. "Are you? Come along." And he began to lead me towards the long mirror that was fitted into the wall by the piano.

"Where are we going?"

"To my—to our own rooms. This way."

"Through the looking-glass? But——"

He twisted a knob at the bottom of the mirror, and stood back as it swung forward and revealed a narrow passage. When he had shut the hidden door behind us, we stood for a moment in the dark. Then he led me on, his arm round my waist.

The secret passage led to the apartments which had been re-decorated for our marriage. We came out into the library through a door concealed by bookshelves. Here the lamps were lit, and by the open hearth, where a fire was blazing, a small round table was laid for two people. I stopped, clinging to his arm.

"How *lovely*—how did you—— Oh! what are you doing?"

He had moved over to the hearth, and was pulling at the bell. Immediately Giulio appeared, carrying a tray on which were two or three smoking dishes. A delicious smell filled the room.

Nikki was looking at me with an expectant, delighted expression. Giulio set down the dishes, bowed, and stood back. Nikki drew me towards the table, and I sat down, feeling as if we were both in a fairy-tale. Giulio placed a bottle of wine beside his master, and went out.

"There you are, my darling—roast pheasant—mushrooms . . ."

"But *how*——"

"This is nothing," he said, piling up my plate. "Giulio can do better still if he's given a little warning."

Still quite bemused, I stared round the room, and began at last to eat. I was ravenous. Then I looked up, to see Nikki gazing at me, his face between his hands, his elbows on the table.

As our eyes met, he said quickly, as if he were a little embarrassed, "Is that what you like?"

I nodded. "Aren't you going to have anything?"

"Oh—yes——" he said vaguely, and poured out the wine. He drank and refilled his glass. After that, he fell to gazing at me again. "You're so beautiful!" he said at last. "I can't believe in this—this paradise . . ."

"It's odd," I said, as his voice died away, "I keep remembering——"

"What?"

"A drunken king—making love to his bride's——"

His face darkened. "It wasn't a very good beginning," he said, putting a slice of pheasant on his plate, and staring at it gloomily.

"It sounds squalid, doesn't it?" I went on, wondering if I dared .tease him a little. "But not to me. I wanted you. I was quite shameless——"

"Christiane," he interrupted, his voice trembling and hoarse, "look at me." As I did so he went on, "Are you telling me that in spite of everything, in spite of my appalling behaviour, you think you—I can hardly say the word—love me?"

"No more, no less, than I've always loved you."

He shook his head, as if he were utterly bewildered. "But you've never even looked at me! Why, I hardly know the colour of your eyes."

"What colour are they?"

He came round the table, and took my face between his hands. "Blue-green—deep as a lake—and shining like jewels."

"Like aquamarines," I suggested.

He drew away, stared at me, and threw up his hands. "This is fantastic!" he exclaimed, with a shaky laugh. "A declaration—a few hours of ecstasy—and a year of hatred and suspicion is wiped out." He began to walk up and down. "No, it's too easy—there must be something behind it."

"Stop doubting," I said gently. "I have."

"You? You're a miracle. Why shouldn't I doubt? Just cast your mind back to that very disgraceful evening——"

"I didn't think it was disgraceful."

"Christiane, listen! I, very drunkenly and very caddishly, tell my fiancée's maid that my marriage is—to put it politely—a marriage in name only, and what happens? I get seduced!"

"You——"

"Oh yes—I get seduced, and why? Because there's got to be an heir. And the next night"—he turned towards me, his eyes shining—"this maid walks into the ballroom, and says, 'You see, the girl you made love to is your Princess—now let's all settle down, and enjoy ourselves.' So we did settle down—but we didn't enjoy ourselves. At least, I didn't——"

"Neither did I."

He put his arm round my shoulders, and pressed my face against his chest. "My darling—forgive me."

I twisted round and kissed him. "Don't—don't be——"

"Well?"

"Morbid. When you talk about forgiveness, it brings back all the sad times——"

"What can I do to make you forget them?"

"Sit down and eat. This is the first happy meal we've ever had."

He wandered vaguely across the room. He needed a shave, and his hair was on end; I had never seen him look handsomer.

"Do sit down, Nikki," I began timidly.

"It's so heavenly to hear you say that!"

"Why don't you rest a little?"

He sat down, and began to pick at his food. Then he looked up at me rather mischievously. "It's certainly true that I haven't rested much—have I?"

I couldn't answer. I felt my colour rising as I looked at him, half smiling, a little shocked.

"Tell me," he said, after another silence, "why did they call you the Snow Princess? I can't understand it."

"Nikki!"

"I really want to know."

"Oh, I don't know—it's a hateful name. I used to be rather a prig, I think," I said, in a confused manner.

"Are you still?"

"I don't think so," I said, with a shamefaced laugh. "I've no right to be, have I?"

"People with enormous aquamarine eyes, and beautiful curly hair, and exquisite hands, and lovely legs, have a right to be anything they like—at least, in my kingdom. So you shall be a prig, my angel, if you want to be."

"Is that all you're going to eat?"

"I'm not hungry, to tell you the truth." He pushed his plate away, and thrust his hands through his hair. "Oh!" he said, with a long sigh, "how I've hated this year!" Then he looked at me, with a sly smile. "And how I've hated you. And how I've longed for—Astrid."

"Ah!" I said severely, "that shameless hussy of a maid of mine. I shall dismiss her."

"And I shall sneak her up the back stairs. No, it's no good, I must kiss you . . ." After a pause, he added: "Shall I peel you an apple? You've hardly touched your wine."

"I don't want any more."

"Perhaps you'd rather I sent for some Tokay?"

"No," I said laughing, and leaning back against him, "not even that."

He walked away to the bookcase. I looked at him anxiously. I know now that he was suppressing a great wave of remorse, an outburst of bitterness against himself.

He thrust his hands in the pockets of his dressing-gown and said, rather unsteadily, "You see—I never expected to fall in love with you."

"Of course not."

"And I thought you knew about that paper—you know—the one forbidding Marta—after all, that was my only condition——"

"I know."

"And then, when you came into that ballroom, looking like a cat —no, a very naughty little kitten—that's swallowed the cream, I really *was*——"

"Enraged?"

"Well—humiliated. To be made a fool of by an *intrigante* young enough to be my daughter—no, it was too much." He smiled at me rather guiltily. After a moment he added: "And, you know, all my life—all my early life, that is—I was ordered about, commanded to do this and that—no question, no choice—and it's made me very recalcitrant about certain things."

"I realized that. That was why I——"

"Why you——"

"Behaved as I did," I said hastily.

He glanced at me, and began again to walk up and down. Then he said, in a slightly mocking tone: "You know, this is going to be a shock to a lot of people. Mamma . . ."

"Yes, I suppose it will be," I said, getting up and standing by the fire.

"And what about the faithful Egon?" he said, turning suddenly, his eyes half-closed. "Is he your lover?"

I stared at him speechlessly.

"Well?"

"No, he isn't," I replied, in a matter-of-fact voice. But I didn't feel very secure.

"He must be mad——" he began. I said nothing. After a long silence, he put his hand up to his head, as if he were coming out of a nightmare. "I shouldn't have said that."

"No, I don't think you should."

The next moment his arms were round me. "Oh! my darling—my sweet wife—bear with me. I'm a brute, and a devil. And you're so young, you can't know all the thoughts that whirl and hammer in my head, and make me say these things. But I love you . . ." I made a reassuring sound, and he continued, sitting by the fire and drawing me down onto his knee, "I'd give anything—anything in the world —to make up to you for this year."

In the interval that followed, I tried to think of him, rather than of my own delirious, unbelievable happiness.

At last I said, slipping my arm round his neck: "I want two things. Will you give them to me?"

"Of course."

"It's daylight—we shall have to separate, and dress, quite soon," I said, stroking his cheek. "But later—this morning, perhaps—I want you to come with me——"

"Where, my dearest?"

"To see Paul. I want to see you together."

He kissed my hair. "I will. And the other thing?"

"Oh—that's a—a triviality. I'll ask for it later."

"My darling——"

"I know it sounds rather silly—but there's something else I want to ask you about now," I began, after another silence.

"Go on."

"Are you really—really happy?"

He sat up, and looked at me with a faint smile. "It's odd you should say that. I was thinking just now——"

"What?"

"Of what my old tutor used to say. He told me that was a word for fools and children. Certainly, it's new to me."

"Do you like the sound of it?"

"Happy," he said consideringly. "Happy—yes, I do. Perhaps it's the word I've been looking for all my life."

4

Paul had just waked up when Nikki and I came in. The nurses were dismissed—by Nikki. I was beginning to realize how much he disliked being watched when he was likely to show emotion.

I picked up the baby, who gazed at me rather sternly. Then he stretched out a pink starfish hand, and gripped my necklace. I took him over to the window. Nikki came and stood beside me.

"Why are you looking at him so anxiously?" he said, touching the baby's cheek with one finger.

"I did so very much want him to have your profile—and I see no signs of it at all."

"Let's hope he won't have my character."

At this point Paul turned and contemplated his father. Then he smiled, and put out his arms.

"He knows you!" I exclaimed.

"I've seen him nearly every day."

"Take him. He'll be happier with you. He always thinks I'm going to drop him."

Nikki handled the baby expertly; he smiled at me over his head, and began to walk about the room.

"You did see me holding him once before. I expect you've forgotten," he said, stopping in front of me.

"Yes—it comes back to me now——" I said, and broke off as I saw his expression. The baby wrinkled up his face and began to wail. "There, you see—he doesn't like you to be gloomy either," I went on.

"I don't know what one does to distract them at this age," said Nikki, taking out his watch. "Here—listen to this. No, I think you'd better not have it to play with."

I laughed; the baby laughed. As Nikki swung the watch to and fro, the pale winter sunlight crept into the room and fell on them both.

A new happiness, one I had never imagined, filled all my heart. At that moment I had nothing more to wish for; the dark head bending above the fair one, the pleasure on both faces, made a picture that nothing has been able to take from me. I have carried it with me since that day.

There was a rustle and a murmur; a gust of perfume filled the room. Queen Elena stood in the doorway.

The spectacle that greeted her must have been a shock, and, as I now know, not altogether a pleasant one. She took a few seconds to adjust herself. Then she came up to us with an air of pleased surprise.

"How charming!" she exclaimed.

A few moments later we were doing our best to amuse the baby, and discussing him with the absorption peculiar to all orthodox parents and grandmothers.

Our conversation was neither interesting nor memorable; but there was one aspect of it that remained with me, and that was the change in Nikki's attitude towards his mother. He teased her; she replied with her usual gaiety and animation. Now there was no acidity, no playing of parts, on either side.

There was something in Queen Elena's temperament that rejoiced, quite simply, in the health and vigour of her grandchild, and in the sight of Nikki and me apparently reconciled and affectionate towards one another. Her family feeling—above all, her desire that the surface, at least, of our relationship should be smooth and pleasant, whatever damage may have been done to her plans by Marta's departure and her son's reconciliation with me—was appeased.

"You look perfectly radiant, my dearest child," she said, as the nurses were summoned and we all three prepared to leave. "Have you—are you looking forward to something?"

"Yes," said Nikki, before I could answer. "I'm taking her away for a change. Tonight—we leave for Kalacz."

"My dear boy, how unpredictable you are! I thought you were overwhelmed with work, and——"

"It can't be for very long. But I settled everything at the conference yesterday, and we shall have five clear days to ourselves."

"I see—no mothers-in-law invited."

"Nor ladies-in-waiting. Christiane will have to make do with a local peasant girl for a maid. We are going to be quite alone."

"And what does Christiane say to all this?"

I laughed, and murmured something about a treat that had been well earned; and so we parted.

Now, I am well aware that most young women of today would have been put out by Nikki's apparent disregard of my convenience. But I was the kind of girl—there may still be some left—who liked to be dominated in such matters as these. I was delighted to be ordered to make ready at a few hours' notice; indeed, I should not have minded if I had been told that I was bound for an unknown destination.

During the afternoon of that day Marta Karillos left Murania for the last time. The knowledge that I should never see her again made me rather uneasy. Of course, it was better that she should go, if only from the point of view of Nikki's reputation; and yet I could not help wondering whether we had lost a valuable friend. It was during the journey to Kalacz that Nikki, acting on a caprice that I found rather daunting, described to me how he had spent the evening of Paul's birth. It was almost as if he wanted to blacken himself in my eyes—but I knew how remorseful he was; his dry and merciless account of his behaviour made me love him more dearly than before.

We set off as dusk fell, and reached the castle of Kalacz at four o'clock in the morning. It was a medieval fortress, a stronghold in the mountains that stood between this part of the country and the Eastern Province. Nikki's grandfather had repaired it; since his day it had been little used.

The castle stood on top of a high, steep hill that was a small edition of the mountains that surrounded it. It had all the trappings of its period—moat, drawbridge, dungeons, solar chamber, inner and outer courtyards. The interior had been very little modernized, and was extremely dark; most of the rooms were hung with hunting trophies and decorated with frescoes of the fourteenth century.

In Kalacz the Orosvars had conducted some of the most ruthless of their family feuds. Within its walls one king had killed himself, another had tortured his heir to death, a third had surprised his wife with her lover and put them both to the sword. It was a place of fearful memories and contained a number of family and other ghosts. These didn't worry me in the least; I was quite immune to any manifestations of dead Orosvars—perhaps because I had had so much trouble with the living members of that family.

I was rather frightened by the frescoes, especially by those in my bedroom, of which the decoration was a story in pictures, commemorating the discovery, by her husband, King Paul I, of the false Queen Geltruda in the arms of her lover. It was in this very room that the killing had been done. Here the Queen had had to watch her lover's slow and agonizing death; here she had been executed; and from this window both bodies had been thrown down to rot in the outer courtyard. King Paul, then in his forties, had immediately married again; his second wife was a girl of thirteen. A Tartar princess. She had been brought to Kalacz for her first confinement; and she gave birth to her eldest daughter surrounded by these crude and yet horribly vivid presentments of her husband and his victims.

"An awful warning—medieval manner . . ." said Nikki, glancing from them to me. "If they really upset you, though, we could——"

"No, no," I said hastily. "I suppose they're rather interesting," I added, in an uncertain voice.

We had reached the third evening of our belated honeymoon, and I was resting before getting ready for supper. We had been hunting most of the afternoon, and I was pleasantly tired. Nikki, half undressed, was leaning against the bedpost. He looked down at me thoughtfully.

"You don't like them a bit," he said. "But if they give you night-mares——"

"You will tell me not to be silly."

"Women are extraordinary," he said, as I broke off. "They have everything planned in advance."

"Don't call me 'women.' It's very——"

"What?"

"Saddening."

"You've been married to me for a year—we've spent three whole days together—and you expect happiness?"

"I've got it," I said, with a laugh. "I've got everything I want."

"No complaints?"

"None."

"No longings and pinings for a nice, safe, respectable husband with a clean record?"

"No—at least——"

"Ah! I thought there was something."

"I can't—quite—see into your mind."

"Do you want to?"

"Sometimes."

"I have a terrible suspicion that you know all about me already."

"I used to think I did. Now—I've found out a great deal that I never dreamed of."

"Disillusioned?"

"No—I'm serious."

"Your eyes get much greener when you're serious."

"Please——"

"Well, go on."

"I used to think," I said, after a moment's consideration (in which he continued to look at me with the same disturbing, tender, half-mocking expression), "that you were idle and selfish. It's only just dawned on me that you work very hard, and think a great deal about other people."

"It sounds fearfully dull—like a missionary, or a politician."

"Well, aren't you a bit of a—a politician? All the time we've been here you've got up early and worked at your letters. That poor secretary of yours doesn't have much fun." He raised his eyebrows in pretended horror. "And once you told me that a king was to be pitied. At least, that was what you implied——"

"I implied, did I? That must have been pretty tedious."

"I think you like being a king," I said, sitting up and taking his hand.

He kissed my fingers, rather absently. Then he wandered over to the dressing-table. After fingering my brushes, opening one or two boxes, and abstractedly examining the contents, he said, in a low voice: "Yes, I do—now. No one can work alone. Now I've got you."

"You mean, I might help you?"

"You mightn't want to. It isn't a very encouraging job, on the whole."

"But you've a great many plans, haven't you? I want to know all about them."

"Not just now."

I held out my arms. As he put his head on my shoulder he muttered, in a grumbling voice: "I dare say you won't believe it— but I lived like a monk after that evening with Astrid. We've got a lot of time to make up, you and I."

"I'm afraid I'm a bad influence."

"Yes—very bad—*shocking* . . . Why is everything you wear tied up with white ribbons?"

"It's supposed to be correct—one's first trousseau . . ."

"You won't be having another while I'm alive—you must make up your mind to that, I'm afraid . . ."

Later on he said, "By the way, you never asked me for that second thing—what was it? You said it was a triviality."

"I want you to give me a present," I said, putting on my dressing-gown and going over to the mirror.

I looked at him gaily, and his face fell a very little, as I had hoped it would. I knew that his mind was travelling back over his early days, and the women who had tried to make use of him.

"Of course, my dearest; anything you want——" he began.

"Well—it's a book. That old play, that had characters with such odd names—an English play——"

His expression brightened; still he looked a little puzzled. "I don't remember."

"One was called Lyndaraxa—the false Lyndaraxa."

"Oh yes—why do you want it?"

"Because it will always make me remember that your voice is so lovely, especially lovely when you read aloud. Will you say a bit of it to me again?"

" 'O that you still could cheat, and I believe!' " he repeated, his eyes on my face. "It's the exact reverse of what I feel now," he added.

I laughed, and went on brushing my hair.

Then Nikki said, in quite a different tone, "There's another bit that's rather applicable." He paused, looking at the ground. "Wait a minute—yes.

> 'The King! The poor Usurper of an Hour,
> His Empire's but a dream of Kingly Pow'r.
> I warn you, as a lover and a friend,
> To leave him, ere his short Dominion end.'

What about that for——"

"Don't be depressing," I said, turning towards him with a smile. He glanced at me with a slightly haunted expression; then he got up and went out.

The next day we rode along a bridle-path that wound through the mountains, to a lake where there were wild duck. Giulio followed at a distance with the guns. As the track divided into a clearing, we came upon the same gipsy encampment that Egon Stanieff and I had seen in the woods round Dhrevin. They surrounded us in much the same way.

They knew Nikki; one or two of them had seen the new coins. They treated him with what seemed to me a strange lack of reverence; he might have been no more than the leader of their particular tribe. I told him how I had met them, and about their dancing. He insisted on asking them to dance for us at the castle on the following night—and then on having his fortune told.

Some remnant of superstitious fancy prompted me to persuade him against the fortune-telling; but he wouldn't listen. He leaned down from his horse, bareheaded, his hair tossed over his forehead, and laid his hand on the old woman's skinny palm.

As we rode on he said lightly: "She wasn't altogether optimistic.

She said I must 'enjoy what I could, while I might.' I don't care for the sound of that, do you?"

"It's all nonsense," I said abruptly, and we began to talk of other things.

A few minutes later, when we fell into silence again, I glanced at his face. And then I saw that there was—perhaps there always had been—a shadow behind his joy. I could not get rid of the notion that it was growing thicker and darker, and that it might one day spread over all his life.

CHAPTER ELEVEN

How We Did What We Could

THE RETURN JOURNEY to Bledz occupied the whole of one day, from dawn until midnight. It was a much more leisurely progress than that to Kalacz, when I, completely exhausted, had spent most of the time in a doze. Neither the pitch-and-toss movements of the coach, nor the cold, nor the stopping to change horses had roused me for more than a few minutes. When we reached Kalacz, Nikki had carried me to my room and put me to bed himself.

Now I was rested, and able to enjoy the spectacle of my husband as a paternal and popular ruler. Here, in the remote villages and little walled towns that marked the road towards the capital, he was known only as the Prince who had succeeded his despotic and dreaded father, the husband of a youthful and amiable Queen-Consort, and (I think I'm not exaggerating) the trustee of his people's happiness.

I first became aware of what would now be described as the feudal attitude of the country folk when we stopped for breakfast in a village some fifteen miles from Kalacz. We were expected; as the coach rattled up the steep, narrow street, it was surrounded by a shouting crowd, ragged, dirty, but not starved or degraded, like the inhabitants of the slums in Bledz. As we drew up at the little posting inn, and Nikki handed me down from the coach, we were surrounded. The women who held up their children to see us, and the men who stood in front of them, waving their caps or clapping their hands, created an informal but friendly atmosphere. It was rather embarrassing not to be able to speak to

them in any but a few set phrases that I had learnt before I
left my own country.

As Nikki paused on the threshold of the inn, the landlord and
his wife ordered the crowd away; Nikki forbade this, and commanded breakfast to be served by the window, so that the people
could see as much of us as possible.

Giulio, a democrat of the first order himself, very much disapproved of these free-and-easy ways, and remained on the box
with the coachman. Just as we were going in, a young woman
burst from the crowd and flung herself at Nikki's feet, the tears
running down her face. She spoke at length, between sobs and
gasps of despair.

Nikki raised her gently, stopped the flood of talk, and asked
a question or two. She replied in short, agonized sentences, and
then relapsed into a passion of tears.

"What is it?" I exclaimed. "Can't we do anything?"

"I'll tell you in a minute," said Nikki, and, taking the girl aside,
he smiled, and spoke to her in a reassuring voice. She seized his
hands, and covered them with kisses. Then the landlord dragged
her away, and ushered us indoors. Looking back, I saw that she
had rejoined the crowd outside in a fresh outburst of grief, and that
one or two of them were trying to comfort her.

"She and her grandparents are being turned out of their farm
in two days' time," said Nikki, in what seemed to me a remarkably
carefree tone, as he drank his coffee. "She had a baby last week.
Her husband died six months ago."

"But how *awful*—who——"

"Oh, it's the old story," he said, glancing out of the window at
the staring crowd. "The landlord wants the farm for his steward."

"Who's the landlord?"

"Old Count Stanieff—your admirer's father."

I ignored the tinge of satire in his tone, and said hotly: "It's
monstrous! You must stop it. You can, can't you?"

"I can, of course," he said, in the same negligent manner. "The
question is whether I should."

"Can there possibly be any question?"

He looked at me as if he were assessing my powers of comprehension. "You want me to save their home for them?"

"Naturally. Don't you?"

"It's rather more complicated than you suppose," said Nikki, buttering a roll. "Incidentally," he added, "the girl's family have worked that farm for five generation."

"That makes it all the more——"

"Wait a minute. If what I hope to do—and intend to do—materializes, such injuries as these will never be done again. You remember what I was talking about yesterday?"

"Yes, yes—your reforms. But that's in the future. This is now. After all, it may be years before——"

"It won't be," he interrupted decisively. "The lid's off the cauldron already. I mean to carry through these agrarian reforms in less than a year. The scheme's all worked out. If Rell were alive . . ."

"But this girl and her family! You can't——"

"If I make a gesture—as, of course, I can—on her behalf, it will be just another piece of absolutism—benevolent absolutism. The only difference is that it will be directed against Stanieff, who's a very nice old fellow."

"He can't be—turning out a helpless——"

"My dear girl, Stanieff doesn't know everything that happens on all his estates. This will be his steward's doing."

"Then tell him—and he'll dismiss the steward."

"I don't think he will, you know. And by the time I get in touch with him, and he gets in touch with his steward—who probably lives hundreds of miles from here, and gives his orders to an agent——"

"Oh, Nikki—don't!"

"I'm trying to outline the position for you—that's all," he said coolly.

There was a short silence. Then I said, "So you're going to let the helpless—the downtrodden—suffer?"

He looked at me steadily. I saw that he was restraining an impatient answer.

At last he replied: "If I put myself in the wrong by riding roughshod over Stanieff's rights—I can, of course; I'm not a constitutional ruler—I shall risk the security of hundreds, perhaps thousands, of other downtrodden families."

"But how?"

"If I do what you want, it will be used against me in the Assembly. They'll make a case of it. They'll use it to show I'm irresponsible—sentimental."

"But you're not! They won't have a leg to stand on. And how can one individual case——"

"My dearest child, all these people have grievances. If I keep this girl and her family in their farm, I shall have to do the same sort of thing all the way back to Bledz. I can't refuse one plea and accept another."

"Surely you can justify——"

"I can justify one action, but not a half dozen."

I was silent. I felt, and must have looked, miserable.

Nikki patted my knee under the table. "Well?" he said, with an odd smile.

"I don't know what to say. If we drive on, and do nothing, that girl's face will haunt me for the rest of my days."

"Suppose I left it to you to decide?"

"Oh! I couldn't—the responsibility——"

"I thought you were brought up to take responsibilities," he said, in a faintly ironical tone.

"I was. But all this is so complicated. Can't one just do good, and—and——"

"And sow the whirlwind, and reap the cataclysm? You might, of course. You might also find yourself thrown out, with no powers left—for good, or evil. No king is stronger than the nation he's supposed to guide. I'm very much disliked by a certain section of the landlords. They've got a great many weapons. I don't want to give them another."

"Well," I said, after another silence, "I see that it's not easy."

"No—it's not," he said, rather grimly. He had eaten nothing, and his expression was as I had seen it all too often—cold and self-contained.

"Couldn't we risk it?" I said timidly, twisting my hands together. He looked at me, and smiled. "You're irresistible. It's not fair."

"I didn't mean——"

"All right—we'll risk it, Christiane. This whole game is a gamble, after all," he said, getting up and moving restlessly about the room.

"You don't really look on your work as a gamble?"

"Sometimes one must. This is one of the times."

He walked out onto the steps of the inn. Count Stanieff's victim, now a little intimidated by her boldness, had taken shelter in the back of the crowd.

I came up to Nikki, and said, in a low voice, "What's she called?"

"Tania Semara."

I stepped forward, flushing a little, and called out the name. The girl—she could not have been more than sixteen—was pushed towards me. I took her hand, and led her up to Nikki. He spoke to her briefly. She covered her face with her hands, and burst into tears. Then she flung herself on her knees, and, picking up the hem of my skirt, kissed it passionately. There was a cheer from the on-lookers.

"We have set a precedent, you see," said Nikki's voice in my ear. "Let's hope we don't have to carry it through all the way home."

Naturally, we had to; I don't know how it was that the news of the Semaras' good fortune outstripped our horses, but it did. During the course of our journey to the capital, Nikki righted many other wrongs, some of them crueller than that already described.

I would not let myself believe that this first arbitrary action of mercy—or, indeed, any of those following it—would be reckoned against Nikki. I would not let his warning echo in my ears; and he did not again refer to it. To me it was wonderful to see him so sought after, so trusted. He seemed to know an enormous number of the people by name; he had achieved this during his tours of the country with Stefan Rell. At the time, my ignorance of the language made it impossible for me to follow all that was said; afterwards, when we were alone in the coach, I gathered that the roars of delighted laughter that followed Nikki's brief greeting and farewells were caused by his understanding of the popular humour and of the mood of the moment, and by his touches of pleasantry. His sardonic references to the poaching and thieving tendencies of some of those who came out to meet him were especially appreciated.

As we started on the last stretch of the journey, he said casually, "I told them you were learning Muranian—I couldn't think of anything to say that I hadn't said already."

"Of course I'm going to," I replied. "Will you find me a tutor from the University?"

"Certainly not. Do you imagine I'm going to have some hard-working, innocent man's heart broken, and all the wrong ideas put into his head? You shall have a governess."

"I won't."

"A schoolmistress, then," he said, putting his arm round me.

I laughed, and leaned back against him. The country seemed to fly past us. It was nearly the end of our honeymoon. Five days!

"We shall have another, some day, shan't we?" I said later on. "It's been such a very short time."

"Yes, my darling," he said absently. "Don't ask me when, though."

"What does that matter? We're going to have all our lives together."

He said nothing. Presently I fell asleep, my head on his shoulder.

2

Two days after our return from Kalacz a Court ball was given to celebrate my birthday. By this time Nikki was plunged in work from morning till night. For the next few months I was to see very little of him during the day.

On the afternoon of the ball, we spent some time with Queen Elena. She was in one of her most inconsequent moods. She asked me what I was going to wear that night, and when I had described to her my gown of white bengaline, trimmed with knots of black, chestnut, and rose-coloured ribbons, she murmured: "You're becoming sophisticated, Christiane. A few months ago those ribbons would have been pink or blue"—but it was plain that she was thinking of something else.

A few minutes later she said to Nikki: "Do you remember General Brancovan? I heard he was in Bledz, and I've sent him an invitation."

"Isn't he rather old for that sort of thing?"

"Well," said Queen Elena, with her slightly feline smile, "we old fogies can amuse each other."

"I'd forgotten he was your contemporary," said Nikki. He added to me, "He was one of my many tutors—not quite the most disagreeable."

"Now, Nikki, that is unfair. Your father and I were most particular——"

"Nonsense, Mamma. Those unfortunate men were used as weapons in your quarrels with my father. I had four, between the ages of six and eighteen," he went on, turning to me.

"Which one did you like best?"

"The Englishman—Colonel Hyde-Menzies. He encouraged me to read English—he gave me all those old plays. Menzies was an eccentric—at least, so I was told—and we got on very well. He wasn't at all like the Englishmen I met on my travels."

"What about the women?" put in his mother.

"If you mean poor——" He paused, with a slight frown.

"Mary Wynne."

"Yes—it was on the tip of my tongue."

"Why was she poor?" I inquired.

Nikki looked slightly embarrassed. "As a matter of fact, she was an heiress. I'm supposed to have treated her badly."

"I can hardly believe it," I murmured, and he pinched my arm.

"At least, she encouraged you to travel," Queen Elena went on.

"Only as far as London."

"What's it like?" I asked.

"Terrible. I went there *incognito*. Dirty—noisy—and nobody talked about anything but their illnesses and their dogs. I enjoyed their plays, though; I went to the theatre every night. And yet Mamma wants Paul to have an English nurse, as soon as he's a year old."

"Now, please don't think I'm trying to interfere," said Elena, glancing at me. "But it's always been done——"

"I'm not going to have the child turned into a polyglot," Nikki interrupted.

"My dear boy, you found it rather useful, surely?"

"I don't intend him to be driven into exile if I can help it."

"How do you know he won't prefer it?" said Queen Elena, sitting up and speaking with sudden vigour. "If you succeed in all your schemes, you'll make the country too hot to hold him."

Nikki smiled. "I'm sorry you don't approve."

"If it wasn't dear little Christiane's birthday, I should give you a piece of my mind. You're playing with fire!"

"Really, Mamma, can't you think of anything more original than that?"

"How can you expect to keep these people in a contented state if you spoil them, and take them out of their proper sphere? And what's all this I hear about everyone speaking Muranian?"

"This system of languages is splitting us into two nations. It wasn't so in the old days."

"I suppose you expect me to take lessons in that barbarous——"

"Of course not."

"And what about Christiane? Why should she?"

"It's wonderful how much you manage to find out," said Nikki gently. "Perhaps you also know that she's beginning her lessons tomorrow."

There was a short silence. Then Queen Elena said plaintively: "Well, I can see that I'm not wanted. It's time I retired from the world. I think I shall go to Mornavitza for the summer."

"I shouldn't."

"Why not?"

"Your information seems to have run out, all of a sudden. I'm handing over Mornavitza to the Council of Bledz. We shan't be living there any more."

"You're not giving it away?" she exclaimed.

"You might call it that. The castle is to be turned into a hospital, and the land is going to be divided up into small holdings."

"How absurd—and dangerous——"

"I think the whole thing's going to be a success. And how can we live in six places at once? I'll find a hole for you somewhere, dearest—one with ten conservatories, and several thousand acres of garden."

"You're most undutiful, Nikki. Why wasn't I consulted about Mornavitza? Christiane, I do beg you to use your influence."

"I'm afraid——"

"There, you see—the poor little thing is too frightened of you to protest."

Nikki said nothing for a moment. Then he began: "Christiane is more interested in Kalacz. We're going to make that our country home, and——"

"That barrack!"

"And I'm planning a festival there for the summer—music and dancing, from all over the country. I shall insist on your being present, Mamma. Now, think of the opportunity for a series of very simple but enormously expensive gowns . . ."

"It's all very well, but I'm serious."

"So am I, oddly enough," said Nikki, and began to talk of other things.

When I went to dress for the ball, I found that he had sent me a bouquet of white roses. I couldn't help smiling a little, as I remembered his mother's superstitious alarm, just a year ago.

Nikki had said: "I wish you could wear the same dress as on that first evening. But that's too much to ask, I suppose."

I replied that I was too young to begin breaking the really important rules, and told him of his mother's warning.

He said vaguely: "Oh! she has to remind one of her Italian background every so often. It's quite a harmless pose," he added, with a smile. "I remember when I was a boy, the tutors she didn't like were supposed to have the evil eye."

And then he plunged into reminiscences of his tempestuous childhood.

"You always disliked your father?"

"No—that was the trouble. I used to admire him when I was a child. It was the disillusionment——" He broke off, looking rather depressed.

Nikki found the ball more of a strain than I did, partly because he was beginning to look on such functions as a waste of time, and to dwell mentally on the mountains of work piling up while he danced, and made conversation, and allowed himself to be drawn aside into semi-official talks with this or that foreign ambassador.

After supper I found myself sitting out with Vanescu in one of the antechambers. There was a half-circle of these small, elegant rooms, all leading into one another, at the back of the ballroom. I was in a chair by the fire, and Vanescu was standing by the mantelpiece. He looked handsome and distinguished, as always, but it seemed to me that underneath his suave assumption that we were all doing the correct thing, and rejoicing in doing so, he was worn and nervous. We had been skirting round the subject of Paul's education—a matter on which we could not, for an instant, have seen eye to eye—when Queen Elena's voice was heard from the next room. Vanescu drew himself up.

Then I heard her say: "Now, that's very charming of you. Tell me—how is your father? Is he well?"

"Considering his age, Your Majesty."

It was Egon Stanieff's voice. I was about to get up and go back to the ballroom when I saw that Vanescu had forgotten all about me. His strained, agonized expression was that of a man who expects to hear some ghastly news.

Queen Elena went on, "And what is his age?"

"He admits to sixty."

"Impossible—he was a contemporary of mine."

"Then, Your Majesty—he cannot be more than forty."

"Then you must be ten! You're rather big for your age. Do you dance? You look as if you do."

"I have been dancing, Ma'am. But now——"

"Well?"

"There is only one lady in this room with whom I will consent to dance."

She laughed softly. Then she said, "My dear young man, my place is in the chimney-corner." He made a protest that I could not hear, and she went on, rather breathlessly: "I hear you're in love with the Queen. That's so delightfully romantic—is it true?"

"Ma'am—I fell in love quite hopelessly when I came to my first Court ball. It was almost immediately after I had the honour of being presented to Your Majesty."

"Your father has taught you well," said Queen Elena, in a low voice. "I will save a waltz for you—later." There was a pause. Then she said thoughtfully: "I think we shall have to find you some more duties about the Court. I understand you are with your regiment now?" There was another murmur from the young man. Queen Elena said briskly, "Well—you had better take me back to the ballroom."

Rather impressed, and very much amused by Egon Stanieff's aplomb, I glanced at Vanescu. He looked absolutely ravaged, and was apparently speechless.

Then he became aware of my horrified scrutiny, and, turning his head away, said hoarsely, "Forgive me, Madame. I——"

"I'm afraid, you're ill."

He looked at me without speaking. At last he said, in the same strained, unnatural tone, "There is no cure for my sickness—none."

"Count Vanescu——"

He put his hands to his head, as if he were afraid of falling. I did not know whether to get up and leave him, or to encourage him to talk. I had never liked him; but now I began to feel sorry for him.

Suddenly he said, speaking as if the words had been forced out of him: "Thirty years! It's been thirty years since I——"

"You have given all those years to your country," I said, trying to prevent a confidence that I knew would be regretted later.

He seemed not to hear me. He went on, in a fierce whisper: "She has no pity—none. It's been worse lately. Sometimes I think she delights in my misery. She knew I was here. She saw me go in with

——" He stopped, looked at me, and added brokenly, "I beg your pardon."

"I am sorry that you are unhappy."

"I hope that you will never know what it is, Madame, to be so used, and to love a heartless——" Again he stopped, trying to master himself. Then he said, in a low voice, looking at the ground: "I was a clever young man—ambitious, hard-working, quick to decide. It has brought me—nothing."

"You have a great position."

"Yes—and an empty life. I'm alone. I've been—but I'm mad to talk to you like this. I must apologize again, and beg Your Majesty's confidence."

After a moment's silence I said: "As you've been used so ill, why don't you come over to the other side? To the King's side?"

In the pause that followed he seemed to be pulling himself together.

Then he said, "We all work for the good of the State—His Majesty, myself——" with a return to his impenetrable Court manner.

"Very well," I said, getting up. "I shall say nothing of this to anyone—not even to the King."

After a moment's silence, in which neither of us looked at the other, he offered me his arm, and we went back to the ballroom.

3

For a long time Nikki had intended to take me with him on a tour of the Eastern Province. When at last we set out, we took with us a very small train of attendants. The nucleus of unrest in this part of the country was situated in a sprawling industrial city, of great squalor and ugliness. Here Nikki had begun to build tenement houses for the factory hands, and our first duty was to visit them. We stayed with one of Nikki's most important agents, who was reorganizing the management of all the factories in this district. He urged Nikki not to exercise his privilege of arbitrarily righting such wrongs as came up during our journey; and this advice was taken, much to my disappointment.

The last and most exhausting part of our visit consisted in our inspection of a factory that had not yet been rebuilt. Just as he was preparing to set out, Nikki was warned that there might be "hostile demonstrations," possibly an attack. He took me aside, and said, "You need not go with me. In fact, I think you should not." For a moment I hesitated; the thought of my son being brought up by his grandmother was in my mind. Then I said that I was ready to go. Nikki said nothing at all. But as he handed me into the carriage, he gripped my fingers so hard that the rings cut into my flesh.

This visit was successful. Our venturing alone, unprotected, into this stronghold of discontent (for Nikki would allow none of our suite to go with us) was a more effective gesture than the promises of Nikki's representatives. To this day I don't know, and can't guess, how great the danger really was. We were received in silence, and left to the sound of vociferous cheering.

All Nikki said was: "You're a brave girl, Christiane. I knew you'd insist on coming, and, of course, it made all the difference."

He had been brought up, as I had, to take such bravery for granted. The look that accompanied the words and the quiet cheerfulness of his demeanour during the journey home were my reward. For some time after that, he seemed to be able to get through his work without the fits of bitterness and despair that made his days so arduous and so fatiguing.

Then the preparations for the Kalacz festival began. It was at this time that Nikki won Vera's heart; they planned the programme together, and from that moment onward she became devoted to him. She had had some experience in organizing singing ballets and folk-dancing displays, and now she came into her own. Each district was to send a team to Kalacz. Those who did not sleep in the village would be housed in the castle.

At the last moment, just after Nikki, his mother, and I had arrived, we were told that the gipsies had come back, in order to take part in the festival. So the programme had to be rearranged; and in the late afternoon of that long, hot summer day, Nikki, Queen Elena, and I found ourselves alone on the terrace. The first part of the festival was to take place in the outer courtyard, by torchlight. We were dressed for it, all three of us, in what I can only describe as consciously simple, *bal masqué* versions of the peasant costume.

Nikki was in his happiest, most tolerant mood; he threw me a glance of amusement as Queen Elena, looking round her, said thoughtfully: "It's very peaceful here. I think I could stay about a week."

"Why don't you?"

"My dear Nikki, just because you're being a country squire, it doesn't mean that we can all sit about and twiddle our thumbs. I've brought down a whole pile of papers for you to sign, and you won't even look at them."

"That's because I can guess what they contain."

"And you're so set on this festival that you're leaving the country to govern itself."

"If only you would let it, Mamma."

Queen Elena threw up her hands. "I, my dear boy! I'm just a pensioner, nobody takes any notice of me—ah, well! Time was . . . I don't know what I'm going to do."

He crossed his arms behind his head, and looked at her with a faint smile. "I think you've a pretty good idea."

"I don't know what you're talking about."

"Your latest scheme: a new castle with a hundred bedrooms, and fifty thousand acres—your own Court, in fact."

She gazed at him innocently. "And why not? It only needs your signature."

"Which it will never get. That estate is another that is being given back to its rightful owners—the peasants who have worked on it for two hundred years."

She gave her trilling laugh, as if he had said something delightfully witty. "Dear boy, your eccentricities!"

"I mean it, I assure you."

"You must be mad," she said sharply. "They'd let it go to rack and ruin in a month."

"Not if they owned it," said Nikki calmly.

"You'd give it to them?"

"Unconditionally."

She got up, and stared at him. Then she said in a dramatic manner, "Now I know exactly where I am."

"I wish I knew where you were."

"I never thought," she continued, with a horrified upward look, "that I should have to ask favours of my own son."

"You never thought they'd be refused."

"Christiane!"

"Yes, Mother Elena?"

"Tell Nikki not to be ridiculous about this—or perhaps you don't know anything about it?"

I came up to Nikki—I had been leaning over the parapet—and put my hand on his shoulder.

"I know everything about it," I said gently (for I could not help feeling a little sorry for her)—"and I think he's perfectly right."

She put her head on one side, and said, in a pleading voice: "How odious of you! Oh dear—why did I have to choose a daughter-in-law with character? There were several idiotic princesses who would have been clay in my hands. You haven't said good-morning to me, dear," she added, extending her cheek for my kiss; then she drew back, and went on, glancing at Nikki, "Oh well—I have my friends."

He laughed. "Stop intriguing, Mamma, or I shall have you exiled."

"Ah yes—like poor Marta."

He looked at me, and we both burst out laughing.

Queen Elena continued idly: "I must write to her. We might set up house together in Paris—that would be amusing."

This was a little more than I could accept, but Nikki continued to laugh.

Then he said, "As you grow older, Mamma, your taste gets worse and worse."

"Poor Nikki!" she said, with a sly look at me. "Are you still hankering?" He leaned forward expectantly—how well they played this game of theirs!—and she went on: "Christiane, you should put a stop to this—it might develop. Habit is strong, you know."

The words were provocative. But there was no malice at all in her tone. She seemed to be asking me to enjoy the joke with her. I shook my head, and smiled.

"You know," said Nikki, glancing from one to the other of us, "I think it might be a good idea if you cut short your visit here, Mamma, and returned to the capital. You're far too wicked for us."

"A reformed character!" she exclaimed, gazing at him in affected horror. "How dull—what's the time?"

"Nearly six."

"Heavens! I brought Mr. Svenson here, quite against his will—his wife's having a baby—and he's been waiting an hour! He's quite attractive," she went on abstractedly, adding, "He tells me all the gossip while he pommels me into unconsciousness—you should try him, Christiane——"

"She'll do nothing of the kind," Nikki interposed.

"I thought——" Queen Elena continued, looking at me with her

head slightly on one side. "Perhaps it's only that white gown—but you seemed to have put on a tiny bit of weight." She swept to the end of the terrace, as if she were in a great hurry, then turned, and added, "What time's this terrible performance?"

"It begins as soon as it's dark, and goes on for several hours."

"And all the next day?"

"And all the next day."

She clasped her hands admiringly. "You've all worked so hard—almost like professionals—only you're not, are you?" She gave us a radiant smile, and disappeared.

4

After a pause, Nikki said: "Poor Mamma—she's so afraid. It must be difficult taking second place—another castle, indeed!"

"Aren't you being a little bit drastic?" I asked, rather surprised by my own question.

"About her wild extravagance? Darling, I've got to be! She could ruin the country—every bit of ground we've gained she could lose for us."

"I suppose so."

"You see," he said, sitting up and taking my hand, "the more I work at it, the surer I am that this country can be well run—a little more for the majority, a little less for the privileged——"

"In our lifetime?" I interrupted.

He leaned back, his face clouding over. "Perhaps not—but in Paul's."

"Then all your plans will——"

"Oh! one of them should materialize almost immediately," he said, in a reassuring voice. "The big one—the People's Rights, the Charter."

"You're sure?"

"Very nearly. I shall force it on the Assembly. They'll fight—but I think I shall get it through."

"And if you don't?"

"Then"—he said lightly—"then I shall threaten to abdicate."

I looked at him. He was smiling. We might have been planning a picnic, or a hunting expedition.

"If they take you seriously——" I began, at last.

"My dear, they've never taken me seriously!" He paused. Then his expression changed, and he drew me down beside him. "Christiane——"

"Yes?"

"If anything were to happen to me—as it might have, when we went to that factory——" He put his arm round me, and held me tightly to him. "Hold on to Paul—with all your strength. Don't give an inch. You must have absolute control of him—promise me."

I swallowed, and then said, in a shaking voice, "But what could happen?"

"My darling—how your heart's beating!"

"Tell me—don't hide anything."

"There's no danger that I can see for the moment. I didn't mean to frighten you," he added, kissing me. "But—I might go too far with my reforms—or too quickly."

"You mean, we shouldn't have granted all those people their requests—we were advised not to——"

"No, no—it's just that they're a hard, obstinate lot, the old régime —and they'll fight to the death for their privileges."

"I see."

There was a long silence. Then, bending down to look at my face, he said softly, "That's enough of the outside world—it does encroach sometimes, doesn't it?"

"We can't hope to control it all the time," I said, trying to speak cheerfully.

"I wonder if you realize how much I depend on you."

"And I on you."

"But you're so wise. Why are you so wise?"

"I don't think I am."

"Tell me—were you very frightened when you first came here?"

"Yes," I said, drawing a long breath. "That week was—I felt so lonely, I nearly gave up. If you hadn't come that night——"

He interrupted me sharply. "And how charming I was when I did come! That should have finished everything."

"It very nearly did," I said, with a smile. "Do you remember the music under the window?"

"That made me feel like a play-actor."

"I thought it was beautiful. That is—I couldn't really think, at all."

"Neither could I."

"The light's beginning to fade—we should go in," I said, after another silence.

"Not yet," he said, drawing my head onto his shoulder.

We stayed there for a long time, in silence. In the distance I heard the murmur of voices from the courtyard below. Someone began to play on a violin, an old melody that I knew. I put my free hand into Nikki's—our locked fingers looked grey and shadowy in the gathering dusk—and hummed the tune. Then, suddenly restless, I got up and walked about, singing under my breath, while he sat looking at me. The music stopped, and the voices came nearer.

"Come, my darling—we must go to the terrace below this one. They're waiting for us."

We walked slowly down together.

I don't know what happened to me that night. I enjoyed and was amused by the first part of the entertainment—Vera's singing ballet, danced by some of the boys and girls from the University School in Bledz. I can even remember the words of the chorus—"Take Your Girl." But it was later, when the gipsies, with their daggers, their heavy, swinging earrings, and their brilliant draperies, began to whirl and spin that my blood was suddenly fired. I was too young and too desperately in love, I suppose, to be queenly, gracious and smiling, all the time. I forgot everything as the wild music went to my head; I gripped Nikki's hand. (I don't know how I should have behaved if Queen Elena had been there; but we were alone: she was watching with her ladies from another balcony.)

"What is it, my sweetheart? Are you all right?"

We looked at one another. A long, wailing, unearthly cry came from below. The torches that lit the terrace where we were sitting flickered and went out as a gust of wind swept over our heads.

Moonlight was pouring into the courtyard. We stared down into rings of changing colour. The flutes shrilled, the drums beat in my head. My cheeks were burning, my hands were icy cold.

"Take me away—take me in your arms . . ."

He stood up, and looked about him; then he lifted me. As he carried me away, the music seemed to follow us, speeding us on; I opened my eyes and saw the glare from below lying ahead, a wall of fiery light. Then we were alone, in the dark; but beneath us, still, those pealing voices sounded like an incantation, shutting out all the other noises in the world. . . .

Some hours later I woke up with a start. I slipped out of bed and listened; far off, from the woods that encircled the castle, I heard the hooting of an owl. Turning, I looked at the dark head on the pillow. Then, suddenly, the sound that had waked me seemed to creep across the room—a little sound—a tapping on the window-pane.

"Who's there?"

There was no answer. I stood in the middle of the room. I saw Nikki turn in his sleep and throw out his arm; his hand hung down over the side of the bed. Then a voice stole across the silence, from below the open window.

"Be wise—stay here—in Kalacz. Don't go back to the city."

Terrified, angry, I ran to the window and leaned out. The moon-light fell on my hair as it slid forward over my shoulder. Everything below was in shadow.

"Who are you? Who's there?"

There was a faint rustling movement—not another sound. I leaned over, and peered down. I could see nothing but the sharp outline of the terrace, steel grey under the white radiance, and a black river of shadow beneath it. As I drew back into the room, Nikki opened his eyes.

"What's the matter?"

"I—I heard something——"

"You'll catch cold," he said drowsily, stretching out his arms. "What are you doing?"

As I came towards the bed, his eyes closed. For a long time I lay awake, gazing at the strip of moonlight by the window. Then, as it faded into the stealing mists of dawn, the voice, the warning, the terror, became part of a broken dream.

CHAPTER TWELVE

How We Came to the Dark River

AFTER SOME CONSIDERATION, I decided not to tell Nikki about the warning—if, indeed, it was one. Kalacz was full of irresponsible, wild young men and women; any one of them might have thought it amusing to try to frighten me in this way. And I knew that Nikki would not take the least notice of such vague advice as this. By the time the festival came to an end, he was already impatient to be back in the capital; in a fortnight the Assembly was to debate, and then vote, on the Charter.

Within a week of our return, it became plain that the hopes for the People's Rights had risen; the number of merchants, small land-owning squires, and enlightened aristocracy on whose support we were counting had greatly increased; and a large number of waverers had come over to our side.

About a fortnight before the meeting of the Assembly, Nikki surprised me a little by accepting an invitation to a regimental dinner at the Guards' Barracks the night before he was to make two speeches and attend a committee meeting and a Ministerial conference.

"You're disappointed in me, I'm afraid?"

I was, a little; but I had hoped to conceal it. We were walking by the lake, after an extremely tiring day and a rather taxing dinner with Queen Elena. The light from the Palace windows shone on the path behind us; I could only guess at Nikki's smile, as he took my hand and put it to his lips.

"I'm afraid you'll be so tired," I said.

"I may, but that's no great matter. One thing is quite certain—I shall be horribly bored. Regimental dinners are for the very young, or the very old. But my reason is impeccable, naturally," he went on, bending to peer into my face. "Otherwise I shouldn't be going—should I?"

"I'm sure you don't have to have a reason for everything you do. Aren't you going simply because you want to?"

"Yes—I am." After a short silence, he went on: "I intend to get in touch with some of the young men whose fathers are my opponents. One or two of them have seats in the Assembly, but never go there."

"I see."

"And Cyril is to be there, and I have a feeling that if I get him at the right moment—however, we'll see. You'll wait up for me, dearest? I shall come back perfectly sober, and rather irritable."

I made the reply expected of me, and after that we spoke no more of our duties, or of the future. But, just before Nikki left, I did tell him about the warning at Kalacz. He said I had been quite right to take no notice of it at the time.

"Was it a woman's voice?" he asked.

"That was what surprised me," I said. "I think it was."

Nikki made a joking remark about his own unconsciousness of the whole affair, and we parted.

I waited up for him until very late, in the little library where we had often supped, privately, with no one but Giulio to wait on us, during these last busy weeks.

Suddenly Giulio burst into the room, leaving the door open; he was dishevelled and breathless. He stood in front of me without speaking. I became aware that the outer corridor was full of people.

"What is it? What has happened?"

"The King!—the King——"

Almost at the same moment there was a heavy knocking on the inner door, and Captain Volkov—whom I barely knew, for he had but recently been appointed as Nikki's equerry—appeared. He was in a state of suppressed agitation.

"Your Majesty——"

"He's been killed," I said, in a small inward voice.

"Madame, no! He sent me to you——"

"He's badly hurt," I said slowly. "He's dying."

"No, Ma'am, no—there was an attack as he went to the carriage with Count Stanieff—he sent me——"

"He's hurt—and you're here?"

"Your Majesty—for God's sake—he said I was to come straight here, and remain with you—and tell you——"

"Where is he?"

"Madame——"

"Where is he?"

At this point Giulio broke into a long explanation in Italian. I raised my hand to silence him.

"Captain Volkov—I order you to take me to the King."

With a desperate gesture, Volkov retreated, and placed himself between me and the door.

"How dare you!"

"It's all right, Volkov," said Nikki's voice. "You can stand back." And he came in, shutting the door behind him.

There was a moment's silence. Then I saw that Nikki's uniform was stained with blood, and that he was panting for breath.

I rushed into his arms.

"I'm not hurt," he said, gently and rather coldly. "A little bruised —that's all. I was knocked down—but you must compose yourself. Christiane! do you hear me?"—for I had burst into a fit of hysterical sobbing.

It had become an instinct with me to do what he told me. His mild sternness had an immediate effect on my nerves. He dismissed Volkov and Giulio.

Then he said, looking round him: "You haven't been disturbed? You've been here quietly all the evening?"

"Yes—— Oh Nikki——"

"You're quite sure?"

"Perfectly sure. But——"

"This is what happened," he said, in a harsh, strained voice. "I came out of the mess into the inner courtyard of the Barracks, about a quarter of an hour ago." He glanced at the clock, and went on, speaking more calmly: "We were talking—Stanieff and I—and there were several others near, but they were behind us. There'd been some joke"—he drew a long breath, and put his hand up to his head— "something about Stanieff asking me a private favour. We'd been teasing him all the evening. I can't——"

"Go on—please go on."

"As we came into the courtyard, two men ran out of the arcade. We had no swords, of course. The officers behind me started to run too. It was quite dark, except for the lights of the carriage. Stanieff"—he paused, and looked at me steadily—"Stanieff got in front of me and pushed me back. I fell on my knees. He was wearing full dress, with orders. I was"—he glanced down at his plain grey-blue uniform—"as I am. I'd come straight from the City Hall. They mistook him for me—they shot him. By the time I got up, we were all in a bunch. There were two more shots. Young Koslav is wounded, in the arm. Then one of the two men shot himself—his revolver was jerked up in the struggle. I heard him shout to the other one, 'It's not the King!' a second before. They surrounded the other man, and took him."

"And Count Stanieff?"

"We carried him back through the underground passage. The doctors are with him. He's badly hurt."

Suddenly sick and faint, I sat down, and covered my face with my hands. "Could he have suspected an attack?"

"He'd have told me if he had. The Barracks were strongly guarded."

"But it was almost as if he knew——"

"I was looking behind me. I'd just turned round, and was telling the others to keep back. We were all—I can't quite remember—but when we were in the mess, there'd been some joke about his being under arrest. We were all laughing and talking at once——" He broke off with a gasp.

"Where was he wounded?"

"In the chest. Two shots."

He looked down at his stained tunic, as if aware of it for the first time.

Then he said, in a dead, dry voice, "I think there's not much hope——"

We stood in silence for a moment or two.

Nikki muttered, "I must go to him—I'll let you know," and moved towards the door.

"Let me go with you—where is he?"

"In the Stewards' Lodge—it was the nearest place."

We walked quickly along the corridor together.

I waited outside the room where Egon Stanieff was lying while

Nikki spoke to the doctors. When he returned, I gazed silently at his stony face.

"He's conscious. He wants to speak to you."

"Is there—what do they——"

"Half an hour—perhaps less."

I went forward into a narrow, high-ceilinged room. All the light seemed to be concentrated on the head of the bed. Two doctors were standing together by the fireplace. I heard one of them say something to Nikki about Egon's family, and his answer—"None of them is in the capital." I knelt down by the bedside, and put my hand on the clenched fist that lay nearest me.

The face was shining, and of a smooth, greenish pallor, as if it had been painted; the lips were drawn back from the teeth in a faint grimace.

I said "Egon——" very low, and he opened his eyes. He was gazing at me heavily, without recognition. I said, raising my voice a little, "You wanted to see me?"

For a moment he looked at me with the same dull, staring expression. Then his face lightened, and became more human. He said, in a thick, slow whisper, "You were there—weren't you?"

"When?"

"Holding my hand."

"I'm holding it now, Egon."

There was a short silence; he gave a deep, snoring breath, and shut his eyes again. Then he said, in a louder, more insistent voice, "In the forest—you were in the forest."

I looked up, and saw Nikki standing at the foot of the bed. The doctors were talking to one another in whispers behind me.

Egon opened his eyes again, and saw Nikki. A look of distress came over his face; he tried to speak, and failed. Immediately Nikki was bending over him, on the other side.

"What is it, my dear boy? What do you want?"

Stanieff smiled. Blood was trickling slowly out of his mouth at the corner. He said, "Just—to see——" His voice stopped suddenly; then he moved his head in my direction.

Nikki bent down still farther, and put his ear to the lips that were now moving silently, as if in a mask.

"Can you tell me again? I can't quite——"

With an immense effort, the dying boy tried to raise himself.

Nikki slipped an arm round his shoulders, and lifted him a little. "Is that better?"

"Yes——" said Egon, in a slightly stronger voice. "You won't leave me?"

"I won't leave you."

"But she—she mustn't——" Again his voice failed.

Nikki glanced at me, and I got up from my knees.

One of the doctors came to the other side of the bed, put his fingers on Egon's wrist, and said to Nikki, "I think perhaps that Her Majesty——"

I withdrew to the door. As I opened it, I heard Egon gasp out, "I haven't got long—have I?"

There was a short silence. Then Nikki said, in an infinitely gentle voice, the voice that I had heard him use to his little son when he thought no one was listening—"Not very long."

I suppose I must have waited for about ten minutes, when the door opened, and Nikki came in. We looked at one another without speaking.

Then he said: "He's dead. He died in my arms."

I stared at him speechlessly. I put out my hand. He looked at the ground and turned away.

At last he said, with an icy, cutting intonation that made me shrink back—"He was lucky."

2

A few days after Stanieff's funeral, Nikki and I were sitting in a little room that led into his cabinet. We had not seen one another alone since the night of the murder; he had been working all day and most of the night, taking such rest as he needed in his own rooms, and I had thought it best not to disturb him. He looked haggard and weary, but calm.

Taking my hand, he said, in a low voice: "This attack was planned some time ago. It's the work of an organization."

"The man has confessed?"

"He won't give away the others. He travelled from the coast just before—that's all we know. His name's Kolomai."

"How do you know about the organization if he won't speak?"

"Oh! he glories in that part of it," said Nikki, with a return to his satirical manner. "It's called the League of Piety. It's been in existence for some time. Vanescu gave me to understand that it had ceased to function."

"Are there—is it a large group?"

"It wasn't. Now—it seems that they've enlarged their scope a little."

"Does Count Vanescu think they can be dealt with?" I said, rather bewildered by his tone.

"He hasn't told me yet."

"Why did they want to kill you?"

"They don't approve of the reforms. It's their intention to destroy, first me, and through me, the Charter."

"But who are they? What sort of people?"

"Religious fanatics, with medieval minds."

"What are you going to do?"

He got up and walked away. Then he said deliberately, "I'm going to interview Kolomai—now—in my cabinet."

"But won't that look as if you were going to let him off?"

"I might—if he changed his politics. He may be of more use alive than dead."

"An assassin——" I began, and stopped as he smiled—not very pleasantly—and shrugged his shoulders.

"We're not democrats yet, you know," he said, in the derisive tone that I knew and dreaded. "We rule by expediency, and by the sword." Then he went on, in a kinder voice: "It's all right. You can't be expected to understand all the complications—why should you?"

"What will you say to him?" I asked timidly.

"You can hear, if you wish."

"How?"

"You remember the door behind the panels? You can listen, and watch. No one will see you."

"I remember—but——"

"You don't care for the idea?"

"Naturally I don't," I said, after a moment of hesitation. "But this is one way of teaching me how you—how to——"

"You must do as you wish," he said wearily. "It's all horrible, of course. But you may learn something."

"I've got everything to learn—I realize that," I said, and he smiled.

A few minutes later, I was standing in a sort of cupboard, behind a tapestry panel. I remembered then that Nikki's grandfather, who had rebuilt this part of the Palace, had had made both the secret entrance and the spyhole through which I was looking.

This room was one not often used. It had an official character, and was plainly furnished, except for a huge, high-backed, very ornate gilt chair, topped with a crown borne up by two eagles, and the Orosvar arms—a throne in miniature. Nikki sat in it; in front of him was a large Empire table on which stood an inkstand and a tray of the same period. The tray was full of papers. The inkstand looked as if it had not been used for the last fifty years.

Kolomai was brought in by two guards. He was a small, slight man of middle age, with thinning hair and a neat beard. He looked shabby, respectable, and harmless. He might have been a doctor, or a schoolmaster, or a confidential clerk. His light, prominent eyes were fixed on Nikki, who, without raising his head, continued to go through the papers in front of him. Then he said abruptly, without looking up, "Take off his manacles, and leave us."

There was a clink and a rattle, a shuffling of feet, then a long silence.

At last Nikki looked up, and said, in an even voice, "Well? Do you know why I have sent for you?"

Kolomai drew himself up, and said respectfully, and with a certain dignity, "No, Sir; I should be glad to hear."

Nikki tossed the paper he had been reading to one side, and, leaning forward a little, said, in the same expressionless tone: "I could have sent you to the gallows without an interview. The verdict was, of course, a foregone conclusion." Kolomai began to speak, but Nikki continued, raising his hand: "Don't imagine for one moment that this is the preliminary to an act of mercy. You showed none—why should you receive any?"

"I expect none, Your Majesty."

"What did you hope to achieve by putting me out of the way— you and your gang?"

The little man's eyes brightened. He said, in a loud, peremptory tone: "We are no gang, Sir. The League is an honourable, ancient covenant of patriotic citizens."

"Since when have they included murder in their activities?"

Kolomai ignored the sarcasm, and began to speak in a high, ranting voice. "It is expedient that one man should die for the people—I am that man. My ancestors——"

"Who were they?" Nikki interrupted sharply.

"In my veins flows the blood of those great ones who were not afraid to take their lives in their hands and to stand in the face of the enemy—I——"

"And I'm the enemy?"

There was a short pause. "You are the enemy of all the people of Murania," said Kolomai, sinking his voice to a whisper.

"How have I offended them?"

"By raising up the hewers of wood and the drawers of water to become princes in the land. For this you shall not be permitted to live, nor any that support you."

"How is it that you, a professor in the University of Bledz, have associated yourself with a band of assassins? The League existed in my father's time, and since then it has become quite negligible, politically."

Nikki spoke with contempt and derision. Kolomai rose to the bait immediately.

"We shall soon be as powerful as your Assembly!" he shouted, waving his arms. "Another year, and you and your kind will go down before us, and then there will be a real King in Murania! We are strong! We are watched and encouraged by those in high places——" He broke off, and his arms fell to his sides.

"Who is behind you? Who are these fine friends?"

"You will never get that from me—not a single name. If you were to tear the heart from my body——"

"We don't torture criminals any longer," said Nikki coldly. "I suppose you think that's a pity?"

"In the great days, the Kings of Murania feared nothing—not even their own cruelty."

Nikki brought his hand down on the table with a bang. "No lectures, Kolomai! I'm not one of your half-baked students. I've had some trouble with them already. You have money behind you, then, as well as great names?"

"Yes—we have money," said Kolomai gravely.

Nikki leaned back in his chair. Then he said slowly, "Does the Count Misia Vanescu allow his name to appear on your records?"

The shot went home. Kolomai started. "I know nothing of His Excellency's sympathies," he said at last.

"That's odd—because it was he who urged that I should sign the warrant without seeing you. Could it be that he was afraid—afraid of a betrayal?"

Kolomai stepped forward and shouted: "I am no betrayer! I have said nothing! I was ready—he should have known——" He stopped, and put his hand over his eyes.

Nikki stood up. "Well—you have said what I expected you to say. There is still a chance for you."

"I have nothing to ask of Your Majesty," said Kolomai, with a return of his rather pathetic dignity. "If I had the means, I would kill you now—and take the consequences."

"Is that all you have to say?"

"That is all, Sir."

Nikki sat down, took a paper from the tray, and signed it. Then he rang the handbell at his elbow. The guards came in, saluted, and placed themselves on either side of the prisoner.

"Take him away."

As I buried my face in my hands, I heard the door shut and the footsteps die away along the passage.

In the silence that followed, Nikki said, in an abstracted voice, "Push the knob in the middle."

I did so. The door opened in front of me. I stood still for a moment. Then I looked at Nikki. He was writing busily.

"Oh! by the way"—he said, after a minute—"we've found out who gave you that warning at Kalacz. It was the wife of one of Kolomai's confederates. They both gave themselves up this morning. They seem to have lost their faith in the League."

I said nothing. He looked up at me, and said harshly, "Well? Have you learned anything?"

I could not answer. I had seen—though I could not learn—how one rules by expediency, and by the sword.

3

Within a few hours of his interview with Kolomai, Nikki had made arrangements for Paul to be sent into safety. I had never imagined that it could be so quickly, so secretly, done; such an action as this would not have been possible in my own country. It was given out that the young Prince had measles—this ensured his grandmother's avoiding the nursery, for she had never had the disease—and he was sent to one of the castles on the coast with his nurses and attendants and one of Nikki's most reliable secretaries. From there the whole party was conveyed by sea to Norseland. Paul was safely installed before the Assembly met to discuss the Charter.

I knew very well that Nikki's indifference to the fate of the fanatic was superficial. He said nothing about it to me until the night of the execution, when he asked me to sit in the little library with him while he went over the notes for his speech to the Assembly.

For an hour or more we sat in silence. I was embroidering a frock for Paul, and wondering vaguely whether it would be possible for me to go and fetch him, when the time came for his return.

Suddenly Nikki put aside his papers and walked over to the window; he pulled back the curtain, and stood looking out. Then he said, in a low voice: "I've given Kolomai a sentence of imprisonment. He earned it, I think."

"Oh! Nikki—I'm so glad—I was——"

"He's a pitiable creature."

"Why did you take him up about his ancestors?"

"All I knew about him was that he was the illegitimate son of a noble. Those are the sort of people who become obsessed with their own grandeur—their potentialities—and so get led into the struggle for power. He saw himself as a feudal lord, running the country."

"And the moment you undermined his vanity he gave himself away," I said, recalling that skilful attack with an inward tremor.

"He gave away the one man I wanted to trace."

"Vanescu—did you suspect him before?"

"I didn't think he'd go so far as to turn the League into a terrorist organization."

I was silent. I thought of Vanescu's subjugation to Queen Elena, and wondered how much she knew—how often she shut her eyes to what he was doing. Then I saw Nikki looking at me, and knew that the same conjecture was torturing him.

He walked across the room, and pulled violently at the bell. When Giulio came in, he told him to bring some brandy—that much I understood. Giulio appeared to make an objection. Nikki turned on him and shouted: "Go! Go! Do as you're told!"

Giulio, much less perturbed than I should have been, shambled out of the room, grumbling under his breath. I went on with my needlework, not daring to look up.

Nikki came and stood by me. Then he said, in a breathless voice: "I shall have to get rid of him—old idiot. He's past his work."

I put down my embroidery, and appeared to consider.

Nikki went on, "Lazy—dishonest—incompetent——" and began to walk up and down. Feeling as if I were shut up in a cage with an angry tiger, I trembled, and said nothing.

After far too long an interval, Giulio came in, carrying a decanter and glasses. With what must have seemed to Nikki an infuriating slowness, he put them down; then he took out a not too clean handkerchief, and, still more slowly, began to polish the glasses. This was a habit of his that I had tried to discourage, without success, and that Nikki had always ignored.

"What the devil are you doing?" he now exclaimed.

There was no answer. Giulio shrugged his shoulders and went on polishing.

Nikki rushed at him, seized the handkerchief and threw it on the floor. He took Giulio by the shoulders and said, in a shaking voice: "Don't do that! Get some other glasses!" Then followed a flood of furious abuse, of which I understood not a syllable.

Giulio shook himself free, and muttered something resentful. When he reappeared, he began a long, complaining speech. Nikki interrupted him with "Get out of this room before I kill you!" Then he hauled him to the door, and banged it behind him.

If I hadn't known how desperate, how miserable, my poor Nikki was, I should have been amused by the absurdity of the scene. Giulio's total indifference to rank and respect, to say nothing of his master's wishes, was not only comical, but somehow engaging; he treated Nikki as an equal—sometimes as rather a tiresome equal. Obstinate, indulged, and slovenly, he yet provided an intimacy, a sort of cosiness, that Nikki found nowhere else, not even with me. Giulio was often used as a safety-valve, and was accustomed to it; he could not know that this occasion was more serious than most.

Nikki poured himself out some brandy with a shaking hand. I drank some too, though I didn't want it, and didn't even like it.

"Vanescu's precious League ought to be here," he said at last, more calmly. "This is going to be one of the times when I really come up to their expectations."

During the next two hours he drank a good deal of brandy. It had no effect at all, except to deprive him of sleep, when he consented to go to bed.

Suddenly he put his head on my shoulder and murmured, "I wish we'd been born in the gutter."

I said, stroking his forehead: "This will pass. Soon everything will be settled, and then you can go on with the work that matters."

Queen Elena's name was mentioned by neither of us—neither then, nor during the days that followed.

When at last the day of the debate on the Charter dawned, Nikki suddenly announced that I was not to go to the Assembly. I was to wait for him in his cabinet. Vera would leave the House as soon as the result of the voting was known, and give me the earliest news. When I protested, he said: "Suppose there's another attack? If we were both killed, what would happen to Paul?"

By this time I had got used to fear and horror—they had been, for the last fortnight, my daily companions—so I submitted without making a fuss.

The debate began in the early afternoon. I saw almost nothing of Nikki that morning; we were never alone. When he left the Palace, his mother was with him, and I was glad of it. If she had not been there, I might have said something that would have shaken his nerve. He was wonderfully calm, I think I never admired him more than at that moment. His last words to me were: "By the way, do try to explain to old Giulio what all this is about. He keeps asking me, and I never have time to tell him."

Nikki had begged me not to wait alone, so I had with me Marita, the personal maid I had engaged in Astrid's place; she was a peasant girl from the Eastern Province, and very pretty. I thought it would distract me to practise talking to her in her own language; I had become fairly proficient in it by this time.

When I came into the room and stood there, looking vaguely about me, the huge gilt chair was more terrifying to me than my own thoughts. The eagles holding the crown were like the familiars of some evil spirit. I began to persuade myself that a fate hung over anyone who sat in that chair.

I looked out of the window. It was pouring with rain. I couldn't think of the future any more; I didn't care in the least what happened to Murania. I wanted to feel Nikki's arms round me, and to hear his voice. I tried to imagine how I should behave if they came in and told me that he'd been assassinated; it was useless. "Whatever happens," I said, half aloud, "I shan't be able to take it in, that's one comfort."

Then I caught sight of Marita. She was looking at me with an anxious expression.

"Marita—have you a sweetheart?"

She smiled, and blushed. "Why, yes, Ma'am."

"Well, then—tell me, what does he think of the King's plan for the people?"

She looked bewildered. "The King's plan, Ma'am?"

"Yes. I want you to forget I'm your Queen, and to tell me."

"I never heard of it," she said, after a pause.

The shock, the disillusionment of that answer, was just what I needed. I felt suddenly calm and clear-headed.

After a moment's consideration, I began: "I shall tell you. For hundreds of years, you and your kind have been kept down, working for next to nothing, so that your lords and their ladies should live like kings and queens."

"Madame—don't you want me to work for you any more?"

"Of course I do. I'm not talking about you as you're placed now—but about the others, who haven't been so lucky. Do you see?"

"Yes, Ma'am."

Rather doubtful, I continued: "Now, the King hates that, and if he has his way today it will all be changed—wouldn't you like that?"

"I don't know——" she said, wrinkling her forehead.

"Are you quite sure you understand what I'm saying?"

"Oh, yes, Ma'am—if you speak slowly."

I explained it all over again, and there was a short pause.

At last she said, in a hesitating tone: "I don't know, Ma'am—whether I should like it or not, I mean. Some of our people try to make trouble—and have meetings—but it never comes to anything."

There was a long silence. Fearing to disturb her train of thought—if she had one—I waited for her to go on.

At last she said wonderingly: "Surely there'll always be the rich, and the poor? The priest in our village——"

"Yes, but not the very rich, and the very poor," I said, preferring not to embark on the question of the priest's authority.

"You've always looked after the poor, Ma'am," she said, after another silence. "They'd give their lives for you."

"But I don't want that!" I exclaimed. "I want them to live their lives. Don't you see——"

The door opened, and Vera came in. As we looked at one another the heavy load of suspense was lifted. I dismissed Marita, and we both sat down.

"Tell me."

"Defeated."

Defeated! That was a history-book word. I had never applied it to anything in my own life.

"And the voting?"

"A hundred and seventy votes to forty."

I sat still for a moment. Then I said, in a dull voice, "And—the King?"

Vera's lips trembled. "Oh Christiane!"

"He didn't—he wasn't——"

"He was wonderful. He just bowed—almost smiled—as if he had known what the result would be—and dismissed the Assembly."

The tears were pouring down her face. The Charter had been very near her heart, I knew—but all that seemed to belong to the past, at Kalacz, when we were so happy together. I remembered Nikki teasing her about her disciplinary methods with the young dancers—and for a few frenzied moments I tried to dream myself back into that time.

Suddenly I saw Nikki's face as she had described it, and began to tremble.

"How long——"

"He'll be some time yet," said Vera hastily. "He sent me a message to tell you not to expect him for a little while. Everything's quiet. There were crowds of people waiting round the House, but they're all quite silent. I had a carriage waiting at the side-door, and came straight here."

"Oh God—the selfishness—the ingratitude—and now——"

"Christiane—it wasn't quite like that. There were those who spoke for him"—she gave me a few names—"and they spoke well. The others—ah! Vanescu's been very clever. We underestimated him."

"What do you mean? What happened?"

"He didn't speak himself, except formally—as if he were above it all—you can imagine——"

"Go on."

"It was the others—the ones behind him. They made a case against —against the King."

"How?"

"There was a great deal of talk about your stay in Kalacz—and about the wrongs you righted. They used those very words—but with mockery."

"How could they make a case out of those? We helped only about a dozen people."

"They made it sound as if you'd helped hundreds."

"But when we went to the Eastern Province we were so careful——"

"I know," said Vera, blowing her nose. "But they muddled it all up—half lies, some truths—it was impossible to disentangle it. I could see, sitting there, the effect it was having. And then they brought up all the obvious things: Madame Karillos—running away for twenty years—then coming back and trying to—to alter laws that had existed for generations——"

"I see. He told me this would happen. But we were sure of a majority, even so——"

"Oh Christiane, the worst part's still to be told." She leaned towards me, and took my hand.

"Tell me, Vera. I'd rather know everything."

"That dreadful murderer——"

"Kolomai?"

"Yes. They said it was irresponsible—sentimental—to let him off— that he should have been executed. And then there was the part about poor dear Count Stanieff——"

"What could they find against him?" I cried, starting up; I was so angry that I forgot everything—even Nikki.

"Well—they made out he was a wild young man, selfish and heartless. They said that he—the friend of the King and the Queen —was one of the very people whose rights should have been limited. You remember that day when we were at Madame Karillos's villa, and two of the guards were killed? They implied that it was Egon Stanieff who killed them."

"But that's crazy! Everyone knows perfectly well——"

"Of course we know—but Vanescu's censorship of the press, and the rumours he's been spreading——"

"How could they possibly prove——"

"They didn't *prove* anything. It was all hints. But I saw how useful the murder of those two guards was—because the King never tried to find out who killed them. So that all the others—his enemies —had to do was to hint that he was protecting Stanieff, who was his friend. So you see——"

"Yes, I see. They had too many weapons."

There was a long silence.

Then I said, in a low voice, "I wonder what he'll do now?"

"He'll fight," said Vera, more hopefully. "You know he will."

"If he has the heart." I went up to her, and put my hands on her shoulders. "Vera—he's given years to this scheme—he tried to put it forward when he was a young man, before his father died. Now he's fought everything—the enmity of the nobles, even the apathy of the very people whom he wants to help."

"I know, I know."

"He may not want to fight any more. He's so tired——"

The doors opened behind me. I turned, and saw Queen Elena. Then I was glad that I had been able to prevent myself from weeping. She looked magnificent, and seemed to be ten years younger. After a smiling glance from Vera to me, she patted my cheek, and began to take off her gloves. As she peeled the white kid from those long, clever hands, I watched her in fascinated disgust, in deadly fear—I could just take in what she was saying.

"Ah! you got here first, Countess—I looked for you. You should have waited; I could have brought you back with me." She gave a happy little sigh, and looked round her. "Well, well! I had *such* a triumphant ride"—she paused, then added, with a mocking intonation—"hardly any stones, and very few hisses."

Vera turned away. I went on staring at Queen Elena.

She said gently: "Christiane, you look pale; you should have come. Nikki spoke well," she went on, rather as if she were describing the opening of a charity bazaar. "But of course it was a losing fight. How could he hope with one speech to wipe out a system that has lasted a thousand years?"

"He hoped to do rather more than that——" I began.

Queen Elena smiled. Then she glided across the room, and, as it were absent-mindedly, sat down in the gilt chair and leaned back.

With a start that was partly assumed and partly the result of rising excitement, she glanced up at the crown, and then at me.

"Aha! This is like old times!" she said radiantly. As I made no comment, she continued: "Oh well—that's over! And now we can go on in the same bad old way, and vastly comfortable it will be too!"

I was now sure of myself. I said quietly, "And what of the courageous minority that voted for him, and the Bill?"

Queen Elena examined her rings abstractedly. "I know this country fairly well, you see," she said, with an air of friendly explanation. "I should think they will be exterminated. One thing you've never understood, Christiane, coming from your own dear little democratic country—here, there is not one King. Every nobleman in Murania has a kingdom—which he rules absolutely."

"That's where it's all wrong—and that's where it will be changed," I said stubbornly.

She threw back her head, and burst out laughing. Her diamonds twinkled, her teeth gleamed; the light shifted, and seemed to run like water over the shimmering velvet of her gown. The room rang with her laughter—she dazzled and bewildered me. I could not move, or look away; all I managed to do was to shut my eyes.

Then suddenly the spell was broken. The footmen flung open the double doors at the far end of the room. Nikki stood there, his eyes on my face. He was lividly pale, and looked tired to the bone. He smiled at me—a quick, mechanical, would-be reassuring smile, that was gone in a second. I knew that he was trying to spare me, and the realization gave me hope and strength. I went up to him, and took his hand.

It was then that I remembered what the old gipsy woman had muttered to Egon Stanieff in the woods at Dhrevin—"something about a dark river." But only Egon knew what she had really said: and he had taken the secret with him to his grave.

4

"Was it very bad?" I said, in a low voice.

His eyes were fixed on his mother's glittering figure—she had got up as he came in—and he seemed not to hear me at first.

Then he said quietly: "Bad—yes, it was bad. I'm glad you weren't there. I should have hated you to see me defeated."

"No—never defeated."

He was now standing opposite Queen Elena. She contemplated

him with raised eyebrows, as if a great fuss were being made about nothing.

"Oh, by the way, Mamma," he said evenly, "thanks for the smile you gave me when the result was made known. I shall remember that smile."

She seemed to be making up her mind as to what attitude she should take. Then she made a slight, graceful gesture of acceptance, and said lightly, "Well, it's time somebody smiled." He gave her a long, grave look. She went on, in the faintly peevish tone of a spoilt charmer. "Oh Nikki—you used to be so gay. It doesn't suit you to be serious and high-minded."

As he continued to look at her without speaking, she added hastily: "Very well—you've been defeated. After all, it's only politics—dreary things!"

"It's not politics!" he burst out. "It's the hearts and souls and bodies of a million people, and their children, and their children's children—it's the whole future!" She shrugged her shoulders pettishly, and moved away. He went on, more calmly, "I could have left Paul a heritage he could have been proud of, but what now—what will he be?" He walked over to the table, and leaning against it, added under his breath, "Just a king, in a land of kings."

No one said anything. A footman came in. Nikki turned on him sharply, and said in a quivering, furious voice, "Yes?"

I had never heard him speak in that tone to any of the Palace servants before, and began to fear that he might give way to one of his violent rages.

"Your Majesty, His Excellency the Prime Minister is here, and begs an audience."

"Vanescu, already——" Nikki began. Then he pulled himself together, and said, in his ordinary voice, "Tell the Prime Minister I will receive him."

He got up, and sat in the gilt chair. I turned away—at that moment his situation was too bitterly ironic to be contemplated—and Vera curtsied as if she were going to leave.

Nikki held up his hand.

"No, Vera, don't go. There will be nothing private. On the contrary—there may be something that I should like you all to hear."

Vanescu's entry was greeted in silence. He bowed very low, and then stood in a respectful attitude—there was no sign of the relief he must have been feeling—opposite Nikki.

"Well, Mr. Prime Minister? Have you come to condole?"

Vanescu made a deprecating gesture. He had the appearance of deploring the harsh manner in which the question was put, and the general atmosphere of tension and hostility. I, at least, he seemed to be thinking, am going to behave like a gentleman.

Aloud, he said gently, "No, Sir. I have come to sympathize."

Nikki looked at him for a moment without speaking. Then he said quietly: "Then please be seated. I suggest we all sit," he added, glancing at me. "I personally feel as if I had been beaten with rods."

After a short silence he went on, "Now, Mr. Prime Minister."

Vanescu allowed another pause to elapse before he said, "Sir— a very grave situation has arisen."

"I quite agree with you. This country has just slid back five hundred years."

The Prime Minister gave Queen Elena the fraction of a glance, and said smoothly, "When, Sir, you were gracious enough to dismiss the Assembly, the Assembly refused to be dismissed—in fact, they are still sitting, and awaiting my return."

Nikki's face darkened. He seemed about to speak. Then he leaned back in his chair, his lips pressed together, his eyes half closed.

Vanescu continued, with an air of diffidence and embarrassment, "They have sent me to—to——" He broke off, slightly changed his position, looked at the ground, and added, in a low voice, "This is very painful to me, Sir."

It was a perfect performance—that of an old and faithful servant, forced into an impossible position.

"Yes——" said Nikki. "I remember my English tutor used to say much the same thing before he lifted the cane." Vanescu drew himself up, as if deeply shocked at this levity. Nikki added, "What were you saying?"

Vanescu rose, in the manner of one who throws away the scabbard. "Sir—the Assembly demands your abdication."

Nikki leaned across the table and looked at him, much as he had looked at Kolomai.

He said, in a very low voice: "Demands? *Demands?*"

"They have the means in their power to enforce your consent," said Vanescu quickly.

"Nothing can enforce my consent."

There was a pause.

Then Vanescu said, in his silkiest tone, "Not even the safety of the Crown Prince?"

"You would never dare!" I exclaimed, before I could stop myself; although I knew that Paul was perfectly safe and well, I looked imploringly at Nikki. His eyes were on Vanescu, who turned to me.

"Madame, half an hour ago a company of Hussars left for Kalacz, to take the Crown Prince into protective custody—what happens to him depends entirely on what His Majesty decides to do."

Queen Elena stood up, the embodiment of offended dignity. To this day, I have no notion as to whether she and Vanescu had planned this scene between them, or whether she was giving expression to a genuine concern.

"Vanescu, you go too far!" she exclaimed.

Nikki looked from one to the other.

Then he said, raising his voice a little, "No, Mamma, not far enough!" He turned to Vanescu, and went on: "Your Hussars will ride to Kalacz. I should like to see their faces when they get there. They will return empty-handed. The Crown Prince is already in protective custody."

He paused, as if to see the effect of this statement on Vanescu—there was none.

He continued, in a lower tone: "He has been for the last few days with his grandfather, King Peter, who assures me that he is well, and happy. So, if your Hussars need a long ride, let them ride to Norseland—it will take them, roughly, three months."

He took my hand in his and pressed it; for a few moments I was aware of no one else. I looked at his sunken eyes, with the dark shadows beneath them; but it was impossible to read his mind.

For the first time he hesitated a little; the pressure of his hand became stronger. Then he said, rather wearily, "A week ago, I had already decided that if the Assembly defeated me on the Charter, I should abdicate."

I had been prepared for those words; I ought to have been able to behave as if they were part of a scheme of my own. But the first shock was physical. I felt as if someone were running a red-hot bodkin into my side. I cried out something—some protest—and very nearly fell forward; then once more I felt the steady, calming force of Nikki's hand. He did not look at me; but he seemed to be giving me some of his strength and determination.

"My decision remains unchanged," he said. Now his voice was

coming from a long way off. As he went on, it grew fainter, then suddenly louder, then almost inaudible. By the time he had finished, I was able to stand beside him and listen with a tranquillity that was a poor reflection of his own.

"I abdicate freely—but on my own conditions."

"Your Majesty is not in a position to make conditions."

"On the contrary, I am in the most powerful position. The most popular figure in this country is in my hands. One threat to my little son, and you and your Assembly would be torn to pieces." He waited for a reply, but none came.

Then, looking across the room at his mother, he continued, speaking directly to her: "As a King, I've failed. I've tried to put humanity into hearts that had no room for it—how could I hope to succeed? I was a fool to think I could." He turned again to Vanescu, and added, in a sterner voice: "But by the time my son attains his majority, you and your kind will be swept away. You're old and rotten, and you smell of decay."

Vanescu said nothing. There was something about his attitude, the set of his shoulders, that indicated an intense satisfaction.

"Doubtless you have some official document," Nikki went on coldly, "by which I can sign my kingdom away?" Vanescu rose, bowed, and took a paper from the inside pocket of his coat. Nikki watched him with a faint smile. "You have—already? I might have known. Let me see it."

He took the paper, and scanned it rapidly.

"Ah! I thought so—'Her Majesty the Queen Elena to act as Regent.' I shall delete that."

Vanescu remained where he was, his eyes lowered.

Queen Elena started forward. "Nikki——"

Nikki ran his pen through the sentence, and continued, without looking up, "For that, I shall substitute 'My beloved wife—Queen Christiane.'"

At last Vanescu was impelled to catch Elena's eye, and for the second time I could not help feeling a little sorry for him.

He began, in an uncertain voice, "But, Sir——"

"That is my one and only unalterable condition. Witness the alteration, please. Thank you."

As Vanescu signed and drew back, Nikki glanced again at Queen Elena. She was standing still; her head was turned away from him.

"And now"—he said—"all that remains is for me to sign." He

drew the paper towards him. "I hope my hand is steady. I should hate posterity to say, 'How drunk he must have been!' There."

He took off his single order—the star of Saint Jerome—and put it on the table; then he leaned back, and the shadow of the crown fell across his forehead.

Vanescu took up the paper. "We may publish this immediately?"

Nikki shook his head. "In one hour from now—when I'm across the frontier. I don't want any disturbance—people are apt to be sentimental about abdications."

There was a short silence. Then, as Nikki's glance fell on Vanescu, standing in front of him, obsequious and self-contained, the blood rushed up to his face. He said harshly: "And now—my last command. Get out of this room—get out!"

Vanescu's presence had helped me to control myself. As soon as he had gone, I knew that I was about to break down. I fell on my knees beside Nikki's chair.

It is impossible to write of that moment without some recollection of the waves of fear and sorrow that rose over my head, one after another, choking me, forcing me into the depths of loneliness and terror. His hand was on my hair; his voice was in my ears, soothing me, expostulating a little. For once, his help was of no avail. I wanted to be brave, to make things easier, to appear worthy of that frightening, dreaded position—Queen Regent of a country in which I was still a stranger.

In shame and torment, I heard a voice cry, "I can't believe it— I'm afraid—Nikki, I'm afraid——" and knew that it was my own.

Queen Elena said: "Of course she's afraid—it was an outrageous thing to do. And the affront to me——"

It only needed that to bring me to myself. It was horrible to think that she had seen me behaving like an hysterical schoolgirl. I stood up and dashed the tears from my eyes.

Nikki was staring in front of him. As she broke off, he said, the faintest tinge of satirical enjoyment in his voice, "You'll get over it, Mamma—you'll have an admirable life, free to come and go." He paused, and added dryly, "They might even regard you as a martyr, if you behave yourself."

She said, looking pityingly at me, "Of course, Christiane can depend on me to help her in any way I can——"

"That's the one thing I'm afraid of——" Nikki put in.

She drew herself up, and walked to the door; I had never seen her look so beautiful, or so majestic, as at that moment.

"If you're going to be insulting," she said icily, "I shall go to my apartments." At the door she turned, and added, "I shall expect you to come and say good-bye to me."

Nikki got up, and walked towards her. I felt an arrow of jealousy pierce my heart—how was it that he could forget everything else when he was with her? I waited bitterly for him to take her hand and make some joking reference to her impossible ways, her frivolity, her imperious demands.

He did none of these things. He stood there looking at her with a sad irony, an odd detachment, as one contemplating a stranger. "Oh, no, Mamma," he said, very gently. "Don't you remember? We said good-bye twenty years ago."

She received the accusation as it had been made, quietly, and let it go. Her eyes on his face, she began to sink into a stately Court curtsey—the kind she made to him on formal occasions. In the middle of it she drew herself up, and said sharply, her voice shaking, "Well—that's one thing I needn't do any more——" and went out.

Nikki came back into the room with an impassive face. He seemed very far away from me.

Then he turned to Vera, who was in tears. "My dear friend——"

"Yes—yes—you must be alone—I'm going——"

He took both her hands. "But not before I tell you how deeply I appreciate your love and your loyalty." She tried to speak, failed, and began to sob again. He went on, in a low voice, as if they were alone: "I shall know that she has one true, dear friend. Please —no more grief."

She gave him an adoring look, and went out.

In the silence that followed, I felt the tears running down my cheeks; but that first wild, desperate panic was gone. Already I seemed to be weeping for something that I had lost a long time ago, something that had been mine in a dream only—a joy I should never know again. I was gazing into the past. As Nikki put his arms round me, I wondered dimly what I should say, how to conceal from him that there was nothing left for him to love.

"No, my sweet—no," he murmured, as if I had been a child. "Don't—don't. It isn't good-bye—we shall meet. You'll come to me when you can——"

He got out his handkerchief, and dried my eyes, holding me away from him so that he could look into my face.

I don't know what he saw there—perhaps a dumb, animal misery that alarmed him. He dropped his hands, and clasped them together.

After a moment's desperate consideration, he took me in his arms again, and said in an urgent, rapid tone, "We'll meet secretly, of course—that will make it more exciting." I was still speechless.

He went on: "Christiane, listen to me—I've got so little time. I want to speak to you, just for a moment, about Paul."

Yes. That name had the power to rouse me. I raised my head; I must have glanced at him with a gleam of intelligence, for his worn face brightened a very little.

"I want him to be—everything that I'm not. I've only thought of myself. He mustn't do that. He's here to serve—and you must teach him. As soon as he can understand the very simple things, he must begin to learn how to be a King—the kind I never could have been."

With an immense effort, I forced myself to answer. "I'll try— I'll do the best I can."

My tears had stopped. I was staring at him vaguely. I tried to remember what I had meant to say to him, when I was preparing myself for the worst. Now that it had come, the power of speech, and of grief too, seemed to have dried up altogether.

And I think that, as he looked at me, and tried to find some word of comfort, he saw and understood; he may have realized then, for the first time, how much I loved him. His face was suddenly convulsed, and his eyes filled. As he flung his arms round me and we clung to one another, the waves broke over his head also, and he wept as I had wept, without hope, without thought, in misery and agony and despair.

He whispered brokenly, "Kiss me, my love, my darling—and re-member——" He faltered, and his sobs broke out again; then he went on, "My only true happiness has been these few short months that you have given me—it was the only thing that mattered, Christiane—if it hadn't been for you——"

I felt his tears on my cheek; then he kissed my hands and drew away, his eyes fixed on mine. There was a long silence.

When at last he spoke, his voice was steady. "Christiane! Now— head up—fearless eyes——"

I obeyed him automatically; what he told me to do and to feel, I did and felt as if I had been a part of him; at that moment I had no existence but in him. He wanted me to be brave, and I was brave. It wasn't difficult, because words had ceased to have any meaning, and everything round us was swaying and reeling. It occurred to me, with a heavy, cold surprise, that he was looking at a dead person, and that he didn't know it.

"That's how I shall remember you," he said, his voice shaking and very low. "With love—and deep, deep gratitude——"

The door shut behind him.

I stood there for a long time before I realized that I was alone. Then I looked round, and saw where I was. I gazed curiously at the great chair, at the table in front of it, and wondered why no one had come in to draw the curtains. Dusk had fallen, and the rain was streaming down the blue-black panes of glass.

It came to me then, with a jerk of recollection, that Nikki had gone on a long journey. It wouldn't be very pleasant, travelling in the rain. . . . How strange, I didn't even know where he was going!

I went over to the table. In the centre, just as he had left it, lay the eight-pointed star of the Order of Saint Jerome. I picked it up and held it in both my hands.

Now I remembered everything that had happened. I pressed the star against my breast; and the pain burnt into my heart—into my mind—into my soul. And then I heard his voice, coming faintly to me through the sound of the rain—"That's how I shall remember you . . ."

CHAPTER THIRTEEN

How We Learnt to Endure

THIRTY YEARS after Nikki's abdication there came into my hands the diary that he began to keep on his departure from Murania. It seems to me that excerpts from this fragmentary record provide, more adequately than any descriptions of mine, the counterpart of my story.

Nikki left Bledz without any idea of where he was going. By the time he reached the frontier, he had decided to retire, temporarily, to his villa on the Gulf of Naples; this was part of a property that had been left him by one of Queen Elena's sisters when he was a young man. He had been there a week when he was writing as follows:

. . . and it isn't so much the fact that I've left her to bring up Paul alone as the thought of her resentment, her not understanding, that haunts me. Why doesn't she write? If she'd written the day after I left, I'd have had the letter by now. I suppose she's finished with me. I don't blame her. A year of insensate, perverse brutality—a few months of heaven—and then she's left, at nineteen, to "do the best she can." And yet, somehow, I did think she'd send me one line of forgiveness— that's all I can hope for. She must have got my letters. I know for a fact that the first one was given into her hands as soon as I was out of the country. I didn't expect this awful, empty silence; I can't accept it. She can't doubt that I worship and adore her. Oh God! let her understand and forgive me. Then, if it's possible—and I feel that it is —she can forget me. Perhaps tomorrow I shall hear.

[*A few days later.*] Nothing from C. I can't believe it. They must be keeping back her letters. And yet she knew—I told her how to send me word. She's decided to cut me out of her heart, that's all. . . . It's wonderfully beautiful here. Too beautiful. I shouldn't have come; it's a place for lovers and forgetfulness, and what one of my tutors used to call "all the fascinating *morbidezza* of the South." I see no one; I speak to no one but Giulio; I sit for hours staring out over the bay. *Dolce far niente,* indeed—it's hideous to be idle; and yet I'm so tired—so tired. I can hardly drag myself to bed. But when I'm lying in the dark, with nothing but the sound of the sea in my ears—then it all comes back: Christiane, my mother, Paul, the faces in the Assembly, that endless, ghastly drive through the streets, Vanescu's look of triumph, the tears, the agony, the remorse. For of course I could have stayed and submitted and schemed and wheedled my way back into favour as the kind of King they want, and in a few years' time presented them with a meaningless version of the Charter. I couldn't. It would have broken me. I explained that to Christiane; I thought she understood that when one loses the last throw one must leave the game. She seemed to understand; she agreed with me. What's happened? I telegraphed yesterday. Christiane, for God's sake . . .

[*A few hours later.*] Why do I write down all this rubbish? Why don't I do what Giulio hints at, and have some of the country girls in to dance, and choose the prettiest to keep me company in this hellish eyrie between the cliffs and the sea? I walk up and down in the orange groves and wish I were dead and buried. That's easy. One could do it in a minute. But there's Paul—and Christiane—one day, she might—what am I maundering about? She's done with me, she's made that clear enough. But it's not like her—to do nothing, nothing at all, while each day seems longer, and each night—last night it was very bad, one can't grind one's teeth and behave sensibly for more than a certain time. Oh! my darling, forgive me, forgive me, try to understand how much I love you—try! Answer me! *Write*—one word, even of hatred, and I could bear this pain, I could indeed. Christiane! Christiane! . . .

[*Three days later.*] Still nothing. I've thought over all the things I could do. I could drink myself senseless—but the idea sickens me; I couldn't get the stuff down. I could follow Giulio's advice—but I swore to myself, after that time in Kalacz, that I'd never again take pleasure without love—and anyway, what pleasure could I find? I could jump over the parapet—but I'm not so blind with misery that I can't see ahead, to a day nine years from now, when I might perhaps be needed. I thought I'd gone through the worst when I saw her standing there alone, trying to smile—but this is the worst of all. I can't eat, I can't read, I can't rest. Dear Christ! help me, have pity on me, help me to lose her love without going mad. But perhaps this is what I deserve. There's a long account against me, I know that now. . . .

[*Two days later.*] . . . and it hasn't been so bad in the daytime. I know at last that I shan't hear, and that we shall never meet again. It's only at night that I curse and weep and walk up and down, calling her name. And then sleep comes with the first light. And then one has to wake up, of course—and then the whole miserable round begins again. There's something bitter and hard about good women. They know how to stab to the heart, all right—and they let you bleed slowly to death while they're praying for your soul.

[*One day later.*] I'm quite collected as I write this. I want to set down the word I could never bring myself to say to Christiane— honour. If I'd stayed, I'd have lost it. And then—a king's oath. I gave them my promise that they should have their Charter if I remained on the throne. I was defeated, and so I had to go. It's as simple as that. She must have known that I couldn't do anything else. Odd—for the first time today I realized what a common word honour is here in Italy, like a false coin that gives a tinny, flat sound when you ring it down. *"Parola d'onore? Non c'e nient' altro?"* I heard Giulio say this morning, when he was talking to Maria about the laundry. Honour—love—defeat. They add up to one thing—despair. If C. had been ill, Vera would have written; at the worst, I'd have seen it in the newspapers. So it's finished. And yet I must go on living; I know that too. . . .

I did not write to Nikki because, within a few hours of his departure, I collapsed, and couldn't move a finger, even to feed myself, for a fortnight. Vera didn't write, because I had sent her to fetch Paul. The country was quiet, and I had a feeling that he ought to be among his own people. The doctors said that his return was the best hope for my recovery, and they were right.

As soon as my letters began to arrive, Nikki left Italy, and went to Paris. After a little while, he started to go about and see some of his old friends. Then he too fell ill; he caught cold, developed pleurisy, and was in bed for several weeks. Now his journal must speak for him again.

. . . I got up today and sat on the balcony. I've been wondering, since I got here, what to do with my life. I'm not rich any longer—but that doesn't matter, the life I lead costs very little. I've had in mind a plan for a book on "the future of kingship"—that sounds pretentious enough—on the lines that Stefan Rell indicated to me when I was a young man. I can't do more than think it over just now. . . .

[*A few weeks later.*] Another invitation from the Princesse de Vailly. She still runs that roaring dinner-factory, with a few exhausted "hands" (her nieces) to tend the machine, and I might do worse than be caught up in its wheels for one evening. How pointless and boring it all is, though! I can't go on pretending that C. is with me, and that I'm talking to her, any longer, and though her letters are just like her, they're horribly tantalizing. Sometimes a whole day goes by before I can bring myself to open the envelope. But to think of her having "her own party" is encouraging—and touching. God bless her, my own darling. . . .

(I must explain here that the Muranian Cabinet was not entirely united behind Vanescu and Queen Elena. Three of the Ministers—in our private language Nikki and I called them the Three Graces, because they were all so remarkably hideous—were pro-Charter, and working for the future he had planned.)

[*Two days later.*] I might have known that Marta would be at the Vailly dinner-party. We had a few words together in the latter part of the evening. She was obviously rather appalled by my appearance. I suppose I do look like a ghost, and I certainly feel like one. She suggested that we should meet. She's a dear sweet woman. And hers is the kind of beauty that's inherent—nothing to do with age.

[*Three weeks later.*] We both shrank from the meeting and kept making excuses to put it off. Then everything came right, and we talked for a long time and I told her the whole story. I felt as if it had all happened a hundred years ago. I don't know what to do. She said, "Don't decide now, think it over. I'm here, if you want me." Seeing her, I've a horror of being alone. We always got on so well. And the love affair's over—it would be a case of two old friends keeping one another company along a rather dreary road. And yet, is it fair? I'm not sure.

[*A month later.*] Marta's the only person in the world who understands about C. She really does seem to want—but women can deceive one completely for love's sake—and I'm not much of a friend, or even a companion, these days. In less than nine years—eight years and seven months—it will be Paul's tenth birthday, and then (it's strange how the thought of that time obsesses me). . . . I shall see Christiane in the spring—it's all arranged. I can't picture it. I'm assured—by Vera— that she's quite strong again, and, with the help of the Graces, taking her place, as it's called.

[*Two months later.*] . . . for another long talk with M. She's very religious—she always was, but now it seems to have taken hold of her—and she did convince me that companionship is all she wants, and all I want. She is a darling. I found myself laughing, after she'd gone, at her descriptions of her farewell tour. Well—her work's finished, and so is mine. We're not going to set up together in the same house; neither of us wanted to, and each was afraid of confessing as much to the other—rather amusing. She's taken a house at Fontainebleau, and I shall go to the Trois Couronnes. We shall ride in the forest, and there'll be some old friends and a great deal of music. . . . I've started my book. M. and I are both sick of Paris.

[*Three months later.*] I never want to see Paris again. I've been helping M. with her charities—I'd no idea there were so many of them —and my book's going well, but I've had to rewrite the first chapter. Christiane's letters—it's no good, I can't even write about them. The last photograph of Paul had a look of Mamma! C. would say I was getting morbid, but I can see it, and why not? Marta said he was like Christiane—but she's nothing if not tactful, bless her.

[*A year later.*] I suppose C. and I both live from one "honeymoon" to the next. She's older: a beautiful woman, not a girl any more. It was—as I'd dreamed of it. The parting wasn't as ghastly as I'd expected. I suppose we behaved quite naturally, but it seems, in retrospect, rather queer that Mamma wasn't so much as mentioned. We talked about Marta. It's odd—she and C. might have been friends. . . .

[*Three years later.*] Of course she's right; I mustn't write to Paul, it might make trouble. I think he must be rather intelligent for his age, from what C. tells me. That was very amusing about the pony. Only four years now before—but it must be some sort of atavistic instinct that makes me dwell on it like this. I must be there. I will be. I may be running a risk—but it will make all the difference to C. if she knows that I'm in the background somewhere, thinking of her, praying for her and for Paul. I'm glad she tells him as much as he can understand about me. . . .

[*Two and a half years later*.] Marta's going to Buda-Pesth to see her people, and Christiane's going to be there on a State visit. They'll meet —secretly, of course. I think, I hope—but what can I hope for? The only way of getting through this sort of life is to exist in a vacuum. *Il faut vivre*, but why? I trust Christiane doesn't guess what a misanthrope I've become. When I'm with her, it's as if I came out of my grave into the sunshine. She made summer in my heart—even at the beginning, when I thought I hated her—and she always will. She'd done her hair differently last time—well, I suppose she must follow, if not lead, the fashions—but it made me feel as if we'd grown apart. And yet it wasn't the hair really. . . .

[*A month later*.] There's a bigger gulf between Christiane and me than there was when I left Murania. That's natural, perhaps. But just lately, her letters haven't been—I don't know, I can't define it. Perhaps when she and Marta have met, it will be better. . . .

[*Two months later*.] . . . and I didn't like to go on nagging Marta about C. There must be, after all, a limit, even to her patience. Sometimes, when I'm alone, I feel that things have gone wrong—irrevocably wrong, and that it's my fault. It's like that time in Italy, starting all over again—God! that was a nightmare. But why should her letters have changed? I can't ask her till I see her, and that's ten months from now. . . .

[*Three months later*.] I must wait, that's all. There's nothing to be done. God knows I've had plenty of practice at this sort of thing, but it's misery and torture not to know why. I think I can guess. She's beautiful and vital and young, and Bledz is full of handsome young men, ready to be devoted. Poor Stanieff—how desperately jealous I was!—but I think C. never guessed it. Sometimes I wish I'd never had anything to do with her. But she shan't know what she's doing to me —what's the good of making two people wretched? I can't talk about it to anyone, not even Marta. When I see her, I shall know—and if it is what I fear, I shan't make a scene. I've no rights over her—none. We've brought one another a great deal of grief and anger, she and I—and I know very well that I deserve every sleepless night, every tear, every stab of pain. . . .

2

In Murania, the first eight years of Nikki's second exile went by uneventfully. Queen Elena, who had renewed her friendship with old Count Stanieff at the funeral of his son, behaved with an extraordinary lack of discretion. When the invalid Countess Stanieff died, they were seen everywhere together; they spent a great deal of time in the country, or abroad, for which I was very thankful. It can be imagined what effect this had on Vanescu. For a time he went on with his work, as if nothing had happened; then our Paris Embassy fell vacant, and he became Ambassador there. At about this time Princess Anna died, and Cyril married again—morganatically; his wife was a Swede, and a very intelligent woman. It was she who influenced her husband towards my party in the Cabinet; she even succeeded in effecting an improvement in Prince Michael's character. He grew up into a *gauche* but kind-hearted young man, very much attached to Paul and to me.

I hope and believe that I did my best for Paul. I know that I didn't spoil him; but, as I look back, it seems to me that the faults in his upbringing resulted in overseriousness, and an almost too deeply ingrained sense of his responsibilities. As soon as he was of an age to take it in, I told him about his father's failure to establish democratic rule in Murania; and he took that to heart, although I wasn't aware of it at the time. He was fascinated by his grandmother, who was, of course, at her best with him; perhaps it was as well that they did not see too much of one another. Paul had not—I realize it now—the brilliance, the moody, passionate humours, the freakish sense of fun by which his father had entranced me. He was a high-spirited, affectionate child; he grew up (but that doesn't bear thinking of) into a hard-working, just, and popular King. Although we spent a great deal of time together, my affections were unfairly divided. I did my duty as best I could; I worked very hard; but all the time I was living another life, in another country.

It was quite true that my letters to Nikki had changed in tone. As the time came near for our next meeting—which was to take place at his villa in Italy—I realized, with growing dismay, that I dreaded seeing him. When we did meet, we were, for the first time since his departure, ill at ease. We discussed all the usual subjects—Paul, the affairs of the country, Nikki's book (he had just completed it), Cyril's marriage: but distantly, and without any of the allusions and jokes which had become a part of our private language. We had six days together—and already many hours had been wasted

I saw that his anxiety and depression were increasing; and so I decided to say what was in my mind.

We were sitting in the loggia, looking out over the bay. The islands faced us, purplish-black, against a stormy sky and a green sea. The heat was tremendous, the atmosphere heavy with approaching thunder. Nikki was leaning against the parapet, his back to the sea.

"Is it too hot for you? Would you like to go in?" he said, avoiding my eye.

"I like it—as long as I don't get sunburnt." I wrapped the long scarf that was a part of my white chiffon *négligée* round my neck, and drew the ends over my hands.

Then I said abruptly: "Something is wrong. Isn't it better to admit that?"

He looked at me darkly, and did not answer.

"Can't we—isn't it possible to clear it up?" I went on.

There was another silence.

Then he said, in a flat voice: "Last night you were tired from the journey. It seemed best not to disturb you."

I waited for him to speak again. At last he said, "I knew—at least, I should have guessed—that this would happen."

"That we should become estranged?"

"Yes."

"My feelings haven't altered," I said, in a low voice. "It's sometimes rather difficult, after these long intervals, to take up just where we left off——"

"It used not to be so."

"Perhaps something—or somebody—has come between us," I said, after another interval of silence.

"Why do you say, then, that your feelings haven't changed?" he said angrily.

I was silent.

He went on, with rising bitterness: "You're not thirty yet. Why should you waste your time——"

"How can you say that?" I exclaimed. "You know, as well as I do, that I live for these times together."

"You've drawn away from me. Your letters are different."

"I didn't know——" I began, rather bewildered. "You never said——"

"What could I say? This had to happen," he interrupted, turning away. "Ours isn't the sort of relationship that goes on happily. Naturally you——"

"Well?"

"You're—you can't be expected to exist as I do. I'm bitterly, desperately jealous, and unhappy, of course. But I don't blame you."

"Jealous? Of whom?"

"God knows," he said, shrugging his shoulders. "I was once even jealous of Stanieff. Now . . ."

"Now, what?"

"I don't know who it is. I don't want to know."

I got up, and came towards him. "But there isn't anyone. How could there be?"

"Oh! I know what you're going to say. You love me just as much as you ever did—perhaps even more, because you've found a more normal happiness with someone who——"

"Listen to me!" I interrupted. "I tell you, there's no one! You've no right to think so—especially when it's you who——"

As I broke off, angry and breathless, we stood looking at one another.

Then Nikki said coldly: "What have I done? Are you going to drag in Marta?"

"I'm not jealous of Marta, and I'm not in love with anyone but you," I said deliberately. "Until you've taken that in——"

In the pause that followed, he began to look rather sheepish. "I did think—perhaps it was foolish—but you see——"

"You don't know what I'm like—even now."

There was a long silence.

"I know you're sweet—and lovely—and kind," he said, in his most insinuating, persuasive voice, putting his hand on my hair. I jerked my head away. He went on gently: "It's my fault, perhaps. I've written you some suicidal letters."

I walked away. It was impossible to say what I had in my mind when he spoke in that tone.

"Tell me, my darling—what was it?"

"Well," I said, after a pause, "it was a rumour—a piece of gossip. Perhaps I should have ignored it. But I couldn't."

"About Marta and me? You know that we see a great deal of one another. Surely——"

"It wasn't that," I said, trying to speak steadily. "I know—I'm always glad she's with you."

"Then what can it have been? Who told you?"

"No one. No one speaks to me of you—except Vera."

"Not my mother?"

"I very seldom see her. When we do meet, we talk about Paul, and—and things like fashions. I read this—in a newspaper."

He began to laugh. "My darling child—the newspapers! Really, you——"

"This was—it had the appearance of truth. No one could have made up such a thing."

"Well?"

"It made me very unhappy."

"Go on, Christiane," he said authoritatively.

I shrank back, half braced, half intimidated, by his tone.

"You and Marta were in Fontainebleau. She had a house, and you were at the inn near by."

"That's all perfectly true."

"It's known that you and she—that you're not——"

"Lovers? No, we're not. You knew that already," he interrupted sharply.

"But it is thought that she—that she couldn't hope to keep you without—I can't say it——"

"Go on. This is all new to me," he said, in his derisive, ironical manner.

"Well—she had parties—at least, that's what I read—and asked younger women—quite young girls—chosen for their beauty—and——"

My voice died away in the silence. I couldn't look at Nikki. Suddenly I heard a burst of laughter. I turned, and saw that he was really amused; I hadn't heard him laugh like that for a long time. In the distance, lightning flashed over the islands; as he began to speak, thunder drowned his voice.

"Oh, Nikki—it's not true, is it?"

He stopped laughing, and held out his arms. "No, my angel, it isn't! What induced you to believe such a thing?"

"I don't know. I—sometimes I get very miserable, and then—then I feel—I can't——"

His arms were round me. I could still hear the smile in his voice as he whispered: "Don't cry, darling—don't. You'll spoil your pretty eyes."

"I'm partly crying—because of the relief."

"You really do believe that it isn't so?"

"Yes."

"You know there's only one young girl in my life—or was—and she led me on in the most shameless manner——"

"Darling——"

"And besides, can you imagine Marta, of all people——"

"I suppose I was dreadfully silly."

He pressed my face against his shoulder; then he said, rather sadly: "It is partly my fault. It's the loneliness. And I've been imagining you in the arms of half a dozen smartly dressed young men . . ."

"How could you?"

"Now, is that quite fair?"

"Oh dear," I said, with a shaky laugh, "what a muddle! And then, when we met, I thought Marta wasn't as friendly—as I'd hoped, I mean——"

"She thought you were angry with her."

"Well, I was."

"Why did you read this filthy rubbish?"

"When I see your name in the paper, I can't help——"

"Don't, my dearest, what's the use? None of them know about me, and you do. And I promise"—he went on, the amusement creeping back into his voice—"that if I start really going to the bad, with or without Marta's help, I'll tell you. You know, you'll develop a lurid imagination, like a lady novelist, if you don't take care."

"I won't. But, you know—I felt so alone."

"I know, I know. It's all right now, isn't it?"

There was panic in his voice—we never admitted our deepest griefs to one another, and I knew just what he was feeling—so I hastened to reassure him. That was our misfortune; we had to keep up a pretence of being contented, and so made a barrier between us that grew more impenetrable as the years went on.

That night the storm burst over the villa in cataracts of rain and tearing gusts of wind. The shutters rattled and flew apart; the doors banged all over the house; the waves rolled up against the base of the cliff with dull, heavy reverberations. As Nikki got up to shut the windows, a blaze of sheet-lightning lit up all the room, and I saw him, white against the blackness, lean, graceful, and strong. That was how I remembered him, all the weary journey home, and for long afterwards.

3

During the first years of Nikki's exile I was to hear many rumours about his way of life, some even more hideous than the one I repeated to him; but I was never again so deeply disturbed. I learnt to repulse such attacks slowly, and with difficulty; in the end, I became immune.

Nikki's letters helped me; he ceased to write, as he had put it, suicidally, and seemed happier. I didn't know that he missed me more desperately as the years went by, but there was something uncharacteristically resigned about his letters that made me very uneasy, so I contrived another brief meeting with Marta, a month before Paul's coronation. This was to take place, according to the ancient custom, eight days after his tenth birthday.

Marta was worried about Nikki, though she did her best to conceal it.

"He's very patient and uncomplaining," she said. "But his life's so aimless. And he frets for you, and for his son."

I said something that was meant to show my consciousness of her value to Nikki.

She shook her head, with a faint smile. "I do what I can. His book was an interest for the first five years. He was quite right not to publish it under his own name—but if he had he'd have been asked to follow it up with another. He hasn't, and so—well, you can imagine."

Later on, she added, "He's so terribly thin, and he doesn't sleep or eat well." I suggested change of scene, and she shrugged her shoulders. "It doesn't matter where he is, or what he does. His thoughts don't change."

And then she described, in some detail, an evening that they had spent at the opera at a gala performance for charity. This occasion seemed to her significant, and has since become so to me.

During the first part of the evening Nikki had tried to give Marta the impression that he was enjoying himself; by the time the curtain had fallen he was frankly listless and bored.

After a short silence he said: "It's so long since I saw the great world amusing itself. How little they all change! Just deeper lines and thicker paint."

Marta glanced over the brilliantly lit auditorium, and said gently: "The Princesse de Vailly is trying to catch your eye. Do acknowledge her."

"Where? Oh, yes." He leaned forward, smiled radiantly, and, murmuring, "Disgusting old harpy," went on, in the same flat, weary tone: "All Paris seems to be here. Can't you hear them whispering, 'So they're together again—how very amusing—what can they have to say to one another after all these years?'"

Marta laughed. "Well, they could say, 'What can she be doing with a man who is madly in love with his wife, and talks of no one else?'"

Nikki continued to lean over the edge of the box. He said tentatively, "Perhaps she's wasting her time?"

"She doesn't think so."

"And what does she think?"

"She doesn't think—she remembers."

He turned and smiled at her. Then he said, "What do you remember, Marta?"

She considered a moment; then she looked at him and said, in a quiet, even tone: "I remember a frightened, bewildered boy tapping on the window of my little room near the theatre in Bledz, and asking me—me, of all people—whether he should run away, or stay."

"And you said stay," said Nikki, leaning back in his chair.

"And yet you ran away—it was always you who made the decisions."

There was a short pause. They had forgotten the fashionable world below them.

He went on, "What else do you remember?"

"Oh"—she seemed to be forcing herself into a lighter mood—"wondering when you'd fall in love, and what I should feel when you did."

"And what did you feel?"

If she thought the question unfair—as I should have—she did not show it.

She said, with a smile: "I think I behaved very well. Sixty miles to Hervat in a closed carriage, without a tear—but when I crossed the frontier, I cried for three days and three nights. I've never cried since," she added briskly, and he smiled. She resumed thoughtfully, "I don't suppose I ever shall—until——"

"Until?"

"I fall out of love with you—then I shall never stop crying——" Her voice shook a little.

After a pause he said, "How can you love someone who's failed —so completely?"

She put her hand on his knee. "You didn't fail, Nikki. You were just a bit before your time, and some day history will bear out what I say." He shook his head, and she went on, getting up and leading the way into the little room behind the box: "We're getting too serious. This is supposed to be a gay, gala performance, and it's a very deserving charity." He said nothing, and she continued, with a nervous look, "Let me see, what's it in aid of?"

He glanced at his programme. "I haven't the slightest idea." They both laughed, more naturally, and he went on, turning to the table, where a bottle of champagne and several glasses were set out: "I'm told that the sale of tickets went with a rush, directly my name was announced as patron. I had no idea I was still of such value to the newspapers."

"You should be gratified."

He appeared not to be listening. Then he said, in a low voice, "Yes —because in five weeks my small son will be crowned." Marta put down her glass and looked at him wistfully. Perhaps he was conscious of her distress, for he went on, in his caustic manner, "And what, may I ask, is that to do with me?"

"You know perfectly well that the whole of Europe wants to know your attitude towards the coronation," she said, after a moment's consideration. "And there are strong rumours that you intend to be there."

She wanted him to look at her. But she could not read his expression.

He stood silent, gazing into his glass; he emptied it before he answered. "And take all the limelight away from Paul? Oh, no— let the poor boy have his day of triumph."

The words were bitter; but the tone was one of suppressed emotion.

Marta, accustomed to these half-controlled gusts of feeling, waited for a moment and then said, in a casual voice, "The Muranian Ambassador has been keeping his eyes glued to this box."

"Vanescu?"

"He's getting up," she went on. "I think he's coming here. If he appears, do you want to be left alone?"

"Good Heavens, no," said Nikki, rousing himself. "Our conversation will be purely social. What else could it be?" he added, rather defiantly.

When Vanescu came in, he was received with smooth cordiality.

"Do I intrude, Sir?" he began.

"No intrusion——" said Nikki briefly, as Vanescu bowed and kissed Marta's hand. "Sit down, Mr. Ambassador. Are you enjoying the entertainment?"

"Excellent," said Vanescu, eyeing him a little suspiciously. "How well Calvé sang."

"You should have heard Karillos in her prime," said Nikki, with a faint smile.

"Karillos?" repeated Vanescu, the slightest tinge of insolence in his tone. "Oh, yes, Madame—you sang?"

"Oh yes, I sang," said Marta, unmoved. "In the dim ages."

There was a pause.

Then Nikki said abruptly: "Well, Mr. Ambassador? What is your diplomatic mission tonight? I feel that you have one."

Vanescu glanced at him and said in his most impenetrable manner, "Purely a social call, Sir."

Nikki laughed. "The first for five years. I wonder why."

Vanescu looked round the crimson damask walls as if for inspiration, and then said, in an extremely casual tone, "There have been rumours, Sir—I know there could be no truth in them, but I wanted to be sure"—he paused, but Nikki made no sign—"that you are contemplating being present at our King's coronation."

Nikki gazed at him with an amiable smile.

"Ah! but not officially," he said at last. "I am a private citizen, you know."

"The Muranians have never considered you as such."

"Which Muranians? The Parliament, or the people?"

Vanescu received this shaft with his usual imperturbability; but Marta saw his eyes gleam under their heavy lids as he replied, "There are still some unruly factions left."

"After ten years?"

There was a long silence.

Then Vanescu said: "Your presence in the capital could easily cause a disturbance. You——"

"I think you exaggerate," Nikki interrupted lightly. "If I am there, I shall be there as a proud father." He paused, and added, with a faintly satirical emphasis, "Even you, Mr. Ambassador, must appreciate a father's feelings for his son, on the greatest day of his life."

Vanescu got up, and so did Nikki. For a moment they looked at one another without speaking.

Then Vanescu said, in his official manner, "I have been instructed by Her Majesty's Government to take every step in my power to prevent your being there."

Nikki continued to smile. He said, "By Her Majesty's Government—but not by Her Majesty."

"Queen Christiane would not act in any way contrary to her Ministers' wishes."

Nikki put down his glass, and locked his hands behind him.

Then he said, in an extremely gentle voice: "That, Mr. Ambassador, is where we disagree. The Queen uses her head, certainly—but where her heart is concerned——" He stopped, and turned away.

After a moment's silence he went on, in a very low voice, "No, Mr. Ambassador—allow me to know all about my wife's heart."

It was plain to Marta that Vanescu was very angry. He seldom condescended to mockery; when he did so, it was not a success.

He said, with an attempt to speak in a light, satirical tone, "After ten years?"

"You are impertinent."

There was something in the indifferent coldness of the answer that Vanescu could not accept.

He said sharply, "On behalf of our Government, I forbid you to go there."

Nikki took a step forward. Marta got up. In the silence that followed, she dared not glance at his face.

At last he said, in a haughty, deliberate tone that alarmed as much as it surprised her—it was, she told me, as if she heard him speaking from the throne, with the whole power of majesty behind him—"Forbid? *Forbid?*"

Vanescu looked at him for a moment without answering. Then his glance wavered and fell.

Nikki picked up his programme and went on, in his ordinary voice: "Mr. Ambassador—the interval seems to be coming to an end. Will you excuse me?"

Vanescu bowed as Nikki and Marta passed before him into their box.

As he went out, Nikki drew back her chair for Marta; when she was seated, he glanced at her vaguely and opened the programme. "The last act of *Faust*. Melba—Plançon—de Reszke. It should be enjoyable."

She leaned forward and put her hand on his arm. "Nikki——"

The lights began to go out all over the house. He went on, as if she had not spoken, "But I always think it's such a silly story."

In the darkness, her eyes filled with tears. In that one trivial remark he had let escape all the grief, all the hopeless pining, that he had meant to keep from her. For it was of his own story, of its mischances, its bitterness, its heavy burden of loss and parting, that he was thinking—his voice made that clear enough.

She said in a whisper, "Why make an enemy when you have no intention of going?"

For a moment he did not answer. Then he said, but not to her— it was as if he were speaking to an unseen presence, rather than to himself: "He'll stand there, alone—no, not quite alone. She'll be there—but not too near. He's on his own now—guarded, and yet so defenceless. The organ will murmur, the incense will rise, he might feel faint—but he mustn't faint, because he's a King." He paused, and she saw that his hands were trembling; then he said, very softly: "They'll hold the crown over his head. It's too big, and too heavy for him to wear. I found it too big, and too heavy—and I was a grown man. He's only a little boy."

The conductor acknowledged the applause, and tapped his baton. The music rose, and filled all the darkened house. Nikki was gazing straight in front of him. The tears overflowed and ran down Marta's face, onto her neck and the gleaming satin of her dress. She sat still, looking at Nikki; his glance was turned towards the stage.

4

As I look at the photographs of Paul which were taken at the time of his coronation, I see a likeness to Nikki that disappeared with adolescence. But it is impossible to recall that day without seeing the father's face behind the son's. When I came to take Paul to the cabinet where Nikki had signed his abdication, it was as if the past ten years had ceased to exist in my memory.

It was the custom of the Kings of Murania to receive the foreign Ambassadors there before starting for the Cathedral. Paul acquitted himself well; better, I believe, than I did, for I had not set foot in that room since the day that Nikki left the kingdom.

When the Ambassadors had gone, we were left alone for a moment or two.

I said, "You'll try to be a good King, Paul?"

"I'll be a great King, Mother," he said; adding quickly, "I'll conquer all my enemies—and my father's too."

This was the moment for a little lecture; but it was not in my heart to quench his ardour.

I smiled rather doubtfully, and he went on, "Why couldn't he have come to see me crowned?"

"I explained why—don't you remember?"

"Yes," he said, looking suddenly grave, "I suppose he'll never come."

"I'm afraid not. But he's thinking of you now, I'm quite sure." There was a short silence.

Then he said: "Did you see the book Grandmamma gave me? It's a history of all the Kings of Murania."

I knew that book; I had been expecting it to arrive before today. It had been written by a *protégé* of Queen Elena's, and set forth, in terms simple enough for an intelligent child to understand, all the principles—or, rather, slogans—of the old régime. Luckily, it wasn't very readable.

I put my hand on Paul's shoulder. "Don't think too much about the past—it's been rather a sad one. Think of the future. Remember what you're going to do, when you're old enough."

He nodded, and pressed my hand. Then I reminded him of one or two points in the procedure that he had rehearsed with the Master of Ceremonies, and took him back to his rooms to dress. An hour later we were driving through the streets to the Cathedral.

I had received a note from Nikki a few days earlier. In his last letters he had spoken at length of Paul; this was to me alone. He said nothing of his movements or his plans—there was always a danger that our correspondence might be tapped—but ended with these words: *"I shall know that you are thinking of me—even if you are not able to give me proof of it."*

Bowing, smiling, answering Paul's excited questions, reminding him every now and then to look this way or that, I was wondering all the time how close Nikki and I were to one another. Had he remained at a distance—or was he somewhere among the shouting crowds? I was horribly afraid. If he were recognized and followed, he might be insulted, roughly handled, embarrassingly acclaimed, even—though this was improbable—murdered.

All through that long day we were together, he and I, and I heard his voice. "You're Northern—nothing dark and deep and devious about you"—we were getting out of the carriage now—" 'If this were love'—well, perhaps it is—one kind of love." We had taken our seats in the choir, and I heard him above the music and the murmur of voices. I looked down at my gloved hands, and saw the raised circle made by the betrothal ring. "Everything Leads Me to Thee"—that was ironic enough; then, as the choristers' voices rose and filled all the Cathedral, one sounded above the rest: "I've been fighting you all my life . . . In spite of everything—can you love me? . . . Your eyes get much greener when you're serious . . . We've so little time, my darling—don't cry—I want to talk to you about Paul . . ." And then, "Christiane! that's how I shall remember you . . ." At last I forced myself out of the dream, and looked across the choir at Queen Elena.

Stately, upright, glittering in gold tissue and covered with historic jewels—could nothing change her? Her poise was unshaken, her beauty almost—but not quite—unravaged by the marks of time. Then again I heard Nikki's voice, "Ah! that's the Italian manner—charm in the morning, murder in the afternoon." How incongruous, how strange those words seemed now—for I was looking at a splendid figure in a pageant: no scheming, sinister, Italian mother-in-law, but a great lady, a majestic effigy.

At last the slow, quietly moving ceremony reached its climax. Paul, who had been kneeling at the high altar, rose, and turned to face the people. The Archbishop of Bledz held the crown over his head. His voice rang through the Cathedral. I could not see my son's face. A cloud of incense hung between us.

Then it was time for me to come forward and repeat the oath of allegiance. And as I knelt and placed my hands under Paul's, I was quite certain that Nikki was near us. I looked up; Paul raised me from my knees—and I remembered how his father had done that, long ago, in another place, another world. This gesture of Paul's was not in the ceremony—it came from him alone, and was, as I now know, one of love and compassion. It was looked on as a delightful, charming piece of courtesy by others, I remember, and much praised, rather to Paul's annoyance.

Queen Elena took the oath after me. Her graceful and dignified demeanour was exquisite, and, even to me, a little touching. As she returned to her place, I saw her put her handkerchief delicately to her eyes.

Dim lights, music, incense, archaic figures, robes, uniforms, boys' voices, sweeping trains, and glimmering jewels—all mingled into a confusion impossible to describe, until the moment came for me to leave the Cathedral. Then, suddenly, I knew how to give the sign that Nikki had required of me.

I was carrying a bouquet of white roses. Before I knelt at the altar to make my offering, I loosened one, and drew it out; it fell on the steps. Then I turned to take my place in the procession.

As we drove back to the Palace, Paul looked at me anxiously. "Was I all right, Mother?"

"Of course, my darling—it all went beautifully."

"And you're not tired?"

"No, dear—I'm very happy."

And that was true. My son was King—one part of my work was done. I began to think ahead, far ahead, to his majority. When he was old enough to be married—then perhaps, I might be allowed to join his father, and we should live happily ever after. Then, surely, they would let me go.

The other events of the day—the banquet, the reception, the appearances on the balcony, the ball, the fireworks—passed with an extraordinary, dreamlike rapidity. When the time came for my release, I sank into a heavy sleep. Next day, things were not so easy. I was expecting a message, a letter, some sign from Nikki— none came. The false ecstasy, the emotional looking to the future, withered and fell away. I sank into a peevish repining—into a fearful anxiety—into agonizing despair.

That night Vera and I dined alone with Queen Elena. We spoke very little. Her manner was gentle and subdued. After dinner we sat on the balcony, looking out over the lake. Beyond it, the windows of La Gloriette flamed in the setting sun.

We had been sitting in silence for some time when Queen Elena's major-domo came in, and asked if he might speak to me. Then he told me that one of the sacristans of the Cathedral had called for the third time with a message of the greatest importance. Would I be gracious enough to receive him alone?

"Which one is it?" I said, as soon as I could speak in an ordinary voice.

"Androv, Your Majesty—the very old man."

I looked at Queen Elena. Vera's eyes followed mine.

Then I said: "I am with Her Majesty the Queen Mother. Whatever Androv has to say must be said to us both."

The major-domo bowed and went out.

Queen Elena said, in a low voice: "It must be from Nikki. Christiane—my poor dear child—would you not rather see him alone?"

I glanced at her, and smiled. Her poison had dried up. I could afford to be generous, although I was not so besotted, or so quixotic, as to be able to forget all the past.

I said gently: "No—please stay, won't you? I should like you to be here. I know that he would have trusted Androv with a message."

She was staring in front of her. "There will be no message for me," she said, after a pause. "We never made it up, you know."

In the silence that followed, Androv was ushered into the room. He was very much agitated, and could not at first speak coherently of what had happened.

Androv had known Nikki since he was a child. He had thought it possible that he might make an appearance, and was on the watch for him. When the procession had made its way out of the Cathedral, the townsfolk were allowed in, to see the decorations; they were followed by a number of peasants, who had travelled from all over the countryside to see their new King drive through his capital. During the afternoon and evening the Cathedral was crowded. Androv stayed there until night fell, and he was alone.

Then, from behind a pillar near the high altar, stepped the figure of a tall man in a cloak. As he came slowly forward, Androv saw that it was his master—"my King," he said—and sank on his knees in the shadow. He did not go any nearer; he watched and waited.

Nikki went up to the altar steps, crossed himself, and knelt.

Then he saw the white rose. He picked it up and pressed it to his lips—at this point, Androv broke down.

"He stayed there—a long time," he said at last, wiping his eyes. "And I waited and looked at him—my dear master."

There was a long silence.

At last I said gently, "And then?"

"Then—he got up—and drew his cloak round him, and stood looking at the altar."

"And you spoke to him first?" said Queen Elena sharply.

The old man looked at her for a moment.

Then he said: "No, Your Majesty. He had no need of me. I watched him go out. It was quite dark, except for the candles on the altar. I stood there till he had gone. He went out by the North Door."

"You followed him?"

"No, Madame. I should have liked to kiss his hand—once more. But he was not thinking of me."

"Then," I said, speaking with an effort, "there was no message?"

"None, Your Majesty. He took the rose in his hand, and went away."

"How did he look?" I said, after a short, bitter silence.

"Madame—he was very weary. He looked like a man who has travelled a long way to find happiness. I think he found it."

"Why didn't you speak to him?" Queen Elena put in.

"He would have looked round, and summoned me to him, if he had had anything to say to me, Your Majesty."

"How do you know that he had not?"

"Madame—he looked neither to the right, nor to the left. He looked at the altar, and at the rose. He was not thinking of me at all."

"You were quite right, Androv," I said, after another silence.

When he had gone, Queen Elena and I remained without speaking for a moment.

Then she burst out angrily: "He shouldn't have come at all, of course—but if he had to come, he might at least have had the consideration—oh! what's the use? He never could behave like anybody else!"

"Will you forgive me," I said, after a pause; "I'm rather tired—I think——"

"Yes, yes—as if you hadn't had enough, without——You must try not to think of this—this *démarche*—and try to sleep."

I left her in the middle of these recommendations.

As we parted for the night, Vera said, "It isn't very long before you'll be seeing him again, Christiane."

"Seven months."

"You'll be so busy that the time will go quite quickly."

"Yes."

"Christiane—don't—don't——"

"What?"

"Grieve too much."

I shook my head, and smiled.

All that night I lay awake. I shed no tears. I was not particularly restless. I was trying to accept, calmly, the fact that some part of Nikki's mind was, would always be, hidden from me—a mystery. I knew now, for certain, that I should never be able to see into its depths. He had come a long way to be near Paul and me—he had kissed the white rose. But he had said nothing, left no single word of hope, of encouragement, of love.

"I shall never understand him," I whispered to the silent darkness. "Never. Not in seven months—nor in seven years. Oh! my darling—help me to understand!"

That prayer was to be answered—soon . . .

CHAPTER FOURTEEN

How We Reached Our Happy Ending

PAUL WAS CROWNED on the seventeenth of April, 1892. A fortnight later a telegram summoned me to Italy, where Nikki was dangerously ill.

He had been living at his villa near Naples; some friends of Marta's had a house not far off, and she spent a good deal of time with them. Nikki's retirement had been partly caused by the need to economize and partly by his increasing disinclination to see any but his most intimate friends.

He had set off for Bledz from Paris. As soon as the coronation was over, he travelled until he reached a point where he could continue his journey to Italy by sea. He slept badly during the voyage, and spent the greater part of the night on deck. By the time he reached Naples, he was already in the grip of the pleurisy that had descended on him once before. Marta was still in Paris; some days passed before she was summoned.

After a moment of indecision, I decided to go to the villa by land. I left Vera behind, so that she could keep an eye on Paul—for Queen Elena had again taken up her residence at the Palace, and was seeing a great deal of him. I travelled *incognito*, with Astrid and one footman.

The journey was alleviated by Marta's thoughtfulness; at certain stops she posted a messenger, who gave me the latest news of Nikki's progress—for it *was* progress. Nevertheless, I reached Naples prepared for the worst; the first face I saw was Marta's, and for a moment I thought that she had come to meet me in order to break the news of Nikki's death. She took both my hands and said, "He is much better—out of danger, or very nearly."

As we drove along the coast, she told me some further details. For a week Nikki had been either delirious or unconscious; then, during a momentary interlude, he seemed to have grasped what had happened, and had asked for me. When he was told that I was on my way, he struggled to keep alive; now he was himself, although dreadfully spent and worn.

"He's a bad patient as a rule," Marta said, speaking with what seemed to me astonishing tranquillity. "But as soon as he knew you were coming, he did everything he was told."

"Are the doctors still anxious?"

"I brought my own physician—Doctor Planchet—with me from Paris," she said, after a slight hesitation. "And Doctor Ricci from Naples, who looked after him before, is there. They both say that the improvement of the last twenty-four hours has been amazing."

"And you're worn out," I said, putting my hand on hers.

"No," she replied, after a pause. "Giulio and I have nursed him between us. We've done it before. Giulio's very quick and clever, although he's getting on for seventy."

It was unworthy—but even then, I felt a pang of fierce and cruel jealousy, as I remembered all the years they had spent together. I said no more, and neither did she. The sun was setting as we reached the villa.

"If he's asleep, don't disturb him——" I began, as we came in through the loggia.

Marta stared at me blankly, and put her hand over her eyes. Terror seized me again, as we stood in silence. Then Giulio came in, followed by Doctor Ricci. Nikki was awake. He had heard the sound of the carriage.

As I came through the dressing-room, I paused, and looked round for a mirror. I wanted to appear as I usually did when we were together, not to burst in upon him, travel-stained, agitated, and dishevelled. I took off my cloak and hat and smoothed my hair. Then I went in to him alone.

He was propped up, facing the door. His eyes were very bright; his face was masked by ten days' growth of beard. That was all I could see at first.

I sat beside him, and took his hand and kissed it. Then I said: "My

darling—everything's all right now. You're going to get quite well—
and I'm going to stay with you."

He looked at me for a moment without speaking. Then he said:
"I'm glad you've come. It's been a long time."

It was then, as I leaned over him to hear what he was saying, that
all the misery of that long journey seemed to gather and settle in my
heart. For the voice that I had so longed and prayed to hear had sunk
into the ghost of itself; I barely recognized it. It was as if he were
speaking to me out of an impenetrable mist.

Still holding his hand, I shifted my position so that he could see
me.

"You mustn't talk," I said, as I saw the signs of effort, even, I
think, of alarm, in his eyes. "I've come to look after you, and you
must be very good and do everything I say."

He smiled. I felt the faintest pressure on my hand. He murmured something that I couldn't quite catch—I thought I heard
"Nothing to make a fuss about"—but I couldn't be sure—and shut
his eyes. They were sunk deep into his head, and the lids were
purple and swollen.

I sat there, holding his hand in both mine, for a long time. He fell
asleep almost at once. His breathing was short and quick; it hurt him
still, for once or twice he opened his eyes with a start, and stared at
me blankly, piteously, as if I were a stranger who had come to add
to his discomfort and pain. His hands and forehead were cool.

I left him when Doctor Ricci came in. A bed had been made
ready for me in the dressing-room. Giulio slept on the balcony;
during that first night I heard him get up several times. After a great
deal of tossing and turning, I fell into the dreamless sleep of exhaustion. I woke to hear that Nikki had slept well. I sat with him a little.
Then I went downstairs to breakfast, as I thought, with Marta. She
had left me a note, in which she told that she had gone back to
Naples. "If I am needed," she added, "I can be at the villa in less
than an hour."

At first I was indignant, then bewildered. A few days later, when
Marta came over, at my request, to spend the afternoon, I was able
to grasp, not without a struggle, the reason for her seemingly capri-
cious behaviour.

Marta was now, she considered, no longer necessary to Nikki's
happiness; and the consciousness of their early relationship was
beginning to weigh heavily upon her. She had given herself up, as I

then saw it, to the most rigorous jurisdictions of her faith. She had sinned, knowingly, and over a long period of time; now she must expiate that sin. She could only do so by holding herself apart from the person she loved best in the world, with a view, as it seemed to me, to ensuring happiness for them both in the next.

I was not deeply religious in those days: I know better now. Then, I could not have given up my thoughts or my will to any but the idolized creature who had been lent to me for a few months of happiness. I had no life, no joy, apart from my husband.

The week that followed the passing of the crisis and my arrival was unexpectedly peaceful. Nikki grew strong enough to talk a little more, to hear such news as I had to give him, even to tease me now and then, in his old ironical manner. We said nothing to one another of the coronation, or of what had happened after it. We lived, for the first time, in the moment. As the wild Italian spring swept over the countryside, scattering flowers and sunshine and the promise of summer, I thought that Nikki grew a little stronger every day. The doctors were very pleased with him; when they congratulated him on his progress, he would laugh and accuse them of dramatizing the situation.

During the second week of his illness we grew very close to one another—closer than we had even been when our love was tempestuous and demanding. One thing puzzled me a little. Giulio, whose spirits I had expected to see rising hour by hour, remained as he had been on my arrival—silent (silent, that is, for Giulio), attentive, rather grim.

Nikki was soon well enough to be shaved; and then I realized, with a sickening return of the terror with which I had first seen him, how ill he had been. Now that the fever had left him, his pallor was transparent; the shadows beneath his eyes were bruised blackish-grey. He swallowed his medicines and pills without too much protest; it was difficult to get him to take the broths and light foods that appeared every two or three hours.

But we were happy—so very happy. It seemed as if his dangerous, embittered mood had drained away with his strength. He was gentle, serene, slightly mocking, infinitely kind. Much that was mysterious, baffling, and as it were withdrawn in his character was revealed to me at this time. I was able to share his thoughts and his feelings, because our lives were, for the first time, simplified, uninterrupted, supremely intimate. There is no place, in a sick-room, for the clash of temperaments or the conflict of views. We were united in a discipline that had been imposed upon us by his fight for life.

One still, sunny afternoon, a fortnight after my arrival, I had been talking to him about the immediate future. We might, I suggested, go up into the mountains, as soon as he was strong enough for the journey; Doctor Ricci was already talking about a change of air. But that could not be achieved until he had spent some part of each day sitting out-of-doors.

The long windows of his room were all open; I had been looking out over the silky glitter of the sea. I turned to Nikki—I had some question in my mind—and was suddenly silent. He was looking at me with a strange, detached, slightly incredulous smile.

Then I knew, at last. This was what Giulio had always known, what Marta had hinted at, what the doctors had ignored. I cried out, "No! no——" and fell on my knees by the bed in an anguish of tears. It was the first time I had wept since I came to the villa, and I couldn't stop myself.

Presently I felt his hand on my hair. "Don't cry, darling," he said quietly. "Try—try to understand—won't you?"

I started up. "But why—why should you——"

"You cling to life," he said, still contemplating me with that remote, tranquil expression. "That's because you *are* life—at its best, and most beautiful. I don't think you'll ever want to leave it, no matter what may happen to you. I'm not made that way."

"You've no right—how can you——"

As I broke off, shaking with angry sobs, he stretched out his hands. "Don't, my dearest, fight against it—we've been so happy. It's just that I can't go on—that's all."

I flung myself into his arms. He held me closely, stroking my hair. He was far from me. The dark river was already between us: he was speaking to me from the other side.

"You could try—you must," I whispered, after an agonized pause. "Couldn't you? For my sake?"

He put me from him, and gazed at me steadily. For the first time since his illness, I saw the cold, weary, disgusted look darken his face.

"I don't know," he said slowly. "I don't think I could."

I got up, and walked over to the window. There, leaning against the casement, I let the tears flow unheeded. I knew that I was defeated. Obstinate, broken, enraged, I continued to struggle.

I said, in a sullen, furious voice, "And what's going to happen to me?"

He said nothing. When I turned, he was still looking at me as if from a long way off, as if the last of all our many partings was already behind him. It was very bitter to realize that neither ruined love nor passionate despair had the power to make him change his mind.

"Come here, Christiane," he said at last. Then he took my hand and smoothed out the clenched fingers, smiling rather sadly. He said in an infinitely gentle, unbearably tender voice, "You know—this isn't nearly so bad as the first time we said good-bye." He paused, and went on, in a lower tone: "Something died then—hope, I suppose. That was like a spring snapping. I went on for a bit—quite a long time. Now it doesn't seem worth while."

There was a long silence.

I muttered, forcing back the last tearing sob, "But I can't—live—without you."

"Yes, you can, my darling. You must. You've got everything to live for."

"But it's you—it's you——"

"Christiane," he said, putting his other hand on my cheek and turning my face to his, "won't you let me go? I'm so tired."

Desperate, speechless, I looked at him. The words of love died in my heart; the appeal trembled on my lips, and was not uttered. I accepted his decision. It was the last thing I was able to do for him.

During the course of that evening, I sent for Marta, and told her what had happened.

She remained silent for a long time. Then she said, "I will say good-bye to him—now."

"Can't you—persuade him? It may be only weakness—the doctors——"

"You have seen them?"

"Yes. Today."

After a short pause Marta said: "He has lost the desire to live. I think I've known that for a long time. Doctor Planchet knows it too, now. I saw him this afternoon, before he left for Paris."

"But mightn't he be wrong? Doctor Ricci——"

She put her hand on my arm.

"He said"—I struggled on—"Doctor Ricci said it was no use worry-
ing him too much—that there was always a chance——"

In the silence that followed, my last defence crumbled away.

Marta said, "May I go in to him now?"

"He's asleep. Perhaps you could wait?"

"I won't wake him—it will be better that way," she said, in a low
voice.

Her face had grown suddenly thin and haggard. The memory of
the night of the ball came back to me; I seemed to see her in white
satin, with turquoises and diamonds on her neck and wrists.

"Very well—go now," I said.

Presently I heard her come out of the bedroom. She stood looking
at me for a moment in silence.

Then she said: "He's still asleep. It's strange. He looks so young—
just as he did when I first knew him."

Three days later, Giulio came for me, very early in the morning.
He would have left us alone, but I told him to stay; he had been
with the master whom he had bullied and pestered and worshipped
for nearly forty years. He knelt down at the foot of the bed, crossed
himself, and began to pray; I saw tears trickle through his fingers.

A long time passed. Nikki seemed to have sunk into unconsciousness. Doctor Ricci was there for a little while—not long, I think.
Then he went out onto the balcony. The sun was creeping into the
room where Nikki came out of that heavy, painful stupor.

"I'm here, darling," I whispered, as he looked round.

He frowned, and moved his head impatiently. Then his glance
seemed to focus on me, and his expression changed.

"Hold me up—I can't——"

As his voice sank to a confused muttering, I put his head on my
shoulder, and held him close. A moment later he asked me what
time it was, and I told him. Then, for a minute or two, he fell asleep
again. His breathing was heavy and loud.

Suddenly he sat up. He looked round at me, and smiled. There
was a faint flush on his cheeks, and his eyes were brilliantly clear.
He said "Christiane——" in a distinct, low voice. Then he gave a long
sigh; his body seemed to slip out of my arms.

I held him against me. His head was on my shoulder. One lock of
hair lay across his forehead. His eyes were open. He was still smiling.
The sunshine was streaming across the room, over the bed. So I had

often held him in the numbered hours of our love: so he had often woken to another day . . .

Epilogue

WHEN I read an autobiography, I like to know what happened to all the principal characters. I will conclude as briefly as I can, and so tie up the threads of my story.

I brought Nikki's body back by sea to Murania; he was buried in the vault of the Orosvars in the Cathedral. By the time Paul had reached his majority, Queen Elena was dead; we saw little of one another during her last years. Two years later my father died, and was succeeded by a nephew who had married my cousin Hulda; they outlived their date as King and Queen, and are now in England. Kirsten married a Romanoff Prince; they escaped the Revolution, and are making a great deal of money in America. Marta became a lay-sister in a convent in Touraine soon after Nikki's death; I believe she is still alive. Vanescu committed suicide shortly after his retirement from the Paris Embassy. Three years after he had begun to rule, Paul carried through an improved version of his father's Charter. He was assassinated during the drive back from the Assembly by a member of the League of Piety—a cousin, I was told, of the man whose life Nikki had spared. Prince Michael refused to take his cousin's place, and settled the crown on his eldest son, Nicholas VIII, whose reign lasted until Murania ceased to exist as an independent kingdom. Soon after Paul's death, I retired, with Vera, to the South of France, to the villa where I live now. Vera died just before her ninety-third birthday. Astrid is still with me. I don't know what happened to Giulio. He refused to come back with me to Murania. He must have died many years ago.

I don't think that mine has been as tragic a story as people think. I love life—I can still enjoy it, as Nikki said I should. And in setting down these recollections, I have found again some of the bewilderment, a little of the pain, and much of the happiness that I knew in my days of undisciplined youth.

THE END

79
83
85